A GEM *of* TRUTH

Books by Kimberley Woodhouse

Secrets of the Canyon

A Deep Divide

A Gem of Truth

Books by Tracie Peterson and Kimberley Woodhouse

All Things Hidden

Beyond the Silence

The Heart of Alaska

In the Shadow of Denali

Out of the Ashes

Under the Midnight Sun

The Treasures of Nome

Forever Hidden

Endless Mercy

Ever Constant

SECRETS *of the* CANYON
—BOOK TWO—

A GEM *of* TRUTH

KIMBERLEY WOODHOUSE

BETHANYHOUSE
a division of Baker Publishing Group
Minneapolis, Minnesota

Published by Bethany House Publishers
11400 Hampshire Avenue South
Minneapolis, Minnesota 55438
www.bethanyhouse.com

Bethany House Publishers is a division of
Baker Publishing Group, Grand Rapids, Michigan

Printed in the United States of America

Library of Congress Cataloging-in-Publication Data
Names: Woodhouse, Kimberley, author.
Title: A gem of truth / Kimberley Woodhouse.
Description: Minneapolis, Minnesota : Bethany House, a division of Baker Publishing Group, [2022] | Series: Secrets of the canyon ; 2
Identifiers: LCCN 2022014470 | ISBN 9780764238017 (paperback) | ISBN 9780764240904 (casebound) | ISBN 9781493439157 (ebook)
Subjects: LCGFT: Novels.
Classification: LCC PS3623.O665 G46 2022 | DDC 813/.6–dc23
LC record available at https://lccn.loc.gov/2022014470

Scripture quotations are from the King James Version of the Bible.

This is a work of historical reconstruction; the appearances of certain historical figures are therefore inevitable. All other characters, however, are products of the author's imagination, and any resemblance to actual persons, living or dead, is coincidental.

Cover design by Create Design Publish LLC, Minneapolis, Minnesota/Jon Godfredson

Baker Publishing Group publications use paper produced from sustainable forestry practices and post-consumer waste whenever possible.

22 23 24 25 26 27 28 7 6 5 4 3 2 1

This book is dedicated to Garry Hogan.
My amazing dad.
The guy my kids lovingly called "The Walking Encyclopedia."
A man of science. A man of theology.
Chemistry Professor.
Genius.
Pastor.
Husband.
Dad. Grandpa. Great-Grandpa.
You taught me what it was to love the written word.
By starting me on The Word.

It hasn't been a fun year for you.
In fact, the past few haven't been all that great.
But to hear you praise God through it all challenges
me to be a better child of God.
So . . . here's to you, Dad.
A man who loved to read the manuals for everything.
A man who loved knowledge and learning.
A weaver of stories.
I learned so much from you. I'm *still* learning from you.
I love you.
Keep on keepin' on.

Dear Reader

I'm so excited to have you join me for another journey back to El Tovar, the Grand Canyon, and the inimitable Harvey Girls.

This time, we not only go back to 1907 and the height of the Harvey Empire, but the story brings in a legend from 1540. The legend is purely from my imagination, but it was *inspired* by a very true story—the history behind the Spanish exploration that brought a small band to the Grand Canyon by accident almost five hundred years ago.

Cibola. (*National Treasure: Book of Secrets*, anyone?)

There's a lot surrounding the legend of Cibola. Because the Spaniards conquered the Aztecs and the Incans and took what was an immense amount of wealth, the legend of vast cities of gold has been fueled for hundreds of years. What happened to the treasure? To think that this expedition of men abandoned a sight such as the Grand Canyon in search of gold completely blows my mind. But they did.

Unfortunately for them and their pockets, they never found Cibola.

It was this rich and fascinating bit of history that inspired my own legend that I use in this story.

So, of course, I used a bit of artistic license to bring this to life. But rest assured, I did the same amount of intense research that I always do for my stories, and I hope you enjoy *A Gem of Truth*.

For more details about the history included in this story and interesting facts, make sure you check out the Note from the Author at the end of the book.

Lastly, I have to mention a best friend from my childhood, Julie Schultz Leavitt. We were thick as thieves decades ago until my family moved away, but I have carried around beautiful memories of her. Then, one day, a few years ago, she came to one of my book events, and we reconnected. She is such a lovely, amazing woman with the most incredible family (four gorgeous daughters!). Thank you, Julie, for allowing me to name my heroine after you. And for not clobbering me when I dragged you to sing in front of the church.

Enjoy the journey,
Kimberley

Prologue

JUNE 1889
DENVER, COLORADO

No child should ever witness a scene as gruesome as the one in front of her.

"Mama!" The scream tore from Julia Schultz's throat, threatening to rip her in two. Tears gushed from her eyes as she bounced along the road, dust stirring in a big cloud and, for a moment, wiping away the scene. "Daddy!" She choked on the word. The ground rumbled beneath the hooves of the horses and the wheels of the wagon. As if it couldn't wait for them to be away from the chaos.

"Hush now, child. They're gone." The words held impatience. And a bit of disgust.

A wiry arm tried to yank her from her kneeling position. The tailgate of the buckboard bit into her hands as she held on with every ounce of strength she had. But it was no use. One more tug and splinters filled her fingers and palms as her backside hit the hay. The burning and stinging produced even more tears. But the pain in her hands was nothing compared to what she felt inside. Her gut twisted in knots, and a deep gnawing made her want to scream.

Clamping her eyes shut, she tried to erase what she'd seen. Just like washing the blackboard in the schoolhouse. She'd always been good at that when Teacher asked. Probably because she was good at making up stories and daydreaming, which helped the job pass faster. Maybe she could do that now.

But she didn't want to make up a new story. Didn't want to daydream about picking apples, or playing dolls, or running by the stream.

The horror of what had just happened couldn't be real. She needed it to go away. To vanish from her mind's eye. She wanted her mama and daddy back.

But that wasn't possible . . . was it?

Imagining an endless blackboard in front of her, she visualized herself with a giant bucket of water and a rag. Every time she doused the rag, she swiped at the pictures in her mind. Until it was all black.

There. That was better. At least she didn't have to see it.

For several minutes, the blank slate behind her eyes helped her to calm down. The tears stopped. She gulped big breaths until her breathing slowed and her limbs stopped trembling.

But then she opened her eyes. Her imagination couldn't change what happened. Or where she was. The road behind the wagon stretched back to where her parents drew their last breaths. She couldn't see them anymore. Couldn't hear the crowd. Couldn't smell the flowers she'd just picked for her mama.

Instead, the smell of sweaty horses did nothing to mask

the scent of the woman beside her. She smelled like liniment and sour milk. Nothing like the sweet smell of her mama.

And the man driving. Well, he was scrawnier than any man she'd ever known, with a mustache too big for his face. He hadn't said a word. Just drove the wagon. Away.

Far away.

Risking the ire of the woman, Julia went back to the tailgate and gripped the rough wood.

Another hard yank brought her back to the hay. "I told ya to sit. Ain't nothin' you can do about them now."

"But it's not right to leave . . . it's not." She clenched her jaw as hard as she could. She had to be the strong one. There was no one else left.

"The sooner you learn about how hard life is, the better. Your parents are dead. Gone."

She dared a look into the woman's eyes. What made her so hard? So unfeeling? She was nothing like her mother, who had always been so full of smiles, hugs, and laughter. Dread built in Julia's stomach. "What're you gonna do with me?" She pulled her knees to her chest and wrapped her arms around them.

The harsh woman let out a huff. "Never you mind. You're just another orphan that needs feedin'. Just keep your mouth shut and your head down. Do what you're told and maybe some family will take you in permanently."

The woman prattled on about rules and such and what a burden it was to have another mouth to feed, but Julia was still caught up on the word *orphan*. An hour ago, that word didn't apply to her. It wasn't true. It couldn't be.

She knew what happened to kids who didn't have parents. Unless some new family wanted them, they were tossed aside. Sent to orphanages. Or worse, left on the street.

The woman before her said she had babies at home and that she needed help. At least that's what Julia had overheard her tell the preacher man when she agreed to take *the child*. Her. But what would happen after that?

Julia didn't want to stay with these people. They weren't nice.

They weren't even happy.

But most of all, they weren't her parents.

Four months later

The pillowcase in Julia's hands held everything she owned in this world. That, and the clothes on her back.

As yet *another* wagon bounced down *another* strange road with *another* set of bedraggled people taking her away, she gripped it tighter.

She slid her eyes closed and made a list of the contents.

A small tintype of her parents that Mama had shoved at her in those last minutes. Two sets of underclothes. One dress. One nightgown. A hairbrush.

If she had any money, she'd take her meager belongings and run away. But where?

Why didn't anyone want her? At eight years old, she was tall and strong. She worked hard. She had good manners. Tried to fit in with each family. But that was just it—they already *had* families. And she wasn't a part of them.

She was a castoff. Another mouth to feed. A burden. An *orphan*.

The awful word kids used to make her feel about as good as cow poop being scraped off a shoe.

The word that caused people to whisper to one another.

The same word that made others cringe and be horrified by the "grotesqueness" of such a child.

Why did grown-ups think that just because she didn't have a family it meant that she was from the devil? It wasn't her fault her parents were gone. She'd tried her best. She had.

But here she was, being carted away at the mercy of yet another couple that looked like they'd been sucking on lemons.

No matter what she did, no one wanted to keep her.

Two hours later, the wagon stopped. The inky black of the moonless night made Julia shiver. At least they weren't in Denver anymore. People wouldn't know what happened to her parents and why. She'd simply be an orphan. And that was bad enough.

"Get out, girl." The man tipped his head toward the shack. "You gotta stay with us a few days before the next family comes through to get ya and take ya to Texas."

"Texas?" Her voice squeaked as she stood from the bed of the wagon. This was the farthest she'd ever been from home. Wasn't Texas hundreds and *hundreds* of miles away?

"Apparently the people who want ya don't have any children of their own. The first orphan they got put a snake in their bed. Wife got pretty sick after being bit. That's why they asked for a girl this time."

What did any of that have to do with her? Did she really have to go to Texas?

This time the wife spoke up. "You won't be a burden to these folks. They actually *want* a child. This will give you a whole new start on life." The woman leaned over the seat and patted Julia's shoulder, as if she'd just said something important.

The problem was, she didn't want a new life. She wanted

her old one back. With Mama and Daddy still alive. But that couldn't happen. Not now. Not ever.

As she climbed the ladder to the hayloft, Julia did her best to shake off the sad thoughts that had been her companions for the past few months. She'd cried herself to sleep every night, missing Mama and Daddy.

She lay back in the hay, the only place this latest couple had to give her to sleep and let out a sigh. What if the people taking her to Texas really did *want* her? Maybe she would have a family again. People who loved her.

Closing her eyes, she allowed her mind to dream. Of something new. Of a mother and father who couldn't wait to meet their little eight-year-old girl. Of a big house with a picket fence and a flower garden on the side.

Of never being called an orphan again.

Of . . . being loved.

1

APRIL 1907
HOTEL CASTAÑEDA
LAS VEGAS, NEW MEXICO

Some days were not predictable.

Which was a contradiction to Julia's life as a Harvey Girl because it was for the most part pretty predictable.

Their uniforms were all the same. Their work hours were long and hard, and they had the same routine day in and day out. Even their customers were predictable—either the regulars from town who made the same orders every day, or the passengers from the train who arrived like clockwork and would be served in the forty-five minute window before getting back on the train and heading to other destinations.

Different faces, same routine.

Predictable.

As the new group of trainees waited for the head waitress to return, it was Julia's opening to regale them with her favorite story. "I couldn't believe it either." She had the whole group's attention now. "There I was, face-to-face with the richest man in the world."

Plenty of gasps rounded the room.

"To think that Mr. Rockefeller himself asked for my assistance in picking out a gift for his sweet wife on my day off. I was flabbergasted."

Amelia had her hands clasped to her chest. "What did you do?"

"Well, I spent the entire afternoon helping the man, that's what I did. The gift had to be perfect, you see." She pulled a Morgan silver dollar from her pocket. "And this is what he gave me for my help. See the eight tail feathers? Mr. Rockefeller said that makes this one of the first ones ever produced."

The six girls leaned in and stared.

Predictable.

"Miss Schultz?" The head waitress's voice made them all jerk to attention. Her arms were crossed over her middle. But at least she was smiling. "Will you wait for me in my office, please? We have something of great import to discuss."

There it was. The *un*predictable.

"Yes, ma'am." With quick steps she left the girls to whisper and speculate as she made her way down the hall and to the office, the silver dollar in her palm hopefully her lucky charm.

Today was different. Julia could feel it in her bones. It had given her a lively bounce in her step from the moment she got up this morning. What could it mean? She took a seat and sat straight, her ankles crossed to the side, her hands folded in her lap.

Her mind could conjure up a thousand different scenarios. But none of them mattered, except for the real one. So she sat. Waiting.

All the years in this work had conditioned her to stay busy.

Sitting in a room with nothing to occupy her hands or her thoughts was just about pure torture. On top of the fact that she hated being alone.

Ever since her adoptive parents died mere weeks after bringing her to Texas, she'd been tossed around from one family to another. Alone meant time with her imagination—a wild and scary place where she could conjure up any of a million scenarios for what would happen next.

The click-clack of steps on the tile floor relieved her more than she anticipated. Julia straightened her back and shoulders as she watched Miss Sue Blaine—the head waitress—circle the room and sit down in front of her. All of a sudden, her throat went dry. She swallowed, the sound reverberating in her own ears.

"Why do you look like I'm about to eat you?" Miss Blaine grinned at her with one eyebrow quirked upward. "It's just me, Miss Schultz. And you're not in trouble. Although your story was quite entertaining."

Julia put a hand to her throat. "What a relief." Even though her brain told her to relax, it took several moments for her heart to stop trying to beat itself out of her chest. She *had* run into Mr. Rockefeller. That much was true. And he *had* given her the coin. What did it matter that she made the rest of it up? "Mr. Rockefeller did give me that coin, Miss Blaine."

Miss Blaine laughed, and her head swayed back and forth. "You do beat all, Julia." She drew in a long breath and tilted her head as her eyes bored into Julia's. "And you are the most meticulous worker I have."

Was there a *but* in there? "Thank you, Miss Blaine."

The woman dipped her chin and folded her hands in front of her. "It will be difficult for me to say good-bye after all these years."

She sucked in a gasp. Did that mean what she hoped it meant? Julia bit her lip and leaned forward. Her heart pounded. Several painful seconds passed.

"Your request to transfer to the El Tovar has been granted, and I give my hearty approval." The woman's smile was a bit teary, and that touched Julia's heart in a way she hadn't experienced. Would this be how a proud mother would look at her? Or a big sister?

She couldn't help it, she jumped out of her seat. "Oh, thank you, Miss Blaine. I know it's because of your glowing recommendation."

But now the woman who had trained her, mentored her, taken her under the proverbial wing didn't look all that happy. "Please sit."

The tone was one Julia knew all too well. Not scolding, but not pleased. There was something else on the woman's mind. So she sat. "All right."

"Julia . . ." The sigh that escaped Miss Blaine was long. She rubbed her forehead and removed her spectacles. "I've known you for many years. We've worked together here longer than anyone else. And while most of the girls come and go every year or so, you have stayed."

Why did her stomach feel like it was being turned upside down?

"We've been through a lot together, you and I." The head waitress tapped her spectacles on the desk for a moment. Then she placed them back on her face, stood, and turned toward the window.

Julia managed a nod, even though Miss Blaine couldn't see it. She was still trying to figure out whether she was supposed to be excited for the news or preparing for something else.

"And while I give you my blessing, I must admit that I am concerned for you."

"Concerned?" Her voice squeaked a bit. What she wouldn't give for a glass of water right now.

"As head waitress, I consider you girls my family. You know that. I teach you, guide you, protect you, and hope that when you leave this place, you have a solid foundation under you. That you will be prepared to take on the world."

"You've done a wonderful job of that."

"Have I?" The older woman turned. While not unattractive, her features were hard. Plain. In her mid-thirties, she was wiry and tall. But underneath her tough exterior, Sue Blaine had a sweet disposition and a heart of gold. "I feel like I have failed you."

Julia felt her brow crease. "Failed me? How? You just helped me get the position I've dreamed about for three years!"

Sue stepped toward her. "You deserve that position. The El Tovar is Harvey's crown jewel, and you will do fabulously, I'm sure. But it's your personal life I'm concerned about. Julia . . ." Another sigh. This one almost sad, as if filled with disappointment. "You don't have any friends."

As the words tumbled out of her mentor's mouth, it felt like a stab to Julia's heart. She *had* friends. Lifting her shoulders, she narrowed her gaze. All the other girls were her friends, right? So what if she wasn't *close* to any of them?

"Don't look at me with such defiance, Julia. It's time to be honest."

Honest. That word was like a splinter underneath her fingernail. All her life, there had been two groups of people. Those who couldn't wait to hear her spin her next tale, and those who rolled their eyes and told her to be honest.

Neither group had been her friends.

Because while the fascination with her stories might get her attention from one group, those people never stuck around. They wanted to be entertained. The other group didn't have time for her. If Julia entered a conversation with any of them, they'd soon tire of her and leave.

Julia felt deflated, and her shoulders slumped. No matter how much it hurt, it was true. She didn't really have any friends. Hadn't for a long time. Maybe not ever.

"That sounded awfully harsh. Forgive me. *I'm* your friend, Julia. I hope you know that, and I'm truly not trying to hurt you—"

"I know that." Julia lifted her chin. Couldn't let the woman continue. "It's my own fault and I know it." She might be a meticulous worker and respected as a Harvey Girl, but that was where all the accolades ended. Ever since she lost her parents, and then her adoptive parents, she'd sought attention and affirmation from others. To do that, she'd told a lot of stories.

Stories to impress. Stories to make people laugh. Stories to make her sound more interesting.

Stories to hide that awful orphan title. Stories to cover up what *really* happened to her parents.

"The girls trust you at work, but they don't trust you to be a friend. And while you have been entertaining time and again, it doesn't help you make deep, abiding relationships." Sue pursed her lips and reached for Julia's hand, taking it between her own. "Everyone loves you, don't hear me wrong. But they won't allow themselves to get close to you because they never know if what you are saying is the truth. More than one girl has come to me about it. I haven't spoken to you before now because . . . well, they don't know you like I do. I thought things would improve over time. But with the busyness of everyone's schedules, most of the girls don't have time to figure out when you're weaving a tale or when you're in earnest."

Even though the words stung, they were true. Julia couldn't blame her mentor for saying them.

"Which leaves me with the fact that this is my fault."

With a shake of her head, she huffed. "No, Miss Blaine, it's *my* fault."

"I should have said something to you years ago, but I figured your stories were harmless. At least to other people. We've all enjoyed them. But . . . they're harmful to *you*, Julia." Sue's face softened, her eyes glistening with tears. "You are gifted in so many ways, and yet you strive to gain standing with your fellow peers. Like you're seeking approval from everyone around you."

Because she was. The question that had plagued her most of her life repeated itself. Why? Why did she have to lose everything? *Why?*

Why didn't anyone want her?

"You don't need to tell stories for people to like you. You're plenty interesting all on your own." Sue squeezed her hand and then let it drop. Her words sounded as if she'd read Julia's mind, and it was unsettling.

Julia swallowed against the tears threatening to build.

Her mentor took her seat again. "A very dear friend of mine is the head waitress at the El Tovar. I will miss you more than you can imagine, but I'm praying that the good Lord has given you this chance for a fresh start."

A fresh start. How many times had she said that to herself? That a fresh start would fix everything. That it was all she needed. To start over. Well, maybe this time she needed to take it to heart.

"I know I can change." Tears stung Julia's eyes, but she blinked and refused to give them their moment. "I've been wanting to for so long, I just haven't known how. My reflex is to tell a story whenever I get into a jam." Why didn't she just come out and say it . . . wasn't it all just a big lie? But her whole life was a big lie, wasn't it?

"I understand that, I do. But what people want to see is the real you. The truth. Living so remotely at the Grand Canyon is going to require that you gain the trust of the Harvey family there."

The question was, *who was the real Julia*? Hidden underneath the layers of stories she'd created to protect her own heart, she wasn't sure if the real Julia even *existed* anymore. If she did, it'd been far too long since she'd come to the surface. Could she start over? Even if she didn't know who she was?

The weight of the new and wonderful opportunity in front of her all of a sudden felt like she was trying to pull a steam locomotive . . . up a mountain . . . all by herself . . . with one hand tied behind her back.

"Can you do that? Commit to telling the truth?" The love and compassion in Sue's eyes brought the tears back to her own.

"Yes. I promise." With a lift of her chin, she took a deep breath and put a hand to her heart.

A smile stretched across her friend's face. "I'm so glad to hear it."

"You're right. It's time I let people see the real Julia." More of a comment to herself than to her supervisor, the words whirled around in her head. How would she keep herself from telling stories?

Sue leaned forward. "Before you go, will you tell me something? Be honest about it?"

Why did that make her stomach churn? She swallowed hard. "What would you like to know?"

"What happened to your parents, Julia?"

The question made her snap her chin up. No one here knew—no one could *ever* know. "Ex—excuse me?" Maybe she could stall. But the lump in her throat grew.

Sue tipped her head, her face still relaxed and caring, but the dip of her brows showed her deep interest. "You've never told me what really happened to your parents. I've heard probably twenty different accounts."

The blunt statement forced her to blink several times as she studied her mentor. Her heart raced. No. She couldn't tell anyone the truth about that. Not now. Not ever. "I'd rather not say."

Williams, Arizona

"Headed to see the family in Albuquerque?"

Christopher Miller smiled at the ticket agent. "Not this time, Ed. I'm headed to the El Tovar." A train whistled a long tone behind them. It had been a few months since he'd gone back home to see his parents in New Mexico. Guess a visit was due . . . but when? Maybe he could convince them to come out to see him sometime soon.

"One of these days, I want to get up to the El Tovar and see it for myself. I hear it's quite the place." Ed stamped the ticket and handed it to him.

"This will be my first time. You know, I've been here two years and have never even ventured up to see the Grand Canyon. Gramps kept prodding me to go, but I found myself always making excuses and staying behind at my jeweler's bench." Then his grandfather got sick and, well . . . he swallowed back the lump that accompanied his grief. Best to get back on track. "Before the hotel was built, did you ever go up to see the canyon?" If he had to guess, he'd bet Ed hadn't seen much outside of this ticket booth all the years he'd worked for the AT&SF Railroad.

"Nope. Been meaning to take the wife there. She keeps bugging me to go. Says, 'We can't live this close and not see it with our own eyes.'" The man's voice as he imitated his wife was funny, yet sweet. "You better tell me all about it so I can go home and tell Gertrude." The man's chuckle couldn't diminish the love written all over his face. He might tease about his wife, but they clearly had a special relationship.

A throat cleared behind Chris. And it wasn't subtle. Impatient was more like it. Must be someone else in line. Someone *not* from around here, who didn't understand their small town where everyone chatted with one another. At the post office. The grocers. And yes, even at the ticket counter. As quiet as Chris was, Gramps had drilled into him the importance of conversation in small towns. Getting to know their neighbors. He winked at Ed. "I will be sure to give you all the details. As soon as I get back this afternoon. Thanks."

Turning on his heel, he gave a bright smile to the throat-clearer. "Have a good day." With his hat in place and ticket in hand, he picked up his leather case and headed to the train platform. Now that he was actually on his way, his insides decided to take that moment to jolt. Like a diamond hit with a chisel. Again and again and again.

He blew his breath out and rolled his shoulders. The invitation from Mr. Owens, the manager of the El Tovar, to meet with him and discuss potential business at the Grand

Canyon was intimidating, yes, but he didn't need to tie himself into knots over it.

While he'd always been proud of the family business and of learning how to be a master jeweler at his grandfather's knee, he wasn't a born businessman. He'd much rather stay in the back of the shop and just create the pieces and work on repairs than come up with any kind of long-term business plan. It was hard enough for him to come out of his workshop and deal with customers. But Gramps had drilled into him how important it was to take *care* of those customers. So, he'd put his best foot forward and banished his shy self to the overwhelming task of greeting the people who entered his shop. Making small talk. Listening to their likes and dislikes. It *had* made him a better jeweler and designer.

His grandfather had given him this business, and he wanted to be the very best steward of that gift he could be. Naturally, when Mr. Owens called from the El Tovar, he couldn't decline, no matter how much he would prefer to lock himself in the store and work with the hand tools. His mandrel, rawhide mallet, bending pliers, and chasing hammer were his normal companions. They understood him.

"All aboard!" Hissing and steaming accompanied the conductor's words.

Chris stepped up into the railcar and glanced at the other passengers. Taking a seat as far away from the others as he could, he settled in for the three-hour ride and flipped through his notebook of design ideas. That was his real passion. Creating original pieces. *Little works of art*, Gramps called them.

With pencil in hand, he sketched out several new ideas as the train chugged north on the tracks toward one of the greatest natural wonders of the world. Ever since the tracks were completed in 1901, the amount of people flooding through his little town of Williams had grown exponentially. Access to the remote canyon was now faster, easier, and definitely more comfortable than the twelve-hour bumpy stage ride from Flagstaff to the rim. Gramps had been brilliant to start a shop in Williams, catering to the visitors on their way to the canyon. While it had been good for his business, it had meant leaving all the family in Albuquerque, which hadn't been easy.

Chris looked up and out the window, letting his mind wander back to home and family. It had been one thing to be here away from most of his family while Gramps was alive. Now that his grandfather was gone, loneliness settled on his shoulders. But he couldn't abandon what Gramps had left him. The legacy was something he wanted to pass on. Still, he missed family. Mom and Dad let him know on a regular basis how much they wished he'd move back home.

Was he just being stubborn in thinking that God still had something in store for him in Williams? He should pray about that. He wouldn't want to get ahead of the Lord and miss what He had for him.

The swaying of the train and the terrain scrolling past his window relaxed him to the point that he couldn't focus anymore on what he had been drawing. Maybe he could close his eyes for a few minutes. Might help him to calm his nerves before the meeting.

Two hours later, Chris couldn't quite believe the sight before him. Oh, he'd seen plenty of pictures of the Grand Canyon and had heard how magnificent it was. But there was something about *seeing* it for the first time with his own eyes. The expanse of it took his breath away. He'd gone from looking out the window of the train at trees and desert brush to walking up a set of stone steps and seeing the hard-carved lines of the canyon. Layer upon layer of rock changed in color from copper-red to dirt-brown. The top of the canyon seemed like a flat line on the horizon. But below that was another world, with mountainous rock formations as far as the eye could see. And far below—so far down it made him dizzy—a shiny silver river.

When he'd exited the train a half hour ago, the view hadn't been that great. Not much different from Williams, if he were honest. But he'd followed the mass of people up the path and past the immense hotel to the rim. As soon as he'd gotten his first glimpse, his jaw had dropped. Where had all this splendor come from? In the middle of dry and dusty Arizona, no one would ever think to find such wonder.

The canyon seemed to have a magnetic pull on anyone who caught sight of it. And just like that, the crowd had moved in rhythm closer and closer to the edge. Gasps and exclamations of awe accompanied their footsteps. It seemed most people weren't concerned about their luggage or accommodations when a sight like this awaited.

But as the train's whistle blew for its return trip to Williams, Chris looked down at his watch. The manager would be expecting him, and he didn't wish to make Mr. Owens wait. Hopefully he'd get a chance to come back and view more of the canyon before he headed home. Why had he never come out here before? To think he'd been this close to such a place for all this time.

Turning away from the rim, he moved back toward the hotel and took it in. The large adobe structure to his left must be the Hopi House. And to his right sat the famous El Tovar. The circle drive held a couple of horse-drawn carriages—

horseless carriages would probably have a difficult time getting out to a place this remote.

He climbed the stairs up to the wide porch and then opened the door. As he stepped into the foyer of the luxurious hotel, he stared. The massive beams in the ceiling, the colorful carpets, and the stone fireplace were all warm and welcoming. Never had he been anywhere so nice. But that wasn't saying a whole lot. Albuquerque had been his home before Williams, and that didn't exactly make him a world traveler.

Two couples walked by. Their light conversation about the wild and untamed West intrigued him. Did people from the East really not understand what was out here? The necklace around one lady's neck was worth more than everything he owned. Probably including his shop.

He was definitely out of his element here.

But he wasn't about to pass up this opportunity.

"Mr. Miller, I presume?" A gray-haired man in a fine tailored suit approached and held out a hand. "I'm Gregory Owens, hotel manager."

Another man—younger and about the same height, with brown hair parted down the middle—also stepped toward him. "Ray Watkins."

"Nice to meet you both. Christopher Miller." He nodded, shook their hands, and tried to steady his breathing.

"Thank you for coming out." Mr. Owens put one hand on the watch in his pocket.

"Thank you for the invitation. This is spectacular."

Mr. Watkins broadened his smile. "The first time I saw the canyon, it was dead of winter, and I almost froze to death because I couldn't tear myself away from the view."

"I admit the only way I could force myself to come inside

was because I knew you were expecting me." Chris returned the smile. *Relax*. The gentlemen seemed friendly enough.

Mr. Owens motioned with his hand. "This is the Rendezvous Room. If you'll follow me through to the rotunda, my office is just beyond."

With a dip of his head, he acknowledged and followed. The dark beams everywhere kept drawing his gaze upward. Whoever built this place was a genius. Numerous fireplaces not only kept the place warm but enticed people to sit in the cozy areas and converse. The atmosphere was elegant and yet intimate.

Welcoming. Warm. Inviting.

He followed the other two men into the rotunda and glanced up several stories. The hexagon shape of the area showed off the stairs and a generous overlook from the floor above.

"It has quite the architecture, doesn't it?" Ray Watkins' voice. "If you'll follow me." The man extended his hand toward the open door.

Chris snapped his attention back to the men he was supposed to be following. "My apologies." He walked into the office beyond the greeting desk, where several posh-looking guests were checking into the hotel, and took the seat offered to him. He set his case down on the floor and waited, unsure of how these types of meetings normally went.

"Mr. Miller, I'm sorry for the loss of your grandfather," Mr. Watkins began. "I had the privilege of meeting him last year when I commissioned a piece to be made for my wife. He boasted of your incredible talent as a jeweler. You two must have been very close." The younger man's tone was friendly and kind.

"We were. Thank you. I couldn't have asked for a better

mentor, friend, or grandparent. He was the finest man I've ever known."

"It was a privilege to know him," the manager affirmed. As Mr. Owens sat behind his desk and straightened his waistcoat, he leaned forward and brushed a piece of lint off the blotter.

Chris doubted the manager allowed for much to be out of place. Not in a hotel with a reputation like this. Everything around him seemed to be perfect, including the appearance of the man. "Thank you, sir."

"Your grandfather is the inspiration behind our proposal today." Mr. Owens tipped his chin toward the other man. "I'll let Mr. Watkins explain."

"Please feel free to call me Ray." The warm and genuine smile from the gentleman made Chris feel at ease. "As you probably know, Harvey has become synonymous with high quality lodging, food, and hospitality as well as celebrating the native artifacts here in the Southwest. Since moving here in 1905, I've been helping Mr. Owens develop new ideas for the hotel and Hopi House. We believe that your jewelry would be a wonderful addition to the handcrafted goods that Harvey sells at the Hopi House."

Wow. Chris's eyebrows felt like they touched his hairline. While he had dared to hope that something like this was the reason behind the invitation, he couldn't quite believe it. "That is quite a compliment."

"What do you say? Would you like to become part of the Harvey Empire?"

2

The clock ticking behind him made the time seem to stretch.

What an incredible offer. It took Chris a few moments to recover his senses. "I'm honored. . . ." Then he had no more words.

Ray looked at the manager and back at Chris. "We'd like to contract you to design and create unique pieces that will only be sold here. In addition to that, we'd like to ask if you'd be interested in teaching some of the modern jewelry-making methods. The Hopi people have been making jewelry for generations and the tourists love to purchase it, but we wanted to add in some higher-end merchandise as well. Items that incorporate your beautiful designs, but also the culture and history here. Do you think you could be away from your store once a week to start? We have many talented artists within the Hopi community. We believe that if you could teach some of them, it would help with your production as the demand grows. In addition, their input in the designs using their heritage would also entice customers. We've already seen the number of tourists to the canyon triple in the time since we opened."

The offer kept getting better and better. Gramps would have been thrilled to be a part of something so unique and prestigious. Trying not to sound too eager, Chris took his time with his response. "I would love to see the Hopi House and what is already offered. To create unique pieces, I need to get a feel for the culture here." A bit shocked that he'd been able to form an intelligent reply, he swallowed down the nerves that threatened to choke him.

Mr. Owens tapped his desk. "Ray and his wife have already arranged for a tour today, and they will be happy to answer any questions you may have." The man's serious expression was difficult to decipher. "We are very excited to work with you on this new venture. If you would be willing to come up one day a week, I believe we could offer you a contract that you will find most advantageous." A packet of papers was presented to him. "For your consideration."

Chris took a quick glance down. For the most part to calm his nerves. Never in his wildest imagination did he think he'd be offered an opportunity like this. To make jewelry to be sold by the great Harvey franchise? What a marvel. As his eyes scanned the top page, the numbers were beyond anything he'd ever known, and he coughed to cover his sharp intake of breath. "May I take some time to read through all of this?"

"Of course." Mr. Owens stood. "Why don't I allow Mr. and Mrs. Watkins to show you around." He walked toward the door. "My apologies, but I must see to the front desk. We are expecting several important guests today."

"Thank you, sir." Chris nodded to the manager as he left and then turned back to Ray.

The man leaned toward him. "Don't worry, he's a bit intimidating, but he is genuine and trustworthy. You'll never find a better man to work for."

A lovely blond woman entered the room, her right hand on her rounded stomach. When she smiled, the room practically glowed. "Mr. Miller, it's so nice to meet you!"

"Mrs. Watkins, I presume." He gave a slight bow.

"Yes. But please, when it's just us, call me Emma Grace. We're all like family around here."

Ray stood and wrapped an arm around his wife's shoulders. "That we are. And we are eager to welcome you. Shall we go on that tour?"

"I'd love that, thank you. As long as you allow me a few minutes to view the canyon again."

The large sandstone structure of the Hopi House was unlike anything Chris had ever seen. Boxy, with small windows and several ladders going up between the levels of roofs, it was like Pueblo architecture but much larger than most. The style was meant to keep the desert sun out and the cool air in. Fascinating how Mary Colter had designed such an incredible replica of dwellings of the Hopi people.

Even at his modest height of five feet six, Chris still ducked as he walked through the door of the structure. Realizing the couple in front of him was watching, he shrugged sheepishly.

Emma Grace grinned at him. "I still duck too, even though I know it's over my head." She walked several paces ahead and hugged one of the native women in a long fringed dress. Their hushed voices chatted for several moments, followed by the sweet laughter of friendship.

Ray stepped next to Chris. "Mr. Miller, may I introduce you to one of our dear friends, Chuma." He turned to the dark-haired woman. "Chuma, this is the man I was telling you about."

Her eyes widened. "The jewelry man?" The young native woman couldn't have been more than twenty.

Chris took the opportunity to step forward. "I guess you could call me that. At your service, miss." He dipped his head toward her.

The woman bounced on her bare feet. "I am wanting to learn everything you can teach me."

Emma Grace's grin broadened. "And she is the most talented artist I've ever known. She'll probably be the fastest student you've ever had. That is, if you decide to come."

Chris shifted his gaze back to Chuma. "I look forward to sharing what knowledge I have."

"May I see some of what you make?" The woman pointed to the leather case in his hand.

"I would love to see some as well." Emma Grace's hand slid back to her stomach as she inched closer. "The little one agrees, it seems."

Ray stepped around his wife. The sheer joy and awe on his face made Chris feel an odd sensation in his chest. Like he was missing out on something wonderful. "Please, go ahead and share with the ladies. We've got plenty of time."

Chris opened his case and pulled out some of his favorite pieces. A necklace with a ruby centerpiece. A pair of diamond earrings that dangled in a swirl design. And a bracelet with inlaid turquoise.

A gasp was followed by oohs and aahs and Chuma's fluttering hands. "I wish the lessons were beginning today."

The pattering of small feet sounded to his left, and Chris turned his gaze to see a petite Hopi girl running toward them.

"Sunki!" Emma Grace bent over as much as she could and held out her arms. As they embraced, the little girl eyed Chris. Ray's wife caught the curious glance and shifted her face toward him. "Sunki, this is Mr. Miller. He might be creating jewelry for the shop here and teaching others how to make it."

"Will he teach you?" The little girl's innocent face beamed as she covered her giggle with a hand.

Emma Grace tweaked the girl's nose. "No. I will not be part of his classes."

The expressive child let out a loud breath. "Good. It took you six months to weave a basket that wasn't lopsided." The girl walked up to him and held out a hand. "Will you shake my hand, mister? I'm Sunki."

"I would be honored, Sunki." He bent down and took her hand. After a hearty shake, he worked to school his features. "It is a privilege to meet you. Please call me Chris. Tell me, do you want to learn how to make jewelry too?"

She smiled and showed off two missing front teeth. "Yes, please."

"I will look forward to it." He held up several of the pieces for her to inspect. "Which one is your favorite?"

Without hesitation, she pointed to the ruby. "The red one. I like things that are red."

"You have very fine taste, Sunki." He grinned at her and tucked the pieces back into his case. "Would you show me something that *you've* made?"

With a nod, she ran off.

"I think you've made a new friend." Emma Grace reached for her husband's hand. "I'm amazed at your work, Mr. Miller. It will be incredible for us to have it here."

"Please don't feel rushed into making any decisions"—Ray held up a hand—"but I'd love to know what you think so far?"

"I'm very impressed," Chris replied. Who wouldn't be? At

this point, he couldn't think of any reason why he wouldn't agree to the business proposition. But he didn't want to commit just yet.

Sunki returned with a beautiful basket in her hands. "I made this one today."

Chris worked hard not to let his jaw drop too far. "You made this? All by yourself? In one day?"

"I sure did." The young girl tucked her hands behind her back and grinned up at him. "Would you like to keep it?"

"I couldn't possibly take such a valuable basket. It's a work of art!"

"Please? I want you to have it and then you can come back and teach me how to make jewelry like the red necklace." Her big brown eyes pleaded with him.

Chris stood straight and nodded. "It would be an honor to have such a gift. Thank you."

"You're welcome." She turned and skipped away to a woman sitting on the floor, weaving.

These people. So warm, loving, giving.

Ray stepped up to his side. "Wonderful people, aren't they?" He tipped his head toward the door. "Shall we continue our tour?"

"Definitely."

An hour later, Chris sat in the lavish dining room of the El Tovar with Ray and his wife. The round table was covered in a bright white tablecloth. The Harvey Girls in their black dresses and white aprons moved around the room in an almost dancelike rhythm. Water, coffee, and tea were served with precision. He'd hardly had time to even peruse his menu because he'd been so fascinated watching them. After taking a customer's order, Chris noticed that the waitress would either leave a cup upright in its saucer or turn it upside down.

He tilted his head.

"You've never been to a Harvey House before, have you?" Mrs. Watkins beamed at him.

With a shake of his head, he smiled at her. "That obvious?"

"You are a keen observer, I can tell." Her eyes twinkled as she leaned a bit forward. "It's what we call the Cup Code."

"What does it mean?"

"Most Harvey dining rooms are along the train routes where passengers disembark for their meals and then get back on the train to continue their journey. Mr. Harvey knew that he could feed people a scrumptious and satisfying meal in forty-five minutes if he implemented an organizational system and trained all of his waitresses with it. A cup upright means the customer wants coffee. A cup turned upside down means tea."

"Brilliant." Chris continued to watch the waitresses move around the dining room.

"But we do things at the El Tovar a bit differently. Here, there isn't a rush for the customers to get back on the train. This hotel was built for guests to enjoy and relax. So while the waitresses will still use the Cup Code to stay efficient, it's not of the same import as it would be at the other locations."

"You know a great deal about the inner workings. How long have you been here?" Chris felt an easy connection to this couple.

"A little more than two years. My wife and I met in this very dining room."

"Really? I'd love to hear that story."

"Mr. and Mrs. Watkins, it's so lovely to see you." A voice to his left made him look up.

"Margaret!" Emma Grace got up from her seat and hugged their waitress.

The young girl took their drink orders and adjusted his cup for tea.

Emma Grace sat back down and picked up her menu again. "Has Chef created anything new and exciting that I simply must try?"

"Have you tried the filets of whitefish with madeira sauce?"

"Oooh, no, I haven't." Emma Grace tapped her chin. "I think I'll try that with the asparagus and roasted potatoes."

"And for you, sir?" The petite waitress turned toward Chris.

Since he still hadn't read a bit of what was printed, he went the easy route. "I'll have the same."

"Make that three," Ray chimed in, then leaned over and kissed his wife on the cheek.

Margaret left, and Chris turned his attention back to Ray. "Thank you both for the wonderful tour. It was a joy to see the canyon and surrounding areas through experienced eyes."

"We were happy to do it." Ray took a sip of his coffee. "Of course, we're also hoping that it helped to convince you to take the offer."

Chris relaxed and leaned back in his chair. "To be honest, I think you've accomplished that. I just want to read through the contract and pray about it before I sign."

"Good to hear."

Chris turned to Mrs. Watkins. "Now, I'd love to hear that story about how the two of you met."

She gave a little smirk. "I was a Harvey Girl, and he sat at one of my tables."

Ray pointed to the table under the window to the left of the fireplace. "That one right there."

"Was it love at first sight?" Chris jumped into the story.

Ray shook his head. "I was smitten immediately, but she wasn't too thrilled with me."

"Oh, stop." She leaned closer to her husband. "That's not how it went at all." She looked back to Chris. "*I'd* better tell you the story."

"You stupid fool!" Of all the idiotic things to do, the man just had to go and run his mouth. Bobby slapped the fool again. "No one else is suppose ta know about what we been doin' down here."

Roger held up his hands, his eyes wide. The coward. "I swear, I didn't tell 'em anything important."

Such a whiner. Most people thought because of his swagger and height that he was strong, arrogant, and put together. That Roger was the brains *and* the brawn. But no, the man was good for nothing. Never wanting to get his hands dirty. Never lifting a finger. With the intelligence of a five-year-old. And that was being generous.

"Come on, Bobby." The appeasing in Roger's tone couldn't cover the fear. His black mustache twitched. "I ain't done nothin' wrong."

Another smack to his curly-haired head. "Nothin' but brag to those lowlifes about our plans."

He waved his hands in a frantic motion. "Nope, nothin' about our plans. I promise."

"I overheard ya, stupid. If I hadn't stepped in, you woulda told 'em all the whole legend!" Another openhanded smack made Roger tilt to the right. "From now on, you ain't gonna speak to any of 'em. Got it?"

Roger ducked as if prepared for another blow.

Stupid weakling.

After several seconds, Roger straightened a bit and narrowed his eyes. "I won't talk to no one." Adjusting his jacket, he stood to his full height. "You just remember your promise. I got it in writin'." With that, he plopped his hat on his head and sauntered out of their shack.

A few quick steps and Bobby was outside, watching Roger walk along the river. The dumb fool was barely useful.

Too many years of small-time thefts, and a couple of stints in jail, had made them both determined to catch a big payout. But the longer they worked together, the more it was apparent that Roger wasn't worth the clothes on his back. And he'd stolen those.

Maybe they were looking in the wrong area of the canyon? It was, after all, hundreds of miles long. At the bottom of the canyon, they'd found access to water, a bit of wildlife for food, and plenty of caves for their searches. But so far, none of the searching had proven fruitful. That needed to change.

Wiping a hand down the canyon wall, Bobby couldn't think of any better way to find the treasure than keep searching. Almost an entire year had passed while they'd looked. And so far? Nothin'.

The letter the old man sold them along with the shack was about as clear as mud. Said the legend of the two brothers was true. Treasure was hidden in the canyon. But details were scarce. And it wasn't like there was a map with an X marking the spot.

But they couldn't give up. No way.

This *had* to be the area where they were supposed to be looking. It took a lot of hiking around, which wasn't fun in the cold and snow, but at least they hadn't had to deal with too many other people around. Now that the weather was warming up again, they'd have to deal with all them rich tourists up top. Which meant they had to stay down here in the pathetic little shack. Out of sight.

Those sightseein' people could mess up their plans right quick. And Bobby wasn't about to let that happen. Not after all they'd been through to get here. There'd been enough investment in this lifetime.

They would find that treasure. By the end of the summer.

And then Roger would get his wish and be let go.

Permanently.

Julia set down her small case and carpetbag and stared at the enormous structure in front of her.

The El Tovar Hotel.

Ever since hearing about it, she'd hoped to one day work here.

And now here she was.

The cacophony of voices around her penetrated her mind. Men trying to direct people toward the hotel. Women's higher-pitched words sounded like birds twittering. And all of it filled with a spark of excitement and delight that couldn't be contained.

Passengers surged past her from the train platform and up the stone steps toward the hotel. No doubt they were wanting to get a view of the canyon, since they all knew the magnificent wonder was mere yards from the edge of the hotel.

But her whole goal had been to get *here*. To work at this place and start a new life.

She took a deep breath and pulled the telegram out of her valise and read it one more time.

Miss Ruth Anniston would be waiting for her. The head waitress.

Julia searched the crowd. She felt almost like a fish swimming upstream. Maybe she should just wait and let Miss Anniston find her. It would probably be easier.

Several moments passed, and the crowd thinned. A small woman—maybe not even five feet tall—approached. But the air with which she carried herself helped Julia to know in that instant that this woman *was* the head waitress. "Miss Anniston?"

The woman's face split in a welcoming smile. "Miss Schultz!" Her steps quickened, and she approached with open arms. Wrapping Julia in a hug, she squeezed, then pulled back. "I'm so glad you made it. After Sue's letter, I feel like I know you already."

Julia bit her lip. Sue hadn't told her new supervisor about her . . . *negative* qualities, had she?

"We're one big family here, so wipe that grimace off your face. You'll do fine." The head waitress hugged her again.

The warmth of the hug helped Julia relax. Other than Sue's hug when she left New Mexico, how long had it been since Julia had felt the hug of anyone else? Especially one saying that they were *family*. Exactly what she longed and hoped for all these years. Could it actually happen? It could if she didn't mess everything up. "Thank you, Miss Anniston. I'm happy to be here."

"Well, we are excited to have you." Miss Anniston picked up one of Julia's bags and tipped her head toward the steps. "Now, let's go get you settled, and then I'll take you out to view the canyon. Normally, I'd want to take you out for a view first, but since you arrived with a train full of new visitors we'll wait until they're back inside." With a giggle, she marched toward the hotel.

"I admire how you think, Miss Anniston." Grabbing the rest of her belongings, Julia followed.

"It comes from years of experience. Everyone is fascinated with their first view—which I can't say that I blame them one bit. It's quite gorgeous and I'm *still* fascinated with it. But then the practicality of settling in and filling their stomachs hits."

Julia listened to the head waitress explain multiple procedures, most of which she already knew after all her years working for Harvey. Thank goodness because it took all her energy to keep up with the woman. Julia's breaths came in larger gasps than normal.

Miss Anniston turned and glanced at her. "I'm sorry. Here I am scrambling at full speed and you're probably not used to the elevation yet. My apologies."

That's right. Julia had forgotten about the information they'd sent to prepare the staff for the seven-thousand-plus feet elevation where the hotel resided. Had she drunk any water today? That was one of the biggest recommendations. How foolish she'd been to overlook that.

"It's all right. I forgot to take the necessary steps like I'd been advised. My eagerness to get here has overshadowed my good sense." She set her case down and put a hand to her chest. "Just let me catch my breath and I'll be right as rain."

Miss Anniston grinned. "It will take you a few months to truly acclimate, but after a few days you should feel fine. Just remember to drink plenty of water. We don't want to take the risk of you getting sick."

Julia returned the grin and picked up her case again as she gave the other woman a nod.

They entered the hotel from a side entrance in what appeared to be the basement. They walked down a long hallway, and then Miss Anniston pointed. "This will be your room. You'll be sharing with Elizabeth for now, but while we have a moment alone, I wanted to let you know that there is an opening for the position of assistant head waitress, which would grant you a room to yourself next to mine."

Julia raised her eyebrows but tried to contain her gasp.

"Sue gave such a glowing recommendation that I believe you would do well with the job. And with your years of experience, you should be a perfect match. I'll be watching you these first few weeks, and if I think you are suitable, I will submit your name to our manager, Mr. Owens, and see what he thinks." The contrast of her blue eyes against the dark of her hair made the woman truly beautiful. Especially when she smiled. Why wasn't she married?

"Thank you, Miss Anniston. I am honored that you would even consider me."

"I'll leave you to unpack for a quarter of an hour. Will that be sufficient?"

"Yes. Thank you." Julia let it all sink in. Was this really happening? It was wild enough that she was at the El Tovar, but now to think of a promotion as well? Her mind couldn't quite wrap around the thought.

Miss Anniston headed to the door and then turned. "I've ordered a picnic lunch for the two of us. It's such a lovely day, I thought you might enjoy having lunch by the canyon. Since it's my day off, we'll have a good chance to talk and get to know each other."

"That sounds lovely." Julia watched as the woman nodded

and left. Then she scurried around the room to put her things away. Elizabeth had left her a note about which wardrobe was hers and welcoming her to the room. When she opened her wardrobe, a neat line of the classic Harvey uniforms waited on hangers. She couldn't wait to start her job here. But even more so, it was a chance to start fresh with the truth.

An hour later, Julia and Miss Anniston had consumed their picnic and were chatting about the weather, the guests, and what was required of a Harvey Girl at the El Tovar. It sounded perfect. Exactly what she'd hoped for.

A lull in the conversation gave her a few moments to let her gaze roam. Julia couldn't believe the sight in front of her. With every fraction of an inch she moved her neck, the view was new and glorious. The rugged landscape was beyond description. Oh, and the depth! She'd been overwhelmed the first time she looked down and Ruth told her it was a mile deep. A mile! Her brain couldn't even fathom it. "I don't think I shall ever tire of this."

"I don't see how anyone could." The head waitress leaned back on her hands and stretched her legs out in front of her on the checkered cloth, crossing them at the ankles. It made her look young, without a care in the world. "No matter how many times I've seen it, I can't wait to see it again."

So far, their conversation had been light, simple. It relieved Julia to no end. "This was a lovely idea, Miss Anniston. Thank you for taking the time out of your busy schedule for me. I'm sure there are a hundred other things you'd prefer doing on your day off."

"When we're not on duty in the dining room, please call me Ruth." She moved from her relaxed position and tucked her feet underneath her. Her spine straightened, and she folded her hands in her lap. "I'm hoping we can become good friends."

"I would be grateful for your friendship." Oh, the thought of having someone to share her hopes and dreams with. Someone she could rely on to help her be a better person.

"Tell me, what's one of your favorite memories as a Harvey Girl so far?"

Ruth's eager face spurred Julia's creativity into action. "I once saved a little boy from an oncoming train. I was outside getting a bit of fresh air when I saw him playing on the tracks." She put a hand to her throat, picturing the story in her mind as she told it. What had she done? Why had she just told that story? *Why?*

"Oh my gracious. What did you do?" Ruth leaned forward.

"I ran to him and yelled for him to get off the tracks, but then I had to yank him away." The compassion and respect she saw in her supervisor's eyes made her go on. What she wouldn't give to have that respect every day. From everyone. "Come to find out, he was deaf and had never been to town before, so he'd never seen a train."

Ruth's brows scrunched together. "Didn't he feel the vibrations of it?"

Julia hadn't thought of that. She licked her lips. "I don't know. I didn't get to speak to him. All he did was cry in my arms. But his mother was so relieved. It was about time for my shift, so I had to go in to change." As the story grew in her mind, she could see it all take shape.

"That must have been quite a day." Ruth reached forward and patted her hand. "I'm grateful you've come to work here."

"Me too." Heat began to build in Julia's stomach, accompanied by an impending sense of dread. Was it so hard to think of a favorite memory? One that was actually true? With everything in her, she had to suppress a groan and keep from smacking herself in the forehead.

She'd promised Sue she would be honest. Now she'd started her new job—her fresh start—with a lie.

3

A new vow to tell the truth had been made that first day, and Julia was determined to keep it. She'd slipped up the one time. But she wouldn't do it again. And she'd hope and pray that Ruth never found out.

Now a second week at El Tovar had passed and she hadn't told a single story. At least not one that she made up. She *had* chimed in a few times when the girls gathered together, talking about their worst experiences waiting tables. But everything she shared was true.

A first for her, if she were to think about it.

In fact, she should be proud.

Except she wasn't.

Not sharing stories was like putting a clamp around her heart and telling it not to beat.

Having an audience enraptured while she spun a tale was one of her favorite things. She'd had a taste of it again when she told the girls at El Tovar about the scorpion she'd had to chase out of the dining room at the Castañeda. She'd been tempted to embellish it, but she'd held to her promise.

Oh, how she'd ached to share more. To have the girls begging for her to continue. To feel a part of the popular crowd.

But at least she wasn't rejected. Wasn't ousted. Wasn't laughed at.

No one called her an orphan or thought less of her for her lack of family. No one knew. And she planned to keep it that way.

But even though her job kept her busy, she still felt very much alone. Just like all her years growing up. Surrounded by people, but lonely.

Elizabeth came back to their room mainly to sleep. She was sweet and kind to Julia. But she had other friends. A couple of other girls whom she spent her spare time with, chatting and laughing in their rooms. Julia had been invited to join them twice. But both times had been awkward. While the others discussed men, hairstyles, and the latest fashion—none of which she could carry on a conversation about—she'd sat there. Uncomfortable and invisible.

But she'd bit her tongue every time the opportunity arose to weave an exciting story. Which was a miracle in and of itself.

She'd made a promise. She couldn't allow herself to fall into her old habits. Her *only* habit. The only thing she was really good at. There had to be something she could do to take her mind off it.

As she walked down the steps to the basement after another long shift, she blew at the hair on her forehead. So far she'd met and learned all the girls' names but hadn't made any close friends. Sue would scold her for not taking the bull by the horns, but she was hoping that someone would approach *her*, seek her out because she was interesting and they wanted to be her friend.

Voices from one of the rooms down the hall caught her attention. The door was open, and a few of the girls were perched on the two beds in Sally and Blanche's room. Laughter filled the air as two girls sat on the floor, having their hair done by others.

There had been a time that Julia would have stopped and joined the frivolity without thinking twice about it. But the way she'd gained entrance before was by jumping in and telling stories.

That couldn't be who she was. She hadn't decided who the *real* Julia Schultz was . . . and until she figured that out, she should probably keep her mouth shut as much as possible.

"Julia!" A familiar voice stopped her.

She turned to see Ruth with a lovely blond woman she'd seen around the hotel. Stopping at her door, she folded her hands in front of her. "Miss Anniston."

"I'd like to introduce you to my very dear friend Emma Grace Watkins." The shorter woman beamed.

Emma Grace aimed a smile at Julia and came forward as if to hug her.

And hug Julia she did. It was like warm sunshine after a week of rain.

"I'm so glad to finally meet you," Emma Grace said. "Ruth has been telling me about you."

For a moment, her heart jumped to her throat.

Ruth rescued her. "It's all good, I promise." The other two ladies laughed. "Emma Grace was my right hand when we opened the El Tovar. The best assistant head waitress ever. Had Ray not whisked her off her feet, I would have begged her to stay longer if I could." The mutual affection between the two was obvious.

"If you will excuse me, I need to use the ladies' room." Emma Grace gave them a little wave and headed down the hall.

Ruth grinned at Julia and grabbed her hands. "You're going to love her. Just wait until you hear her story. I know the two of you will be instant friends."

Instant friends. If only there were such a wonderful thing. "She seems like a lovely woman."

Ruth tilted her head. "You've been awfully withdrawn the past few days, Julia. You aren't coming down with anything, are you?"

"No, I'm fine. A little tired, but that's to be expected." She paused. How could she explain? "I've just been doing a lot of pondering lately."

"Pondering?" One of Ruth's eyebrows raised. "Sounds deep."

Julia giggled at the expression on her face. "Nothing so consequential, I assure you. But Sue challenged me in several areas before I left, and I have been mulling it all over and examining my life."

"Well, you've done an amazing job upstairs. I've already submitted your name for the promotion with Mr. Owens." Her supervisor changed the subject with ease. Whether she didn't want Julia to be uncomfortable with other ears around, or if she could sense Julia's discomfort with the topic, it didn't matter. It was much appreciated.

Julia put both hands to her chest. "The promotion? Already? I'm so honored. . . ." She floundered for words as guilt filled her. What if her new supervisor found out she'd lied about rescuing that boy? "And thank you for the compliment. It truly has been a joy to be here."

"I'm glad to hear that."

Why was small talk such a drain on her? It shouldn't be this difficult, but it felt like every simple phrase was dry and monotonous. Like a tuba stuck on the same note. Over and over and over again. Life always seemed to have so much more color when she told stories. To be honest, she simply wasn't all that interesting without them.

"Julia?" Ruth waved a hand in front of her face.

"Hm?" Feeling the heat rise in her cheeks, she scrunched up her nose. "I'm sorry. I guess my mind wandered."

"That's okay, it wasn't important."

Julia studied the other woman's face. Somehow it seemed like maybe it *had* been important. What a bad friend she was being. No wonder she didn't have any! Resolved to do better, she turned and focused. "Please. Tell me."

The lovely woman's eyes sparkled as she talked about a new embroidery project she'd taken on, hoping to give it as a gift to Emma Grace and her husband for their new arrival, but she wasn't sure if she would finish in time. The way she spoke with her hands and the genuine care she appeared to have for these people made Julia yearn for the same.

"What are you afraid you won't finish in time?" Emma Grace appeared at their sides, a little out of breath. "I can't think of one thing that Ruth Anniston has put her mind to that she hasn't been able to accomplish."

Ruth shook her head and laughed. "Oh, nothing." She linked arms with her friend. "I think we should go have tea and you can tell Julia all about your hiking expeditions."

"Oh, do you like to hike?" The woman's face practically lit up as she shifted her gaze to Julia. "It is my most favorite thing to do around here. And there's so much to explore! Why, the Bright Angel Trail is amazing, but there's so many caves off the beaten path. You could spend a lifetime exploring." She took a big breath. "But just wait until I tell you the legend about the Spanish treasure. You'll be ready to set out the next day you have off."

They reached Ruth's room, and Julia couldn't wait to hear more. "There's a legend about treasure? And no one has found it?"

Emma Grace's chin bobbed up and down. "Yes. Isn't it exciting? It's been so long that most people have forgotten about it."

Julia's heart picked up its pace, and she bit her lip. She was always a sucker for a good story. Especially one about treasure and adventure. She leaned in, eager to hear every word.

Her new friend's brows lifted. "In 1539, a Franciscan priest told some officials in Mexico that he'd gotten a glimpse of the legendary *Cibola*. But it wasn't just one city. According to the legend, there were actually seven so-called cities of gold.

"Working off the friar's testimony, in 1540, Francisco Vázquez de Coronado led a large Spanish army on a hunt for Cibola. The expedition was huge and expensive. Many of these men went into great debt to go. It was reportedly about six months after they left that they made it to the Hopi Mesas, which are east of us here at the Grand Canyon."

"Wow. Six months just to get here? That's a long time to travel and not even start the search!" Julia put a hand to her throat. Of course, that was back in the 1500s. There were no trains, or even stagecoaches, back then.

"It definitely boggles the mind." Emma Grace's eyes sparkled with excitement. She must love adventure too. "Anyway, at this point, García López de Cárdenas took a small group of men—guided by some of the Hopi—in search of the 'great river,' hoping to be able to travel the river for the expedition's search. Cárdenas and his men came upon the Grand Canyon and saw the river. But that was from the rim. After some life-threatening exploration, they realized the river was not just a tiny ribbon flowing below them. The canyon was far deeper than they had imagined, and the river was rapid-flowing, dangerous, and not navigable by their ships. So . . . they left. In fact, as the story goes, the Hopi did a good job fooling the Spaniards, convincing them that the canyon was a wasteland and held nothing of value for them. This was the Hopis' land, after all. I can't imagine they were too eager to have a bunch of outsiders traipsing through."

Julia couldn't help but laugh. "I can't say I would want to give up this land for anyone else either. I can't wait to hear the rest. Go on."

Ruth sat over in the corner, shaking her head at the two of them. "Emma Grace, look what you've done." She waved a hand. "Getting sweet Julia all intoxicated with the thought of finding treasure."

"Oh, pshaw. You love it too and you know it." Emma Grace winked at Julia. "When Cárdenas returned to the larger expedition, he told Coronado there was nothing for them out here, and the entire party headed east, leaving the Grand Canyon unexplored for another two hundred and thirty-five years."

"What about Cibola and the treasure?" At this point, Julia was on the edge of her seat.

"They never found the cities of gold, and most returned home. But they never recovered financially from such a bold venture." A conspiratorial smile covered Emma Grace's face. "*But* legend has it that two of the Spaniards said to be a part of the expedition brought many treasures with them—precious stones that they planned to use to gain them entrance to the cities of gold. You see, these brothers believed that one had to be worthy to enter Cibola. They were part of the group that stumbled upon the Grand Canyon. Even though Cárdenas thought there was nothing there, they believed differently. Because why would God create such a masterpiece if not to hide something even richer?

"Secretly, they made some plans of their own. The two believed *they* would be the ones to find Cibola. But, when the time came to leave, they followed their leader and rejoined the rest of the expedition party and stashed their treasure somewhere in the canyon, hoping to return after they left their counterparts. But when the two men mounted their own expedition and returned, the legend says that they never found the canyon or their treasure again. They were lost to the rugged depths, along with their secrets about the treasure they'd left behind."

Which meant it was still here.

Somewhere within the massive 270-mile gorge. To think that there was treasure—perhaps even the cities of gold—here. Right here! Julia leaned back and stared up toward the window.

Her mind whirled with possibilities and questions. Maybe that was just the distraction she needed. Something to occupy her thoughts and spare time. Now, whom could she convince to go explore with her?

Sometimes being the head waitress was not all it was cracked up to be. There were days Ruth would much prefer *not* being in charge.

Days like today, when it had been nice to simply sit and chat with two girlfriends. But when Emma Grace brought up the legend about the treasure from 1540, Ruth hadn't missed the excitement on Julia's face.

She was clearly smitten with the story. And then she took off, determined to find another girl who had the same day off and would hike with her.

Ruth rubbed her forehead and prayed this wouldn't be a disaster in the making.

"I'm sorry." But the expression on Emma Grace's face didn't *really* look apologetic. Her friend giggled.

"Oh, don't even apologize. We both know you don't mean it." Ruth narrowed her gaze at her. "You knew exactly what you were doing when you told her that legend. In fact, I think you secretly wish you could go off adventuring with her."

Emma Grace put a hand on her swollen abdomen. "It's no secret. I definitely do. But we both know that Mr. Watkins would pitch a mild fit if I tried anything like hiking down into the canyon at this stage of my life."

Ruth laughed and leaned forward. "Only a mild fit? Gracious, he'd have the entire hotel chasing after you."

With a hand to her mouth covering her mirth, Emma Grace shook her head. "I'm glad it's only a few more weeks before our little one is due. Whew. Everything makes me need to use the ladies' room. Especially laughing." She stood with an awkward push off the bed. "No comments about my unladylike stride."

The laughter had been good for Ruth's soul tonight. Helped her relax and not carry around so much tension. "Promise." Ruth opened the door for her friend and stretched her back and shoulders as she made her way to her small desk and chair.

A letter had arrived from Sue that she hadn't read yet. Ruth had been looking forward to a few moments alone so she could read the news. Opening the envelope, she smiled and leaned back in the chair.

Dear Ruth,

Before I go any further, I fear I need to apologize. There's something I should have told you about Julia.

The next few paragraphs made her heart pound. Absorbing the words from her friend, she cringed. So her waitress had lied.

Ruth sucked in a breath and held it. The news wasn't what she expected. She put a hand to her forehead. What to do about this now? Most of the time, she dealt with black-and-white situations. There were rules and they were strictly enforced. Yes, she had to deal with the emotional issues of the girls, and the occasional gossip had to be squelched immediately, but she was usually able to deal with them in a loving yet firm manner.

She'd never had one of her girls be a fantastic liar. This was going to be different. And much more difficult.

Thankfully, for the rest of the letter, Sue returned to personal catching up and then signed off.

Ruth let the hand holding the letter flop into her lap. Closing her eyes, she let out a long sigh and shook her head. Could she nip this in the bud before Mr. Owens approved Julia's promotion? Or should she say something to their manager about the letter? Tapping the missive against her palm, she stood and paced the room. If she spoke to Mr. Owens about it, Julia would likely be fired. And that wasn't what Ruth wanted for the young waitress.

Sue had been correct in her assessment—Julia *was* the best worker she had. Lovely too. But apparently she'd tried too hard in the past to get people to like her. The lies and stories were to gain approval. What was the motivation behind that? There was something deep inside her new worker that she wasn't sharing. Maybe she never would.

The girl was lively and fun. Extremely creative. Ruth hated to squelch that, but somehow she had to get across to her that the truth was paramount.

When Emma Grace had started sharing some of the wild and crazy things that had happened on her shifts as a waitress for Harvey, Julia had entered in several times with stories of her own. Each time, she made sure to look at Ruth and say, "It's the truth. I promise."

Now her words made much more sense.

She'd have to confront her about the lie and explain that Sue had told her everything. Including the promise. And soon. Make sure that Julia knew Ruth would hold her accountable.

Maybe there was a way to encourage Julia's creativity in some other manner? In truth, she was a precious girl. No wonder Sue adored her so much.

There was a tap at the door, and Emma Grace entered. "Oh boy, I see there's a storm brewing. What's happened? How can I help?"

"You know me too well." Ruth's laugh was weak. "You know that I would never want to slander or gossip about one of my charges. But I need some advice. You must promise that you will keep this in the strictest of confidence."

"Of course." Emma Grace sat again. "Why don't we pray for wisdom first?"

With a sigh, she nodded. "Perfect."

After they prayed for several minutes together, Ruth shared her conundrum about Julia. When she was finished, she plopped into her chair. "Sue believed in her . . . and you know what? I do too. In my heart, I know I need to help her. I just don't know how."

Her friend stood and reached toward her with open arms. "It does seem a bit overwhelming at the moment. But I think you *do* know what you need to do. You are exactly the example this young woman needs. God brought her to you for a reason. Just like He brought *me* to you."

Ruth stood and hugged her friend. Gave her an extra squeeze.

"I don't know what *I* would have done without you, Ruth." Her friend held on for an extra second. "You believed in me. I have a feeling that's what Julia needs right now." She pulled away with a sad smile. "Don't be too hard on her. As a favor to me?"

Ruth nodded. "Anything for you."

"Good. We both know there's more to her past and likely a lot of pain. There's only one way through that pain, and it's not easy." Emma Grace yawned. "Sorry to rush off, but all of a sudden I'm exhausted. It's probably best I head to bed. Can we finish catching up tomorrow?"

"I'd like that."

Closing the door behind her friend, Ruth mulled over everything she knew about Julia and Emma Grace's impression of her. If anyone understood the truth underneath the stories, it would be her friend. Was there a difference between Emma Grace's covering up her real identity because she was running for her life and Julia's being a storyteller? The longer she thought about it, the more it made her head hurt.

Ruth stood in the middle of the room with her face lifted to the ceiling. *Heavenly Father, I don't know what to do. I want to honor Your Word and the job that You have given me here. Please give me discernment and show me how to help Julia. And all my girls.*

Weariness seeped into her limbs. As she changed into her nightdress and washed her face, she couldn't make heads or tails out of what little she knew about Julia. Sue—her friend for many years and someone she trusted implicitly—believed in her new charge.

Emma Grace encouraged that too.

She pulled the covers back and knelt on the floor. With a long, cleansing breath, she released it into her Father's hands and lifted up each of her girls by name.

4

The bell over the door to Chris's shop jangled. *"Such a happy sound."* That's what Gramps used to say. It didn't matter if it was an interruption, that bell signaled a potential customer.

Chris set down the bracelet he was working on and wiped his hands on his apron. As he stepped from his workshop in the back to the glistening showcase area, he saw his landlord wave a hand.

"Good morning, Mr. Langford. How may I help you? Perhaps looking for a gift for your wife?" Pasting on a smile like Gramps taught him, he hoped he could be a convincing salesman.

The older man removed his hat and stroked his gray beard. "Mr. Miller, I'm afraid I'm not here to shop."

Why did that make his heart drop to his toes? He wasn't late on his rent for the building.

"My wife and I have decided that it's time to move closer to our children and grandchildren, so I'm selling all of my holdings in Williams and heading to California."

"Oh?" This building was one of the man's holdings. But

they'd had an agreement for years—that they could rent to own. Best not to jump to conclusions.

"That includes this building. I've had two other offers on it the past year, but since I'd made an agreement with your grandfather, you get first option to buy. But I need to have the transaction final within the next six weeks, or I will sell to one of the others."

"Six weeks?" That's all the words he could force out at the moment. How on earth could he purchase a building in six weeks? The longer he stared at the man, the more his gut twisted into knots.

This store was his livelihood. Gramps had been so proud to put his store right here in the best part of Williams. Close to the train. Right in the middle of all the hustle and bustle.

"I know that's a short amount of time and I'm sorry . . . but this is the price I'm asking from you. In accordance with the contract I had with your grandfather, I've deducted the months of rent already paid toward the balance I would ask of anyone else." Mr. Langford's voice cracked as he slid a piece of paper across the shiny glass counter. "Son, you've been a stellar tenant and it has been an honor to know you, but I'm sure you understand the predicament I'm in. It's time for us to think about our futures, and I must admit that I long to spend mine pouring into my grandchildren."

"I understand that, sir." Chris blinked and pulled his thoughts together. He couldn't blame the man for wanting to be near his family. But the reality of it all was like a sledgehammer to a precious pearl.

Should he open the paper now? Or wait? What was the protocol in situations like this?

"I can see that this is a bit of a shock, so I'll leave you to pray and ponder. Just let me know in a few days what you'd like to do. I'd much prefer selling to you." Langford settled his hat back onto his head, nodded, and strode back to the door.

The bell jangled again, but this time it was like a loud gong in Chris's ears.

His fingers covered the paper, which seemed to burn the longer he touched it. Just his imagination. But as soon as he opened that paper, he'd know the impossible amount he *didn't* have. Even with the rent they'd already paid on the building.

With a deep breath, Chris lifted the folded paper and opened it.

$1400.

Fourteen. Hundred. Dollars. The number rolled around and around in his head. Even if he was fortunate enough to have someone wealthy come in and buy every single piece of jewelry in the store, he couldn't come up with that amount. The offer from the El Tovar was even more of a necessity now. Thank God for paving the way. But could he make enough in such a short amount of time? It seemed impossible.

The bell jangled again, and Chris jerked his head up and stuffed the paper into the pocket of his jeweler's apron.

Great. Jeffrey Connors smirked at him from the door. The man was artificial. Fake. Counterfeit. Brummagem.

But a customer nonetheless. "Good morning, Jeffrey. How can I help you?"

"Christopher, I'm so glad I ran into you." The smirk grew into a smarmy grin.

"You came into *my* shop. I wouldn't exactly call it running into me." Sarcasm dripped from his tone, even though he'd tried his best to hold his tongue. What was it about this guy that rubbed him the wrong way?

Jeffrey removed his hat and brushed at the top of it. His shoulders and chin lifted. "Semantics, my dear man. Semantics." He walked around the store, glancing here and there at the items in the displays but keeping his nose in the air and not showing any real interest.

What was he up to?

"I heard Mr. Langford gave you the news."

"How do you know about that?" The words were out before he could stop them.

The slimy man tilted his head and put on an innocent-looking expression. "Everyone who knows *anyone* in this town *knows*." He drew out the last word and rolled his eyes in a very dramatic fashion. The corners of his mouth appeared to be fighting off a smile.

Chris should've known. Mr. Langford didn't have a mean bone in his body, but that didn't necessitate him keeping his plans a secret. But Chris couldn't deny that it hurt. "Langford is a good man. I can't disagree with him wanting to be closer to family."

"I'm sure it was a bit of a shock." The man perused the case with diamonds. "But no one will fault you for not being able to raise the money in time."

What? Who said anything about him *not* being able to do it? Of course, he didn't really have the confidence that he *could*, but no one else should be assuming. "Six weeks gives me plenty of time." Maybe if he said the words aloud, he could convince himself.

"Don't kid yourself, Miller. You and I both know the truth of the situation." The condescending look from Jeffrey made him want to kick the man out. But that would be ungentlemanly. And maybe a bit rude. "Besides, I came here to make an offer."

He didn't want to hear it.

Connors went on without his permission. "I'll buy the building and turn this into a very high-class, prestigious jewelry store. A place where people will come from far and wide to buy our unique pieces. With my father's connections, we can reach the wealthiest of clientele and really make a name for ourselves. I'll hire you on to design for me and you can stay holed up in your little workshop, which we all know is where you prefer to be." He turned to face him. The insincere grin on his face stretched from ear to ear. "See? It's the perfect plan."

Enough was enough. Chris stepped forward and put a hand on Jeffrey's back, pushing him toward the door. "I have no desire to work for you, Connors. Rest assured, I'll be purchasing the building myself. Thank you for stopping by." With a final nudge, he managed to get the man out the door.

The jangling of the bell accompanied the smug look on Jeffrey's face as he turned and walked away.

How on earth could he win against the likes of Jeffrey Connors?

Another beautiful morning.

Julia stretched and reached toward the ceiling. Every day she was here at the El Tovar, she felt a little more alive.

And to think that her supervisor had submitted her as the candidate for assistant head waitress! The prestige of that promotion at a place such as Harvey's crown jewel . . . Wouldn't all the other girls she'd worked with over the years be jealous?

Her roommate frowned. "You do love the mornings, don't

you?" Looking exhausted and haggard, Elizabeth headed toward the bathroom.

Julia giggled. She did love the mornings. Especially with such good news! Nothing could sour her mood—not even a grumpy roommate.

She splashed water on her face and then prepared for the day. This time it wouldn't take her fantastical stories to get their attention. Her position would demand it. *And* their respect.

There was a knock at her door.

Julia grabbed a towel, dried her face, and then tightened her dressing gown around her. She opened the door with a smile.

"Good morning, Miss Schultz. Don't you look chipper today." Ruth's greeting was sweet, but her face serious. Then there was the fact that she'd called her *Miss Schultz*. Had she done something wrong?

Her stomach dropped, and the giddiness of a few moments ago left in a rush. "Good morning, Miss Anniston. Won't you come in?" She held the door with a tight grip and then closed it behind the head waitress.

Ruth stood there with her hands clasped.

Julia took a long breath.

"I don't wish to put a damper on your day, but I need to address an issue so that we can put it behind us."

Just as she feared. She was in trouble. "Yes, ma'am." She swallowed against the lump in her throat.

Ruth pulled an envelope out of her pocket. "As you know, your previous supervisor is a good friend of mine. For many years, Sue and I sent letters back and forth. But they'd gotten fewer and farther in between. It seems that your presence here reminded us of what we missed and we decided to write more often."

"Oh. That's nice." But it wasn't. Sue knew many of Julia's secrets. Well . . . her lies.

"After our picnic your first day here, I was so amazed at your story of saving the little boy from the train that I mentioned it to Sue."

Julia took another large swallow. For some reason, the lump grew. She knew why. She was caught for sure.

Ruth let her shoulders dip and let out a long sigh. "Why did you lie to me, Julia?"

Heat rushed to her face, her limbs, even the tips of her hair it seemed. Tears burned her eyes. "I'm so sorry, Ruth. I just got caught up in the moment and wanted you to like me."

"Sue told me about your penchant for stories and how she felt that she failed you by not addressing it earlier. She also told me about your promise to her."

All she could do was look at her feet. A deep shame flooded her being. "I haven't lied since that day, I promise you. I made a vow not to do it again."

"But didn't you already promise Sue?"

"Yes, but I had a slight misstep. That helped me to see how important it was to follow through with my promise. Haven't you ever made a vow and then realized how hard it was to keep it?"

"I take promises very seriously, Julia. They are not to be tossed around. Honesty is paramount."

"And I have been honest with you about everything else. I pro—" She cut herself off and bit her lip. How many times had she said, "I promise"?

Ruth rubbed her forehead with her left hand. "Listen, I've been praying about this ever since I read Sue's letter. And yes, she told me everything. I understand that you've been hurt quite deeply in the past. Being an orphan and tossed around from family to family must have been extraordinarily difficult for you. I understand that you feel the need to clamor for attention or affirmation." She took a slow inhale. "Now, to your credit, I have seen you restrain yourself several times with the other girls. I do believe that you have been putting your best effort forth to be honest, but that still doesn't negate the fact that you lied to me right off the bat."

"I—"

Ruth lifted her hand and shook her head. "I won't abide any more lies. Understood?"

"Yes, ma'am."

"Even though you are one of the hardest workers and the best waitresses I've seen come through these doors, I will not hesitate to have you dismissed if I suspect you've been dishonest with me again."

"Yes, ma'am."

Ruth lifted her chin. "I've decided not to bring this matter to Mr. Owens' attention at this time, but you need to walk a fine line, Miss Schultz. You have to earn my trust again. Show me that you can be honest. Sue believes in you, and she wouldn't do that if she didn't see your potential." She tapped the letter against her palm. "For now, I need you to check in with me every morning a half hour before roll call and room inspection. It will be good for me to get to know you better and also to hold you accountable."

"Yes, Miss Anniston."

"As for the future, the promotion is still a possibility. Work hard. Be yourself. Take the time to get to know everyone here." Her lips lifted in a light smile. But her tone brooked no argument.

"Thank you. I can do that."

Ruth checked the watch pinned to her shirtwaist. "I expect to see you upstairs before anyone else. Set a good example, all right?"

She nodded.

"Good. Just be yourself, Julia. Be real. I expect you to uphold your promise to honesty and to do your very best." With that, she opened the door and left.

As the door clicked behind her supervisor, Julia leaned against it and slid to the floor. She couldn't risk this job. This was everything she'd ever wanted. Why oh why had she lied that first day?

Ruth's words replayed in her mind. *"Just be yourself, Julia. Be real."*

The only question was, did she know how?

5

Life was good. Exciting. Thrilling.

Julia's day off had started with her feeling hesitant and unsure. She'd barely slept the night before because she couldn't get her mind off Ruth's words. The conundrum of *who* the real Julia was and how to just be herself compared to the Julia she'd always been . . . well, that seemed to be a constant debate raging in her mind.

In the middle of the night, she'd come to a startling conclusion. She didn't have any idea who she was. In fact, all the stories she'd told were more prominent than any of her real memories.

Other than the day of her parents' deaths.

And that was probably why. Reality was harsh and ugly and unloving.

But she'd made a new vow. To figure out who she was. What she loved. What gave her excitement to face the day.

The fact that she still had a job was a miracle. So now she needed to prove that she could change. She *could* be honest. And she would gain the trust of Ruth again and earn that promotion!

She'd met Tessa earlier this morning for breakfast, and

then they'd ventured out together. The scenery alone had taken her breath away and made her appreciate another day to live and breathe.

After a full day of hiking in the canyon, Julia already couldn't wait for her next day off. It was exactly what she needed to keep her mind occupied.

Skipping down the stairs to her room, she felt like she was on cloud nine. "Wasn't that magnificent?" She gripped the elbow of her hiking companion.

Tessa grinned. "Yes."

"Does that mean you are up for some more exploration?"

The other Harvey Girl shrugged. Quiet and a bit mousy, the girl never said much. In fact, the most words she spoke were probably to her customers each day. And that had to be quite a stretch for her. But when Julia had asked around for a hiking partner, Tessa was the only one to volunteer. With a smile even!

The most the younger girl had spoken all day had been about an interesting desert flower and a tree. Maybe enough words to amount to ten sentences added up altogether. *All. Day.* Maybe it just took coaxing to get her new friend talking.

"I appreciated your insight into the vegetation. Where'd you learn those things?" Julia was determined to help Tessa out of her shell. It might take time, but she had plenty of that. Especially with as much exploring as she hoped to do.

"Books." Another one-word answer. Another shrug. With another smile.

"I love to read, myself. But I don't think I've read too many books on flowers and trees and such."

They reached Tessa's room, and her new friend waved a hand. "Thanks. It was fun."

Wow. Four whole words strung together. Might be a record for the day. But it was sincere, and the sparkle in her friend's eyes conveyed more than all her words from the day. "Thanks for going with me. Do you mind if I ask Miss Anniston to line up our days off? I'd love to explore some caves next time."

"Sure." Another shrug. But her grin widened.

Progress. Julia would take it. "Great. I'll see you tomorrow!"

As she walked to her room, her mind filled with all she'd seen. Like a moving picture, the canyon and all its glory passed by in colors and textures. Cracks and crevices. Rock formations. Mountainous peaks rising from the center of the canyon. Layer upon layer of rock. Igneous—granite and basalt. Sedimentary—sandstone, mudstone, shale, limestone. And metamorphic. All three types were visible, a fact she'd learned reading a book she'd snagged from El Tovar's library.

Then there was the glorious river at the bottom. Silver like a mirror and snakelike from the rim of the canyon, but the farther she'd hiked into the canyon and the closer she got to it, the larger and more full of life it became. The powerful flow pushed, charged, and rushed through the gorge and over boulders in white-capped waves. Never in her wildest imagination could she have dreamed of what she'd seen. And that was just along the Bright Angel Trail. There were hundreds upon hundreds of miles to explore up and down the canyon.

Placing her key into her door, her mind shifted back to the legend Emma Grace had told her about last week. It captured more than just a fanciful query in her mind. In fact, if she were honest, she was a bit fixated on it. Her obsession with the legend had taken over every moment of every day when she wasn't needing to focus on work. Which had been a wonderful distraction to keep her from weaving tales. She entered her room and closed the door behind her, then leaned against it.

Instead of being exhausted after a long day of hiking, she couldn't wait to get into her nightgown, crawl under the covers, and jot down her ideas about where to look for the treasure.

With a twirl on her toes in the center of the room, she let out a giggle and then slipped out of the faded and dingy shirtwaist she'd paired with a split skirt. It had been a brilliant choice because she hadn't minded getting it dirty or snagging it on the craggy rocks and prickly brush.

She made quick work of washing up in the basin and slipping her nightgown over her head. Shoving her feet into a thick pair of socks to ward away the chill in the basement, she let her mind daydream about what she might find on her next day off.

Once ensconced in the warmth of her bed, she pulled her notebook into her lap and tapped a pencil to her lips. First, she should sketch out her ideas. Not that she was the greatest artist, but she did like to have a plan, and what better way than to put it down on paper while it was still fresh on her mind.

Where would she hide a valuable treasure? She closed her eyes and went over the details Emma Grace had told her.

A smile lifted her lips. Maybe . . . just maybe . . . she could be the one to find the treasure.

Chris followed the host through the double-door entry to El Tovar's enormous dining room. The scent of fresh-baked bread filled his nose and made his stomach rumble. Winding around the elaborately dressed tables, the host led him to a corner table. To the left of the room's giant stone fireplace, the table sat under a window that looked straight out to the canyon.

Magnificent.

Ray stood from his chair and welcomed him with a hand held out in greeting. "So glad you made it back."

The smile that filled Chris's face as he shook the man's hand couldn't be stopped. The venture was exciting and now needed more than ever. After a few frantic days of crunching the numbers, he had a plan. It was desperate, yes. Out of his comfort zone, most definitely. More aggressive than anything he'd ever imagined. But there was no other choice. "I am looking forward to getting to work."

Ray grinned. "Glad to hear your excitement. Mr. Owens and I are equally excited and wish to get started as soon as possible." He pointed to a chair. "Please, have a seat and we can order lunch."

Chris took his seat and lifted his briefcase onto his lap. Without pausing, he pulled out the contract and slid it over to Ray. "Here's the signed contract."

The raised eyebrows of his lunch companion made him cringe inside. Was it too pushy? Had he overstepped?

"Excellent." Watkins took the papers and set them aside. "The terms were agreeable, then?"

"Yes, very. Thank you." He set his case down and folded his hands on the table in front of him. "I also brought pieces with me that I've been working on. I'd like to go ahead and put them on display so that we can start selling as soon as possible."

"Even better. Mr. Owens will get started on the advertising

now that the contracts are signed. We also have hired ten Hopi who are ready and willing to learn the trade. As you read in the contract, they will be paid by the Harvey company."

It had been one of the best parts of the deal. The Harvey company would give him fifty percent of all sales for his design and expertise. They would split the costs of the materials with him, and they would pay the other employees. Better than he expected! With ten more sets of hands, they could produce a lot more. And with the great Harvey name, reputation, and way of generating sales, it should be a win-win situation for them all.

Even with the commission the company would take for hosting his jewelry displays, he could make a good profit. If he had to stay up every night and work for the next five weeks, he would. There wasn't any other choice.

"Great. I can return on Monday and begin teaching them." Chris gave an eager nod. "I'll also bring more jewelry to sell."

"Sounds like you are on top of things." Ray leaned back in his chair as a red-haired woman in a pristine black dress and white apron poured water into their glasses.

"Would you gentlemen like coffee or tea?" Her voice had a velvety quality to it. The tone was a beautiful alto.

Green eyes connected with Chris's, and he blinked. "Yes . . . yes, coffee please." He could imagine a simple emerald choker around her neck but couldn't decide which would be more beautiful, the stone or her eyes.

"Thank you, Julia. Coffee for me too."

Chris watched as the waitress left their cups upright and traded her water pitcher for a carafe of coffee. In a matter of seconds, she returned and filled each of their cups. Quick. Precise. Without spilling a drop.

"I'll give you a moment or two to look at the menus, and

then I'll be back to take your orders." She nodded at each of them with a smile that showed off a dimple in each cheek.

She walked away, and Chris's gaze followed. Ray cleared his throat.

With a jerk, he brought his head back. What had come over him? Heat streaked up his neck and into his face. He took a sip of his coffee and looked down at his menu. "What do you recommend?"

"You remind me of myself." Ray's deep laughter as he straightened the silverware in front of him made Chris feel even more embarrassed. "I'm not sure if you remember, but this is the table where I met my wife for the first time. Almost exactly like you just met Julia." His eyebrows stretched upward.

A tickle in Chris's throat forced him to take a drink before he could respond. While he'd been curious about the Watkins' love story, it didn't mean he was looking for the same. "Oh?"

"Don't worry. I won't give you a hard time. Just don't go to the head waitress to inquire about her. Neither Miss Anniston nor my sweet wife were impressed." Ray winked.

Allowing himself to relax, Chris nodded. "I'll remember that." He pretended to study the menu but couldn't focus on any of it. He'd never met anyone with red hair before. With her fair skin, freckles, dimples, and green eyes, she was more fetching than any other woman he'd ever met.

Stop. Focus. There was no time to be sidetracked by a beautiful waitress. No matter how much Ray Watkins touted the benefits of marriage and how much he loved his wife. No matter how much his mother hounded him about it every single time they spoke. He had to come up with a way to pay for his building.

"I'm thinking of trying the stroganoff today. Have you

ever had it?" What a dumb question. The man lived here. He probably had sampled everything on the menu. Multiple times.

"I have. It's one of my favorites." Ray set his menu down.

Julia appeared out of nowhere. "Are you two ready to order?" She pointed her sweet dimples at Chris first.

"Yes, Miss . . . I'm sorry, I don't know your name." This wasn't usually the way he met people.

"Miss Schultz." She leaned an inch closer and lowered her voice. "But you may call me Julia. Mr. Watkins' wife has been a gem in helping me to learn all about the El Tovar."

"You're new here?" He would have never guessed. Her skill was impeccable.

Her smile widened enough for him to see her teeth. And another shot of those dimples. "I've been a Harvey Girl for several years now. But I just arrived at El Tovar a few weeks ago."

"It's nice to meet you, Miss Julia Schultz." He dipped his chin at her. "I'm Christopher Miller."

Ray leaned forward. "Forgive my lack of manners, I should have introduced you two. Julia, Chris here is a jeweler. He designs and makes the most beautiful jewelry I've ever seen. We will be showcasing and selling it over at the Hopi House."

"That's fascinating. I can't wait to see some of it." Her eyes were bright and sincere.

Ray tipped his head in her direction. "And from what I hear about Miss Schultz here, she's about to become the new assistant head waitress. Very prestigious."

Julia's cheeks tinged pink. "I don't know about prestigious, but it would be an honor for me to earn that promotion." A clock in the dining room chimed. "Goodness,

I better take your orders now." She raised her eyebrows at him, as if in question.

Chris's mouth was drier than it was a moment ago. He took a sip of water. No woman ever had this kind of an effect on him before, and he didn't have time for it now. "I'll have the beef stroganoff."

"I'll have the same." Ray tapped the empty table setting next to him. "My wife should be joining us soon. She loves the stroganoff, so why don't we just round out the table."

"Sounds lovely. I'll put these orders in right away and bring around a basket of bread and butter."

As tempting as it was to watch her and the other Harvey Girls as they moved with grace and precision around the room, Chris felt a weight on his chest. Honesty was always the best policy. About everything. Even though the offer from Ray and Mr. Owens was generous, he needed to be forthright about his motivation and current situation. On the off chance the worst-case scenario happened and he lost his building, he didn't want to let the company down. "Ray, there's something I need to tell you."

"That sounds ominous." The man took a sip of his coffee and focused on him. "Go ahead."

"My apologies, I don't believe it to be ominous or bad, but I wanted to be forthcoming about a situation I'm facing." He stirred two sugar cubes into his coffee. "The man who owns my building—where my jewelry shop is located—came in to see me a few days ago."

As he relayed the story, the urgency of his timeline made his heart pound. But it was out in the open. "If I can't come up with the amount in time, then I will have to figure out what to do. But I will take it one step at a time. That's the best that I can do."

"We definitely wish for you to stay in Williams, and I'm sure Mr. Owens will agree with me when I say that we don't want to lose you. I guess the question is, if you lose your shop, what will that mean for our contract with you?"

The same question that had plagued him. While the assumed profits from the Harvey Company would be substantial, would he want that to be his only means of income? Where would he live? His home had always been above the store. "I will uphold my end of the bargain. And if push comes to shove, then I will simply have more time to work here."

For years, Bobby had slaved for someone else. Been treated like dirt. And for what? Nothin', that's what.

Turning to a life of stealing had been easy. And it wasn't all that bad until jail. Being locked up for petty theft was stupid and a waste of time. So now it was time to stop working those dumb small jobs. All Roger's ideas, anyway. And he was about as bright as a burnt-out matchstick.

That's why it was so important to find the treasure. Respect and adoration came with money. And with money came power. Lots and lots of power.

Bobby needed it.

As if the stupid tourists weren't bad enough. With all their frills and ridiculous frippery, traipsing all over the place on their burros, asking dumb questions.

Bobby had heard 'em all. Hated 'em all. Wanted to shoot every single one of 'em. But that would draw too much attention.

Stupid rich people. And those fool Kolb brothers with their

cameras and pictures. Always drawing attention, wanting more and more people to hire them to take photographs or whatever the stupid contraptions did. And add the obnoxious Harvey Girls too. Too nosy for their own good. Bobby's blood boiled. Why did everyone have to get in the way of the plan?

Wasn't like they could just go killin' everyone who got in their way. Which was a shame. Life was too short to be dealing with all the distractions. But too many people disappearing would bring the law.

Roger said they should scare 'em all off. Which wasn't too dumb of an idea for the idiot. But how? That would take some serious thinkin'. Because they didn't want anyone to be wise of their presence. That was the secret that needed to be kept. Otherwise someone would try to run them off. Or find out they'd escaped outta jail back in Oklahoma. And that couldn't be allowed.

Bobby wasn't going back. Never.

Time was not on their side. The nicer the weather got, the more they'd be overrun with the hordes of gawkers.

Mountain lions roamed these parts. What if one were to attack a tourist or two? Or say some of 'em got bit by rattlesnakes? It might at least help to keep people away for a bit. If the head honchos who ran the train and hotel sent a hunter down, Bobby could just get Roger to kill the hunter, which might buy them a bit more time, as long as no one found the body and called the law. The canyon was a dangerous place after all. Couldn't have those nice, clean, wealthy people gettin eaten or bit now could they.

The more the idea filled out, the wider Bobby's grin grew.

There was lots of death in the Grand Canyon. What was a little more?

6

The train's gentle sway, in addition to Chris's exhaustion, was almost enough to lure him into closing his eyes on the way back home. If he could turn off all the wheels spinning in his brain.

The weight on his chest had lifted as soon as he told Ray Watkins the truth about his circumstances. And after lunch, they'd taken all of the inventory he'd brought with him to the Hopi House and, with Chuma's help, had a display set up within thirty minutes. By the time the train whistle blew for him to return to Williams, they'd sold every piece of his jewelry.

Which was a huge blessing. But also a problem. That meant there was nothing else to sell until he brought more. There was no way he could keep up with that kind of demand. On the other side of that, at this pace, he'd be able to raise enough money to purchase his building *if* he could create enough pieces to sell.

If he told Mr. Langford that he was doing his best to purchase the building—maybe even give him a down payment—then hopefully that would delay the man in entertaining any other buyers. His landlord had said six weeks. Chris prayed that the man would hold to it.

Four weeks and six days remained. With the sales from today, it seemed doable. But did he have enough precious stones and pearls to create ample pieces to sell? Gramps had purchased a good deal of silver and gold right before his death, so he should have enough of that. He'd have to do a detailed inventory when he returned and try to project how many pieces he could reasonably make with what he had on hand. Everything needed to go toward the purchase of the building. Everything.

He couldn't lose the store. Not after Gramps had sacrificed to give Chris this start. No matter what, he wanted to honor his grandfather and be a good steward. If he needed to sacrifice in other areas for a bit, it would all be worth it in the end. Especially with this huge business opportunity out at the canyon. If the sales today were indicative of the future, then Chris would have no trouble paying for the building and then building up his stock of supplies again.

He'd told Ray he would return in two days so he could start teaching those who wanted to learn. It normally took months to train someone, but even if there was just a little bit of help here and there with some of the tedious, time-consuming things, then extra sets of hands would be great and ever so helpful. Now he just needed to gather everything he'd need to create a job for each person so they could make several of each piece. He'd also have to make one for them to look at as a sample.

His mind spun with all the details. Realizing that rest wasn't possible, he pulled a pencil and notebook out of his case so he could jot down everything and prayerfully not forget any important details.

List after list filled his notebook. Then, when he was sure he had it all planned out, he started sketching out a few simpler pieces that he hoped he could teach some of the Hopi in short order. If he saved the elaborate work for himself and taught them how to make the settings and clasps and do other simpler tasks, then all should run like a well-oiled machine.

The train slowed, and Chris couldn't believe they were back in Williams already. He had much to do, though, so he was glad he'd taken the time and used it wisely.

He disembarked and hurried toward his shop.

"Christopher!"

He didn't slow his steps. If Jeffrey Connors wanted to catch up to him, he could. The man had two legs, didn't he? A twinge of guilt tapped at his conscience. Gracious, where were his manners? Apparently there were none left for the likes of the slimy gent. *Lord, forgive me for my ugly thoughts.*

"Christopher!" the man shouted again.

All right, God. It's Your turn. Glue my lips shut if You need to. Help me to be nice. Whatever I need to do, but I need to get back to work. While he wasn't normally in the habit of telling the Almighty what to do, he still couldn't stand the thought of another confrontation with Jeffrey. Thankfully the good Lord above knew. And He knew Jeffrey too.

Outside of his shop, he finally slowed and turned to face Connors. "How can I help you?"

"I was hoping you'd taken a bit of time to think about my offer." The smug smile on the man's face told Chris that rarely did he not get what he went after.

Gracious. Be gracious. Kind. That's what Jesus would do, right? "I have thought about it, yes." But not the way the man hoped. "While I appreciate your enthusiasm, rest assured, I will be purchasing my building. Have a good evening." He made the move to shift to the door, but Jeffrey stopped him with a hand on his shoulder.

"I find that a bit hard to believe, Chris. Now, don't go trying to put on a brave face. We've known each other for *years*."

The way the fellow drew out that last word made it sound like they'd toddled around together when they were still in diapers, not just been introduced two years ago. Acquaintances. That's what they were. "This isn't just a brave face."

Jeffrey's smile slipped just a little. "Well, I'm glad to hear it, my friend. Glad to hear it. But I'm just a moment away if you'd like to reconsider. Clock's ticking!" He pointed to his watch. "The city council already loves my business plan and is excited to see what I am planning to do with this place."

The man had the gall to speak to the city council? Of course. Jeffrey's father was on the council. Chris pasted on a smile. "Thanks for stopping by, but you'll have to excuse me. I have a lot of work to do." He turned, unlocked his shop, swept in as quick as he could, and closed the door. The lock clicked back into place, and he leaned against the door with a sigh. He'd never been an impatient man. But lately he'd become more and more short-tempered whenever he saw Jeffrey. The man could get under his skin like no one else.

Maybe he shouldn't have prayed for patience after all if *this* was the answer.

The amazing smell of fresh-baked bread wafted from the kitchen throughout the entire dining room. What was it about flour, butter, and yeast coming together that was so tempting? Chef Marques probably had that in his master plan to entice people into his restaurant. Not that he needed any other enticement. His food was the best Julia had ever eaten. But if the scent of baking bread didn't stir people to hunger, she didn't know what else could.

She worked alongside Charlotte to stamp the pats of butter with the El Tovar crest. The other girls polished silver, prepared the bread baskets with fresh linens, and checked the tables to ensure that every setting was pristine.

Expectations were high here. Perfection the goal.

Her stomach growled in response to the browning goodness in the ovens.

"Mine's doing the same. Let's hope it's done soon so we can sample today's batch." Charlotte giggled and stamped a row of butter pats in quick succession.

Julia switched out her completed tray with one yet to be done. "I was just thinking the same thing. Hoping to hear the ding of the timer so we can all converge on the kitchen."

Chitchat with her fellow Harvey Girls had become comfortable. Normal. But for some reason, other than Tessa and their hikes, she hadn't been able to make any real connection with anyone except Ruth. And they hadn't had the opportunity to speak too much this past week, other than her morning check-ins. Julia didn't want to be a drain on the woman who had forgiven her so graciously and who had to be boss, mother hen, big sister, and comforter to all thirty of the girls. Besides, she was supposed to be helping Ruth with all those responsibilities as assistant head waitress. She had at least two more weeks of a probationary period before it was official, from what Mr. Owens told her.

So, she'd watched all the other girls and put her best foot forward with them. But while they were content to just stroll along the top of the canyon on their days off, she yearned for more. She loved hiking and exploring. Didn't realize how much she truly enjoyed it until she came here. And even though it had only been a few weeks since she'd been at the canyon, she was hooked. It wasn't just about the treasure either . . . even though it occupied her thoughts more often than not.

It was this place. Wow.

"What's the sigh for?" Charlotte sent her a grin. "Any particular gentleman you're thinking about?"

"No." She let out a nervous giggle. That was the other thing that seemed to keep the Harvey Girls' minds occupied: men.

"Oh pooh. I was hoping you'd say there was one. You're so secretive, Julia." Charlotte poked her with an elbow.

Secretive? Really? Is that what people thought of her? That was a new one. But in all her work to keep honest, maybe that's what she came across as. "I'm not that secretive. Just contemplative, maybe? I was just thinking about all that there is to explore here." Please oh please, couldn't she find another person who wasn't engrossed with finding a husband all the time?

"I know you like to hike the trails. All the other girls are talking about where you and Tessa have gone so far. But I'm afraid of heights. Even venturing to the rim is a bit too much for me. I don't mind the view—it's very beautiful—but I think I'll enjoy it from here, thank you very much." Even though Charlotte was obviously trying to keep it light, the tint of fear was clear on her face.

Julia set down the stamp and wiped her hands on a towel. Then she reached for Charlotte's arm. "I won't push you to do anything you don't want to do. I promise. But I do enjoy hiking."

Her eyes sparkled with unshed tears. "But the other girls . . . they've started to tease me about not going to the edge."

Ah, peer pressure. It was an ugly beast. Maybe this would give her a good opportunity to become a friend to Charlotte. "Don't let them try to goad you into doing anything. Stand firm and ignore the teasing."

"You think that will work? They keep threatening to drag me out there. They say it will help me." The girl was shaking now.

Without another thought, Julia wrapped the girl in a hug. "Have you talked to Miss Anniston about this? That kind of treatment isn't tolerated."

A quick shake of her head. "No. I don't want to be labeled as a tattle. It's harmless, really." Charlotte swiped at her cheeks with a handkerchief. "Please don't say anything to anyone. I'll be fine."

Julia refused to let it go. "I promise I won't say anything, but you have to promise me that you will let me know if they start in on you again. Deal? You need someone in your corner."

The other girl met her eyes and took a deep breath. "Deal." The slight smile showed the tension release.

With another tray of butter pats at hand, Julia focused on the work to give Charlotte some time to compose herself. It lifted her heart to think that she could be a friend to someone else. Maybe having a position of seniority was exactly what she needed. Not everyone's attention or affirmation for her telling an engaging tale. No. Instead, she could pour into other people.

All these years, she'd wanted to have friends. But for some odd reason, she thought that she would have to be the one to get them and, in essence, *keep* them. By earning their friendship. Earning their love.

Maybe she just needed to *be* a good friend.

Ruth approached with her hands clasped behind her back. "Good afternoon, Miss Schultz, Miss Rand."

"Afternoon, Miss Anniston." With everything in her, Julia tried to keep her voice calm and cool. But more than anything, she wanted to ask Ruth for an audience so they could talk about her little revelation.

"Excuse me, I need to avail myself of the facilities." Charlotte kept her gaze down and walked away.

"Everything all right?" Ruth stepped a bit closer.

"Yes. She just shared something personal and probably needs to splash some cool water on her face."

"Okay. I was hoping we could chat for a moment. There's something I need to tell you." The hesitancy in the head waitress's voice didn't make it sound like it would be a pleasant conversation.

But she hadn't lied again! Had she done something else wrong? Julia nodded and set aside her work.

Ruth turned and walked toward the back corner of the dining room and Julia followed. No one was currently working over there, so at least it was quiet. She wouldn't scold her in front of everyone . . . would she?

"I'm sorry to have to tell you like this, but we have two new waitresses arriving today."

Okay. So far, that wasn't too bad. Two of the girls had gotten married on a whim and put in their notice, so of course they would need replacements.

Ruth's shoulders rose with a breath. "I have to say, Julia, you have done a phenomenal job here. I'm so very proud of you. I even wrote a letter to Sue to let her know how well you are doing and that you haven't told another wild and crazy story."

"Thank you." Hearing the woman she respected most tell her she was proud of her was like balm to her cracked and splintered heart. If she could be like anyone, she wanted to be like Ruth Anniston.

"But I'm afraid that one of the girls arriving today is someone that you know quite well. You've worked with her before."

Every bit of happiness within her seemed to shrivel up. Great. Someone from her past. She closed her eyes and clenched her jaw against the rush of feelings. So much for a fresh start. "Might I inquire who it is?"

Ruth released a long breath. "Florence Nichols."

Just hearing the name made her want to cringe. Not that Florence was a horrible person . . . not entirely. "Florence." She put a hand to her forehead. "Why did it have to be her?" Gracious, did she say that out loud?

"Sue told me that the two of you had several arguments in the past but that Florence had been transferred to another Harvey House." She reached forward and put a hand on Julia's arm. "I'm so sorry. I didn't know that when I hired her. She had the highest of recommendations. It was only after she was on her way here and Sue let me know of your . . . history with her. She felt strongly enough about it to call me."

Memories of those first few weeks in New Mexico flooded into Julia's mind. She wasn't sure if Florence had been transferred because of their obvious distaste for each other or because the company needed her elsewhere, but Julia had never been more relieved in her life. Something about the other girl raised her hackles. Sue had been right to warn Ruth.

If Julia had been in her position, she would have done the same thing. Somehow, she had to show Ruth that she was more than capable of handling this situation. She couldn't risk losing the assistant head waitress position. Or Ruth's hard-earned respect. "Miss Nichols is an excellent worker, as I'm sure Sue told you. She was never a problem as a Harvey Girl. And that was years ago."

"She just wasn't a friend to you." One eyebrow shot up.

"No." Julia lifted her chin. "But I will take full responsibility for that. I enjoyed telling elaborate stories to the girls every night and loved the attention. She wasn't about to believe them and challenged me at every turn. Of course, she was also easy to like and fun, so the girls flocked to her."

"Well, I'm sorry that this will be awkward, but I will have a chat with her as soon as she arrives. I'll make sure to nip this in the bud immediately. She just needs to see that you aren't the storytelling Julia anymore and I'm sure everything will be fine." Ruth patted her arm. "Now, I know we both have work to do."

As her supervisor walked away, Julia allowed her shoulders to sag. While she hadn't wanted to say anything bad about Florence—another new conviction of hers—she hadn't spoken of how spiteful and conniving Florence could be. Why hadn't Sue mentioned it to Ruth? Or had she? No one had ever wanted to be the one to tattle on Florence, for fear of her wrath. So had the head waitress even known the truth?

Dread weighed down her steps as she headed back to her station. Would she never be able to get past who she'd been? Would anyone ever truly love her for who she was?

Time to be honest with herself. No. It couldn't happen.

Because she wasn't worthy.

She wasn't worthy of having parents. Wasn't worthy of having friends. Wasn't worthy to be loved.

This was her lot in life. Maybe the sooner she accepted that, the sooner she could move on and be a different person.

The Julia Schultz she'd tried to be all the years prior hadn't worked. What if the new Julia Schultz *here* wasn't working? If it had worked, she'd at least have some friends by now, right?

At this point, she barely even knew her roommate. She'd avoided the group settings as much as possible, more to keep her tongue bridled than anything else. But did anyone even think of her as a friend? Charlotte had opened up this morning . . . but what would she think of Julia once Florence got here and spread her opinion?

For the first time in her life, she'd thought of herself as someone with value and purpose. She'd worked hard. Earned the promotion . . . well, almost. She loved her job. Had gotten excited about the legend and the treasure. Would anyone ever think that she was worth their time?

As she went back to the butter pats, she used a bit more force than necessary. But the butter didn't protest. Charlotte was over in the corner speaking to Ruth now. What would Florence do to the sweet girl once she arrived? Julia had been the brunt of Florence's gossip too many times. Poor Charlotte didn't have a chance, especially if the new waitress discovered her fear.

So many emotions clouded her thoughts that she couldn't keep focused on her task.

It wasn't fair.

Wasn't fair that her parents were gone. Wasn't fair that she'd gotten tossed around like a rag doll from family to family. Wasn't fair that the one way she could get attention as a child was to come up with outlandish stories.

Wasn't fair that she didn't have anyone. No family. No friends. No one.

Several girls had reached out to her over the years and invited her to come with them to visit their families. Or tried to convince her to go to church with them.

But she didn't need more rejection.

The world had done a smash-bang-up job of that over the years.

The dark cloud that descended over her in that moment tempted her to run outside and fling herself over the canyon walls. Her misery would be over then. For good.

But that's not what she wanted. Not really. She wanted to live. Wanted to be happy.

She craved hope. Craved love. Craved family and friends. The sunny outlook she'd held for several days was now gone. It didn't take much.

"Everything all right?" Ruth was at her side, studying her face. "You look like a storm is brewing in that head of yours. I hope it's not because of the news I shared." Compassion oozed from every word.

Julia blinked several times and looked at the woman beside her. Should she be honest and tell her that yes, Florence Nichols' arrival here would be a disaster for her? The end of her fresh start? Maybe she should just ask to transfer somewhere else. But where could she go where her reputation wouldn't follow her, if she couldn't even get away from it here? The train had made the world accessible. There was nowhere for her to run. Not that she wanted to. She loved it here.

"Julia?"

She couldn't stop the tears from forming in her eyes, no matter how hard she tried. "I'm sorry. Maybe I . . ." Should what? What was the answer?

Ruth tilted her head a notch. "After the dinner shift this evening, you're coming to my room for a cup of tea." She held up a hand. "No arguments. I think it's time we had another heart-to-heart."

7

The phone rang in the front of the store, and Chris made a dash for it. It had taken hours and hours of work and very little sleep to get prepared for the next day at El Tovar. Mr. Holland—an old friend of Gramps who helped out in the store every once in a while—was willing to come work in the jewelry shop on the days Chris would be up at the canyon. Which was a huge answer to prayer. That way, merchandise could be sold at both places. Now he just had to keep up the pace and produce enough items for each location.

He could sleep later. Like next year.

"Hello?" Out of breath, he picked up the receiver and spoke into the mouthpiece on the wall.

"Christopher?" Mom's voice came over the crackling line. "Were you running to the phone? Is this a bad time? Would you like us to call back tomorrow?"

His shoulders shook with a light chuckle. Every phone conversation started the same way. Several questions without a pause for him to answer. "I'm glad you called. Is Dad there too?"

Muffling and more static.

"I'm here. But it's hard for both of us to hear at the same time." Dad's low bass voice rumbled.

"Good to hear your voices. Put your heads together so you can listen. I've got some news."

"Maybe he's met a girl." The excitement in Mom's voice couldn't be denied as she whispered to his father. If the operator was listening in, they'd probably laugh too. Chris could imagine his parents' faces, Mom looking at Dad with a conspiratorial wink as she held up a hand to shield her words from him. "Have you met a girl?" Her voice was louder this time. Obviously directed back at him as if he hadn't heard.

"No, Mom." Well, he had, but he was still sorting that out in his mind. Of course, as soon as he thought about Julia with the pretty red hair, he had a hard time focusing. He shook his head. "It's about the shop."

"Oh?"

"Mr. Langford has decided he needs to move closer to his family, so he gave me a few weeks to come up with the remaining funds needed to purchase the building."

"How much is left?" Dad's voice was steady. Inquisitive. He was a numbers guy.

Chris hesitated a moment. "Fourteen hundred dollars."

His mother's gasp was hard to ignore and then more muffling. Dad must have covered the mouthpiece with his hand.

Several seconds of silence passed. "That's a good deal of money, son." His father's voice came back on and wasn't quite as chipper as it had been moments ago.

"Yes, it is. But you haven't heard the other piece of news. The manager at the El Tovar Hotel invited me up a couple weeks ago and had a business proposition for me. I'm going to be making jewelry to sell there."

"But how will you manage both?" Always the practical one, Dad asked the hard questions.

Good thing he had the answers and had been working on this for a while. "Mr. Holland will work here in the shop when I'm up at the Grand Canyon. Mr. Owens at the hotel has arranged for me to teach some people who want to learn basic jewelry making. I realized what an incredible opportunity it was when everything I brought up there the first day sold out almost immediately."

"Oh heavens! What a blessing!" Mom was clearly enthused.

"Sounds like a wonderful opportunity . . . but . . ." Static filled the line.

"But what, Dad?"

"What will you do if you can't pay Mr. Langford?"

The crux of the matter. "Well . . . I'm hoping and praying that I will be able to. I'm scraping together every dollar that I can. I'm keeping my chin up and my eyes on the Lord. If it's His will for me to be able to purchase the building, then He will make a way."

"That's the spirit, son." At least Dad approved.

"You can always come home and settle down here." Mom was quick to put her two cents in. "I know of several young ladies who ask about you on a regular basis. We sure would love to have you home and see you start a family."

Chris swiped a hand down his face and hoped his parents didn't hear the long sigh. He should've known it was coming but had hoped that his parents would realize by now that his heart was here. In the store that Gramps had given him. He and his grandfather had shared a dream, and now he wanted to follow through with that dream. With everything in him, he wanted that.

"I know you're anxious to have grandchildren, Mother"—he laughed to lighten the mood—"but remember that I need to get married first, and so far, I have been a little busy."

"Well, maybe that's the problem. Maybe you need to spend less time working and trying to make money and get to searching for the right girl. You're not getting any younger."

It amazed Chris that his mother could go from cheering him on to scolding him in a matter of seconds. But he loved her and knew her heart. She really did just want to see him happy. But God had given him this path. He wanted to see it through. "I know, Mom. And I have been praying about it. I promise."

"Good. Don't worry. God knows exactly what He's doing. We will just keep on praying for His will to be done." Her tone was matter-of-fact.

"Even if it means that I stay here?"

A pause. "Even if means that you stay there." But her voice cracked.

Dad whispered something to Mom, but Chris couldn't decipher it. He'd always loved their relationship. It had been an example to him of what a godly marriage should look like. If only he could be so fortunate to find the same.

"We'd better let you go. I'm sure you still have a lot of work to do." Dad's voice did its typical rumble through the line. "We love you and will talk to you soon."

"Love you too." Chris hung up the receiver and backed away from the phone mounted on the wall. Such a funny-looking contraption. The wooden box with two large bells looked like eyes, while the mouthpiece looked like a giant nose. The receiver hanging on the side made it look like the telephone monster had only one ear. When he was a kid and they'd seen a telephone at the fair, he'd thought it was watching him. Now the image stuck with him.

As he went back to his workbench, chuckling, a waitress with red hair flashed through his mind. While there had been lots of women he'd found attractive over the years, there had only been a handful who truly caught his attention. None had been the one God had for him, though. Ever since Gramps passed, he'd been so busy that he hadn't even entertained the idea anymore. Maybe his mother was correct on that account.

His thoughts went back to Julia. Maybe he'd see her tomorrow.

The thought was enough to put a spring in his step as he walked back to his workbench.

The dinner shift had been busier tonight than Julia had ever seen it. So many people had flocked to the canyon, and the dining room at the El Tovar was the very best place to eat and enjoy the scenery all at the same time.

Even if they doubled the size of the dining room, Julia bet they would fill it. Every day. Which made her feet hurt even worse just thinking about it.

But at least it had kept her busy and she hadn't thought about Florence Nichols' arrival until now. Since the day was pretty much over, she wanted to pretend she didn't have to think about it and deal with it tomorrow after she'd had some sleep.

Every inch of her body screamed of her exhaustion. Maybe the extra hiking she'd been doing was a bit too much. Especially after a day like today. She headed down the stairs to the basement and dreamed of a hot bath. She'd added her name to the list, but at this point wasn't sure she could even stay awake long enough to wait her turn.

The boisterous hum of voices greeted her in the hall. A large group of the girls were gathered together. What was going on?

"One of my favorites was when she tried to convince a new Harvey Girl that her bloodline was royal and her family was killed mysteriously so she had to flee." Laughter filled the air.

Heat filled Julia from head to toe.

The laughter was at her expense. She closed her eyes against the pain. Why oh why had she told so many lies about her parents' deaths? Deep shame and embarrassment flooded her stomach. What would all the girls think of her now?

"And the very next week, she told a group of traveling salesmen that her parents were killed in a stagecoach accident that was meant for her because she was a famous actress and she had to go into hiding."

Voices floated all around her. Girls whispering and giggling and shaking their heads.

The walls closed in. Blood pounded in her ears.

She had to get out of here. Now.

But there was no way through the crowd where no one would see her.

Ducking her head, she scooted over to the side of the hall.

"Oh look. There she is now! Julia, my dear!" Florence's singsong voice was as false as the tales about Julia's parents.

Tears stung her eyes, and she kept on walking. Which only made the whispers and laughter louder.

"Julia." Ruth rushed toward her from the basement exit.

"Go to my room right now." She gave her a little shove. "I will deal with this."

"Miss Nichols." The head waitress's voice rose above the din of the crowd. "That is *quite* enough."

The hush that followed Ruth's words was almost *too* quiet. Julia forced one foot in front of the other, but each step seemed heavier than the last. Trying to blink the tears away, she took a deep breath. It didn't help. Everything blurred in front of her.

"If I remember correctly, I gave you strict instructions to report to my room immediately." The tone in Ruth's voice brooked no argument.

"I'm sorry, Miss Anniston." Florence's voice at least sounded contrite. But what good would it do now?

"Your apology is not enough. We have a strict rule about gossip here, Miss Nichols. And I can't imagine this kind of behavior was allowed at your last Harvey assignment. I will make sure to speak with your previous supervisor again." A pin could drop in the hallway and everyone would be able to hear it. "I'm disappointed. In *all* of you. But, Miss Nichols, this is your first warning. You will be on the demerit shift."

Gasps were heard throughout the hall.

"Miss Anniston, please. I wasn't meaning any harm. Just having a little fun getting to know everyone." Florence used that smooth-as-silk tone she used to get out of pretty much anything. Most of the time it worked.

Something that Julia despised. She made it to Ruth's door and dared to turn back and look down the hall.

"This *wasn't* fun. And yes, it *was* harmful. I will not abide it. Make another mistake like this and you can seek employment elsewhere."

No one dared argue with the head waitress.

"Now, everyone to your rooms immediately. I don't want to hear another peep out of any of you for the rest of the night. Tomorrow morning, there will be roll call at five thirty, along with a room inspection, and everyone will be polishing silver and cleaning in between meals. The dining room better look spotless and sparkle. Miss Nichols, you will report to my room at five a.m. sharp."

The girls scattered, their eyes wide.

"Did you hear me?" Ruth had her hands on her hips.

Even from this distance, Julia could see that all the color had drained from Florence's face. "Yes, Miss Anniston."

The sharp tap of Ruth's heels was accompanied by several clicks of doors as the other girls did as they were told. Not a whisper or word.

The only noises she could hear now were Ruth's steps and her own breathing and the pounding of her heart. No one had ever done anything like that for her. Ever.

Ruth took her by the arm and led her farther into her room. "I'm sorry about that."

The shock of it wore off as the door closed, and Julia burst into tears. "It's not your fault." She gulped back the wave of emotion. "It's mine."

Her supervisor steered her toward the bed and made her sit down. "I take it that everything Florence said was true?"

"I didn't hear all of it. But for the most part . . . yes. She may have exaggerated a little, but it's no worse than what I've done in the past."

"I take it that you don't like to talk about what really happened to your parents?"

Julia shook her head.

"Sue told me as much. Would you care to tell *me* what really happened?"

Another shake. "No. It's too horrible to speak of."

"I see." Ruth plopped down on the bed beside her and wrapped an arm around her shoulders. "I can't say that I understand. But I'm proud of you for walking away like you did. That took a lot of courage."

Tears streamed down her cheeks and dripped onto her apron. "I'll never be able to show my face to any of them."

"Yes, you will. Remember, you are about to be the assistant head waitress. You are going to hold your head up high and do your job to the very best of your ability. If the girls show any disrespect, I will take care of it right away."

"But none of them will ever be my friend now. Not one of them." She sounded pathetic. Pitiful. Just like what everyone always expected of a child without parents. Tainted. Downtrodden. Alone. Unworthy. "Since my parents died, I've had to deal with the same thing all my life. I'll never measure up. I'm not good enough."

"Where did those words come from? Did someone say that to you?" Shock was written all over Ruth's face.

"Don't you see? I grew up an orphan, shuffled from one family to another. That's why I got really good at forming interesting answers to questions. Stories. Because then I was worth listening to. Worth being a friend to. Worth being . . . loved." Never had she let it all burst out of her like that. But there it was. Her heart laid bare. The tears wouldn't stop now.

Arms came around her and held her as she cried. "I'm so sorry, Julia. I had no idea."

Julia leaned her head against the other woman's shoulder.

"Perhaps I was too judgmental of you and your stories before. Not that I approve of lying . . ." A long sigh. "But maybe I was too harsh in my words. I didn't understand your past and all you've been through. The way Sue portrayed it, you loved to tell stories to entertain the other girls. She was simply concerned about your well-being, wanting you to have the deep relationships you deserve." A light groan emanated from her throat. "I'm sorry. I don't think I'm conveying this well."

Julia pulled away and sat up, swiping at her face with forceful strokes. "That's just it. Who says I'm deserving? This is my lot in life."

"Why would you say something like that? Life is full of ups and downs for everyone."

"But that doesn't mean that we all deserve love." Twisting a handkerchief in her hands, Julia looked down and shook her head. "Or friends. Maybe some of us truly are bad eggs."

"That's not true. At all. There are no bad eggs, just a bunch of people with sin natures. God loves every one of us the same."

"God? Why does everyone keep saying that God loves us? I don't get it." Julia came to her feet. "I haven't seen one lick of love since my parents died. So how can you say that God loves me? *Why* would He love me?"

What a failure she was.

Ruth climbed the steps from the basement and looked at the watch on her shirtwaist. She had an hour before the girls' curfew. Hopefully she'd scared them all straight and they would stay in their rooms as instructed. They'd seemed to have the fear of God in them as they scurried away after the scolding.

But now she had to figure out what to do about Florence.

There were several of the new hires who were prone to gossip and didn't have the best moral compasses. Hadn't been too big of a problem *yet*, but now it seemed the new girl could be their ringleader. Something that needed to be taken care of immediately or it could be disastrous.

She wiped her hands on her apron. She still hadn't changed out of her uniform, but she needed some fresh air. After sending Julia back to her room without any clear answers, Ruth had some serious soul-searching to do.

The canyon was always a great place to think and reflect. To put things into perspective. Many times she came out here to pray for the charges under her, or, if she needed to make a big decision, she'd simply sit and listen. But tonight, she felt completely inept. Empty. Needing a refueling.

As she took brisk steps to the rim, she poured her heart out to God. *I'm so sorry I failed You. But I didn't know what to say. Help me, Lord. Give me the words I need for Julia. She needs You, but she's so hurt.*

There was nothing left to say. He knew what was in her heart. Understood her struggle. How could she show her new friend that He was there for her? Especially when she had no comparison of love from an earthly father.

Sitting on her favorite bench, she stretched out her legs and crossed her ankles in front of her. Her shoulders ached. Back ached. She felt like she carried a fifty-pound pack.

Footsteps sounded to her right. Probably some of the guests heading back to their rooms for the night. If she was quiet, perhaps they wouldn't notice her and would walk on by.

Tilting her head up, she peered into the full moon that glowed down onto the canyon. It took a few minutes for her eyes to adjust, but it was always worth it to see the expanse of stars and the depths of the canyon.

"Miss Anniston." The familiar voice of the assistant chef caused her to smile. "What a pleasure to see you this evening." Over the years, they'd worked together a great deal and developed an easy camaraderie.

"Mr. Henderson." She turned toward him. He was a man of strong faith. Maybe she could bend his ear. "Would you care to join me?"

"I would love to." He lowered himself to the other end of the bench, removed his hat, and held it between his hands as he leaned over his knees. "You looked deep in thought as I approached."

"I was." Best to just get it out. "I find myself in quite a quandary."

"Perhaps I can help."

"I was hoping you'd say that." Shifting on the bench, she turned to face him. "It's a spiritual question."

His head tilted. "Can't say that I'll have the answer but go ahead."

"One of my girls is an orphan. She can't fathom why God would love her and hasn't seen His love—or *any* love, for that matter." As she poured out the story, all the emotions came with it. Failure on her part. Extreme compassion. And a desperate desire to point her charge to the Comforter.

Several minutes passed as it all gushed out. "I had no answers to her hardest questions. Didn't want to just spout a bunch of platitudes that would be meaningless to her. I feel horrible."

Then she was empty. Of words. Of everything.

Frank reached over and patted her hand. "We all have those times when we are unsure of what to say. And this is a particularly difficult situation."

This man's friendship to her had helped her grow in her faith over the years they'd known each other. And his advice was always spot-on. "Do you have any brilliant words of wisdom to share with me? Maybe one of your theological tomes has some guidance?"

"A few verses come to mind." He looked back out to the canyon. "But I'd like to pray over this for a while, if that's all right?"

"Of course. I appreciate you listening."

His lips lifted into a nice smile. Over the winter he'd grown a mustache and beard. It had taken some getting used to, but she liked it. The short-trimmed coppery hair on his face made him look more like an esteemed university professor than the chef that he was. "Thanks for confiding in me. I know your trust is hard-earned."

They shared a glance, and Ruth took a deep breath. "There are days I wonder why God put me in this position, because I don't have all the answers and, frankly, it's hard. But I'm grateful he put friends in my life to help. I owe you a big thank-you."

He dipped his chin. "You're welcome. Shall I come find you tomorrow evening?"

"That would be lovely." She glanced down at her timepiece. "I need to get back inside." She stood, and he stood with her. With a new spring in her step, she headed back to her room. At least she wasn't carrying the burden alone. *Thank You, God, for sending Frank.*

Now if she could just keep Florence and the other girls in line, she might be able to keep her head above water.

She'd need to spend more time on her knees in the coming days. Because her gut told her there was a storm brewing. This was only the beginning.

8

The next morning, hours before dawn, Julia dressed in her hiking outfit and grabbed a lantern. Tessa couldn't go with her today, and that was probably a good thing, because Julia was in a foul mood and would be terrible company. With very little sleep and the discomfort of knowing that Florence was here—a reality she couldn't change—she had to face facts. The woman from her past could make things very difficult for her.

But in all honesty, it was her own fault.

Ignoring the rule of not venturing out on her own, she decided it wouldn't really matter. Who would miss her? Did it even matter if she got dismissed? Florence was sure to ruin her life here anyway.

But a niggle of guilt made her slip a note under Ruth's door, simply stating that she needed some time to herself since it was her day off. Then she snagged several rolls from the kitchen and a few slices of ham and an apple. That should get her through.

The pouch with her food was crisscrossed over her body from her right shoulder while her canteen was slung over the left. Her steps thudded in the still of the wee morning hour as she fumed her way west across the rim.

Ruth was kind. And she tried. But after spouting words from the Bible for over an hour—words that didn't make any sense to Julia with all the churchy speak—even Ruth gave up. Probably not for good. The woman definitely believed what she said. Julia wished she could too. But they were both tired. Emotional. And they hadn't gotten anywhere.

Julia had too many questions that her supervisor hadn't been able to answer. Her questions were hard. Blunt. Rough around the edges.

Things that sweet and innocent Ruth probably never had to deal with before.

At least her supervisor said she finally understood why Julia was an expert at making up stories. At least they'd come that far.

Ruth might've responded differently if she knew what actually happened to her parents, but if she'd told her supervisor the whole truth last night, all that would have been accomplished was more pity. Which she didn't need. What she longed for was acceptance. Unconditional love.

That wouldn't happen if everyone knew the truth. If people knew the truth about her parents, then she wouldn't just be an orphan. She'd be a pariah.

But wasn't she already?

Stomping her way down the path to the Bright Angel Trail, she muttered her grievances. Julia kicked at a rock and then fisted her hands. Why wasn't she good enough?

The rock disappeared into the dark of the early morning. Like it was eaten up by a silent monster.

The thought made her shiver. This wasn't wise. Being out

here alone and in the dark. Another chill raced up her spine, and she pulled her sweater tighter around her middle.

Deep breaths. She couldn't go back now.

Each step felt uneven and unnerving. Why hadn't she been paying attention? Her toe hit something, and before she could correct herself, she fell forward, palms and knees hitting the ground in agonizing thuds. The lantern shattered a few feet away.

"Ouch." The word slipped out on a groan.

Lying facedown, she stayed where she was and assessed the situation. Though she might be a bit sore, it didn't feel like anything was broken. At least not at this point. Tiny pebbles dug into her hands. Her knees stung from the impact, but she could move all her limbs. That was good.

With another moan, she pushed herself up to sitting and crawled over to a boulder. Looked like a decent enough place to sit for a bit. Get her bearings. And wait for more light.

Which she should have done from the beginning. But her stubborn willfulness got in the way. Again.

At this point, she had two choices. Go back to her room and spend the rest of her day off wallowing. Or wait for the sun to rise and go exploring again. She would be by herself, but she'd have something to get her mind off the fact that Florence had told everyone what a liar she was.

Exploring it is.

Treasure or no treasure, she could at least get some fresh air and keep her imagination occupied. Who cared if she made up fantastical stories in her own head? She wasn't hurting anyone with them. Besides, after last night's escapade with Florence, none of the girls would want to spend time with her anyway.

No matter what Ruth said.

As the first streaks of light rose over the eastern horizon, Julia picked at a piece of scraggly grass that was doing its best to grow between two rocks. That was how she felt. Crushed between forces, pushing with all she was worth just to get a glimpse of the sun.

Why was life easy for some and so hard for others? Why couldn't she have been born to some wealthy socialite family that spent their years vacationing in Europe, on African safaris, or here at the Grand Canyon?

As soon as she thought it, she cringed. Her parents weren't perfect. In fact, they really weren't the best people. But at least they'd loved her. She had loads of fun memories from when she was a little girl. Granted, none of them involved fancy toys or dolls, but she had been loved.

For eight short years, she'd been loved.

If she ever had a family, she'd want to make sure that her husband and children knew that she loved them with all her heart. Never would a day go by without that.

Because she knew—all too well—how it felt to *not* be loved.

The sky began to lighten and the canyon awoke. The sounds around her pushed the dread of the dark away, and Julia got back to her feet. She'd definitely be sore tomorrow from her little tumble, but at least everything was in working order.

When she reached the trailhead beside the Kolb brothers' studio, she nodded at Emery and paid the toll to hike the trail.

"Awful early to be out hiking alone." He chewed on a toothpick.

"I love early mornings." She pasted on a smile.

"Want your picture taken?" He leaned up against the building and propped his foot on the wall behind him.

"No, thank you. Maybe another time?"

"Your choice." He tipped his hat at her. "Have a good hike."

Julia picked up her pace and headed down the trail. The brothers fascinated her. With their home built on the very edge of the canyon, they had a reputation for being daredevils. Taking great risks to get just the right shots, they pulled quite a few stunts. Many of the other Harvey Girls had even talked about assisting the brothers by posing and helping to stage some of their outlandish photographs. The display of pictures in the photography studio brought many oohs, aahs, and laughs for the creativity. While Julia wouldn't want to take the same risks that the brothers did, she had to respect their passion for their work. How many times did they run up and down the trail every day just to develop the pictures in time for the guests? And it wasn't an easy trail. Not by *any* stretch of the imagination.

The trail was quiet except for her footsteps along the well-worn dirt path and a few insects and birds that buzzed and hummed in a little chorus together.

The scent of the canyon always intrigued her. A little dry and earthy, woody, smoky, dusty, with a metallic hint here and there. She imagined there wasn't another place on the planet that smelled like this.

With short, quick strides, she made her way down into the canyon. It was pretty easy on the way down. Heading back up was a different story, especially after a long day of exploring. But she would appreciate the burning in her legs later. It made her feel alive, even through her exhaustion. With an eye toward a long, hot bath and a nice warm bed. Which was about all she had to look forward to from now on.

"Oh, stop." Her scolding to herself echoed down the path

in front of her. "No one likes a negative attitude." She blew a few strands of hair off her forehead. It didn't matter what stories Florence repeated. Ruth said she would put a stop to it, and Julia would just have to trust that would happen. Besides, she might gain more respect from the other girls if she simply let it slide off her. Like water off a duck's back.

That would be hard, but she could do it. Ruth made it sound like the promotion was permanent last night. Julia hoped it was true. She would hold her head up high and be the very best assistant head waitress she could be. If she had to spend all of her time off by herself, then so be it. Even though she'd always hated being alone, maybe now was the time to get over that as well. This was her lot in life.

Easier said than done.

A lizard skittered its way across her path, and she put a hand to her chest. Good thing it wasn't a snake. She hated snakes.

As she made her way down the path, the layers of the gray limestone wall shooting up to the rim changed to a richer red color. The color of the dirt below her feet changed to red. There was also more green in the moss and grasses that seemed to thrive here. The trail had a lot of switchbacks as it made its way down. Every one offering a different view.

Since she was by herself with no one to talk to, she might as well take her time and explore whatever she wanted. Tessa liked to stick to the trail as much as possible since that made her feel safer, but Julia felt adventurous and a little reckless.

After several more switchbacks, she noticed an almost imperceptible trail that took a steep trek to the right. Assessing the situation, Julia ventured out a few steps and peeked around the red wall. Was there anything to explore over there, or was it just a trail the wildlife took?

While the first few yards would be a bit tricky, after that it looked interesting. She squinted and took a deep breath before carefully taking one step at a time. Wait. Somehow she needed to mark her path so she could find her way back to the main trail. But how? It was too dangerous to use any of the food she had in her pouch. First, any animal could find it as a snack and her trail would be gone. Second, she needed the food for her own fuel for the day. What if she used moss or grass? Would the wind blow it away?

Rocks? She could probably make a simple design out of rocks that would help her to see the way back, as long as no critter messed them up along the way. That was the best idea.

Crouching down along the narrow ledge she stood on, she made a simple *X* out of five rocks. As the ledge widened a bit, she breathed a little easier and kept leaving herself *X*s here and there. About a half hour later, the side of the canyon opened up into multiple paths. This looked to be where the local wildlife converged. Narrow trails went in several directions. Perhaps leading to water? Or their dens or nests? Maybe she should have paid a bit more attention in school when it came to studying animals, their habitats, and the like. As much as she didn't want to run into any four-legged creature, she did hope to find something interesting to explore.

Winding her way along the red wall of rock, she gasped. There. What was that? She crept closer.

A cave! A little thrill raced through her. It would take some getting to, but the hole in the side of the canyon wall looked inviting. Just the place to sit and eat a snack.

When she reached it, she saw that the entry was a few feet above where she stood. So, she placed her hands on the edge of the opening and jumped, using her arms to lift her up to the ledge. It worked! She wriggled her way to a kneeling position at the mouth of the cave and looked into the space. Blast. The cave was only a few feet deep.

Oh well. With a sigh, she turned herself around and sat at the edge of the opening, allowing her legs to dangle.

She couldn't beat the view, though. She opened the pouch and dug into some food. Life wasn't really all that bad. Yes, Florence was now at the El Tovar and the girls had laughed at Julia's expense. But she had a really good job. A new promotion. And a beautiful place to work. So what if she didn't have friends or family?

At least Ruth seemed to want to be her friend. Could that be enough?

It wouldn't be so bad to stay here at El Tovar and work for another twenty years or so. Maybe she could ask the Kolb brothers to teach her how to do photography. Or she could take up painting. Or some other kind of art or hobby. Something to help her pass the time and maybe even make a little money. Women were beginning to do all kinds of adventurous things nowadays. Why couldn't she?

She liked hiking, after all. Wonder what she could do with that? Of course, deep down, she hoped to find the treasure. In her wildest imagination, she could see herself as a treasure hunter. The first woman to become famous for finding the lost treasures of the centuries.

The fresh air filled her lungs as she took a long, deep breath. The only thing she'd practiced over the years was storytelling. Perhaps it was time to change things up.

She scooted herself off the ledge and found her footing back on the narrow path. Placing her hands on her hips, she looked off to her right. What if there was another cave not too far? It was still plenty early in the day. Lots of hours of daylight left. As long as she started the trek back up by two or three in the afternoon, she should make it just fine. She could explore at least one more if she could find another.

With a bounce in her step and the sun beaming overhead, she kept her steps close to the sheer rock wall next to her and left herself another X. That should also ensure she could get back to the Bright Angel Trail without too much trouble.

The screech of a bird overhead drew her gaze upward. A bald eagle! She'd never seen one in person before. It swooped down toward her, and she crouched low. It wasn't coming after her, was it? Yikes! But she couldn't tear her eyes away.

Majestic, with a wingspan that looked to be more than six feet, it floated closer and closer until it pumped its wings a few times about ten feet from her head and then landed on a large boulder above her.

She dared to make eye contact with it as the large bird scanned its surroundings. Gracious, the beast must be three feet in height. Massive! Now that her heart had picked a faster pace, she decided it was time to move away from the creature and put some distance between them. The thought of those massive claws clutching her shoulder produced a shiver. Stepping a bit quicker, she moved along the ledge and rounded the corner of another rocky jut, which opened up another incredible vista.

"Wow." The whispered word left her lips as awe filled her insides. The grandeur of this place was beyond anything she could have ever imagined. She'd heard one of the guests say that the river carved the canyon, while another man argued with him and said it was the biblical flood that carved it. It didn't even seem possible that water could make this miraculous place.

As her eyes took in all the glorious cracks and crevices, rocks and ridgelines, she gasped. There! Another cave. Just ahead.

She headed for it and made sure to make lots of noise along the way, hoping to alert any creature of her approach so that it would run away and hide so *she* wouldn't have to. When she reached the mouth of the cave, she had to duck. It was a mere four feet at the tallest point but seemed to go a bit deeper than the first one. Julia looked around the opening. Didn't appear to be anything watching her. No nest seemed to be inside. In fact, the floor of the cavern didn't look like it had been disturbed in a long time. The red dirt was littered with rocks but appeared smoothed by the wind.

No footprint of man, bird, or beast.

With a deep breath for courage, she ventured in. What she wouldn't give for that lantern now. The floor of the cave was covered in inches of dirt, and her boots slid a bit in the sandy surface. How interesting. Venturing forward, she kept one hand on the wall to steady her as she crouched her way forward.

It was too dark.

She snapped her fingers. She'd packed a couple of candles! She dug into her pack and pulled out a candle and a small box of matches. She'd brought two with her. Better be careful of the time. She lit the first candle and stepped deeper into the cave. Pretty soon, she was down on her hands and knees because the space kept getting smaller. But something in her told her to keep going.

After several minutes of crawling awkwardly while trying to hold the candle up, she realized she'd reached a dead end. Well . . . stuff and nonsense. She'd hoped to find something interesting.

As she shimmied herself around in the tight space, a weird-shaped rock in the corner caught her eye. She turned back to it and inched closer. With the rock covered in what looked like spider webs, she didn't want to touch it but reached forward with the candle anyway.

That wasn't a rock!

Wiping at it with her other hand, she bit her lip.

No. It couldn't be. She wiped at it some more.

It was!

What was the name? Oh, she'd read about them. Good heaven, why couldn't she remember what it was called. Wait—a morion! That was it! The curved metal helmet had a flat brim with a crest from the back to front. The drawing in the history book from the library even portrayed Coronado wearing a helmet like this.

Her hand shook as she pulled it toward her and turned it right-side up.

Several things tumbled out, and she dropped the helmet and scooted back with a jump, hoping it wasn't anything alive. Like spiders.

Ick. A shiver raced up her spine.

But when nothing moved, she inched forward again. Five small pouches lay in the dirt. And a thick scroll tied with a strip of leather.

She stuck the candle in the dirt to keep it upright so she could use both hands and lifted the scroll. It was thick. Much thicker than any paper of today. Julia worked to unroll the scroll. The leather was too old. It crumbled and fell away. The edges of the scroll were ragged. Like it was an afterthought to use this material as a place to record something of import.

At first, she couldn't see anything, so she leaned closer to it and then had to get closer to the dim light of the candle.

At the bottom were swirls and loops that might be letters? Someone's signature? Whatever they were, they were burned or somehow etched into the thick rawhide-like material.

In the center were two straight lines. What on earth did that mean?

She tilted the scroll even closer, being careful of the flame. As she moved it from side to side, two perpendicular lines attached to the other two lines appeared.

The Roman numeral for two!

Her stomach did a little flip.

The helmet. The old scroll.

She sucked in a breath and bit her lip between her teeth as she set the scroll down and reached for one of the pouches.

Her fingers fumbled over themselves as she worked the drawstring open.

Dumping the contents into her palm, she swallowed and widened her eyes.

Stones of various sizes and colors caught the light.

Several seconds passed. What should she do now?

Bobby walked out to survey Roger's progress and glared at him. "How hard can it be to build a dumb cage for a trap?" This whole idea to catch a mountain lion and use it to scare the tourists was great, but not if they couldn't pull it together.

"I don't know." The guy looked far too slicked up to be working on a trap.

After all these years, why the need to dress better? Was it practice for once they found the treasure? Or was something else going on?

"Seems it needs to be mighty strong to hold the big cat once we've got it in there. And I don't wanna be on the receivin' end of its wrath when we let 'em loose again."

Good point. But they could deal with that later. "When we move the cage to the lookout point over the trail, we'll leave some wounded animal below to attract it. Then we'll rig up a rope to open the door so that we can be at a safe distance."

"Yeah. I was thinking that too."

Of *course* he was. "Why are you dressed like that? Planning on goin' somewhere?" The fool was more worried about mussin' his suit than the job at hand.

Roger's chin lifted and his eyes darted away. "I got a card game to attend to."

"Better not be using any of *my* money. Did I give you permission to do that?"

"I got my own money. I don't need your permission for everything, ya know." Roger's shoulders squared as his chest lifted. "Besides, once we're done with all this, you said we were *done*. You and me. For good."

The fella better not be gettin' all belligerent and defiant. "But we're not done *yet*, are we?" With a glare that could hopefully sear the threat into the worthless fool, Bobby wasn't about to let Roger think he could take the reins of his own life now.

"Fine." Roger stomped back over to the flimsy-looking cage and tinkered with the door again. "I'll have to buy some better supplies in town. And we're gonna have to put something in there for bait. Should I kill a rabbit or somethin'?"

"Nope. Only a live animal will work. Them mountain lions want to kill their prey." Seeing the tall man bent over the cage with no intention of moving, Bobby grabbed for the rope and shotgun. "You get that trap in working order right away, ya hear me? I'll go get us some bait."

Maybe by this time tomorrow they'd be able to put the first part of their plan into action. If Roger didn't get himself killed in the process. Not that him being gone was such a bad thing . . .

Up the trail, a skittering of rocks made Bobby stop. What was that?

Footsteps.

Someone else was out here.

Probably one of them fool girls. A flash of red hair darted into view.

Only one of 'em. Hm. Wouldn't be too hard to get rid of one. There'd be no witnesses. The animals would eat the carcass before anyone could find 'em.

With the shotgun raised, Bobby aimed at the girl's back.

The blast echoed off the canyon walls.

9

With a rawhide mallet in one hand, Chris positioned a band of silver around the mandrel with his other. "See the groove there?" He pointed and leaned back so Chuma and the others could squeeze in and get a look. "I'm lining it up here so I know this is the size ring I am making. Now I'm going to use this mallet to smooth out the shape. I'm using the rawhide mallet this time and not the chasing hammer that I just demonstrated because I want the finish to be smooth without any markings."

He tried to keep his words as simple as possible and not filled with the terminology that usually filled his brain. Most people didn't understand half of what he said anyway when he went into jeweler mode. Add to that the Hopi people spoke English as a second language. It impressed him how they picked it up so quickly.

So far they'd learned and mastered several techniques today. Which was incredible. They really could help him produce multiples in quick succession. If he did the most intricate parts that had taken him years to perfect, they could handle some of the other tasks. Hope sprang up in him.

There was a light at the end of his tunnel, and it was getting brighter by the minute.

The day passed in long hours of teaching and training. By the time four in the afternoon rolled around, they'd finished five simple cuff bracelets inlaid with turquoise, eight rings, and three sets of earrings. They were all working on the last and most difficult project—three necklaces with turquoise and orange calcite gemstones. The native women had oohed and aahed over his choice of colors, which made him quite proud. Gramps had taught him a lot over the years, but he'd praised Chris for his natural ability at putting color combinations and stones together in an appealing way.

God was the one who deserved all the glory. His creation was filled with beautiful colors that inspired Chris. He never wanted to take any of it for granted.

As he sat at a table using his pinching pliers, he pushed a stone into position in its setting. He leaned back and turned the necklace this way and that. Perfect.

"Mr. Miller." One of the older women approached. What was her name? Humeatah, maybe? It was hard to keep track of all the new names. "Is this correct?" She held up the end of the necklace so he could inspect the clasp.

Not a flaw to be found. Deep respect filled him. "It is. Thank you . . . Humeatah, is it?"

"Very good." She wagged a bent finger in his face. "You learn quick."

"Not as quick as you do. I'm afraid you put me to shame." He sent her a smile.

Her cackle of laughter was accompanied by a wink. "When you reach as many winters as I have, you learn fast." She set the necklace down and reached for another to work on. "Look at Chuma. It's my goal to keep up with her." Her wrinkled grin made her eyes almost disappear.

He could learn a lot from these people. They didn't waste time. Nor did they work themselves to the bone. They took time for one another and for family. Spent time each day listening to their elders and taking care of them. Remarkable.

If only he could learn that same balance.

He bent over his makeshift workstation again and set another stone. Tiny moccasin-encased feet appeared in his peripheral vision. He lifted his head and stared at the little one.

"Hi." She waved. Big brown eyes studied him.

"Hi."

"Pretty." Her chubby little hand patted the necklace in his hand and then went back to her face as she stuck a thumb in her mouth.

His heart did a little swell as he watched her skip away. In his line of work, he didn't see a lot of children. But oh, how they blessed his heart. He glanced around the room and watched the people around him. Many families lived and worked together here.

A wave of loneliness hit him. At thirty years old, he'd always wanted a family, but his introverted ways hadn't exactly helped him meet anyone. Gramps had teased him on more than one occasion, but at least he hadn't hounded him about getting married like his mother did. Chris had the frame of mind that if God had someone for him, He'd have to drop her in his lap. Maybe not literally, but at least a clear sign would be necessary.

A slight tap on his left shoulder brought his gaze to the other side. "Sunki." He couldn't help but smile at the precocious and inquisitive girl. "How are you today?"

Her hands were clasped behind her back as she lifted her chin and tilted her head to the right. "I like watching you make jewelry. But my mother told me not to touch."

Ah . . . so that was why her hands were behind her back. Her mother was one of his best students. She eyed them as she continued to work.

"Would you like to sit beside me and get a closer look?"

Her head bobbed up and down. She sat on the floor.

"That won't do. You'll be too low." He stood and looked around him. A three-legged stool about three feet in height sat in the corner. He fetched it and brought it over to Sunki. "Here." He lifted the girl onto the high stool, keeping his urge to laugh in check as the young girl kept her hands clasped behind her. If only everyone could be so obedient. "Can you see?"

Her eyes lit up as her smile stretched almost to her ears. "Yes."

He tapped her nose. "Good. Now, let's get back to setting these stones, shall we?"

Another vigorous nod.

With the supervision of his small assistant, Chris set three more stones in the jewelry before lifting his head to stretch his neck. Out of the corner of his eye, a flash of auburn hair caught his attention. Miss Schultz.

Her eyes scanned the room and then landed on him. Focused. Serious. She made a beeline for him.

He couldn't help but watch. Her dark split skirt was covered in a layer of reddish dirt. Along with the smudges on her face and neck, she looked as if she'd been digging. What had she been up to?

"Mr. Miller." Her voice was a bit breathless.

He stood. "How may I help you?"

She stepped closer. "Might I have a few moments of your time this evening?"

"Certainly." He checked his pocket watch. "Perhaps during dinner if you're not working?"

She bit her lip.

Oh dear. She didn't think he was implying something intimate . . . did she?

"Could we perhaps meet privately before then?"

That made his eyebrows shoot up. Privately?

"Maybe a brief walk outside when you are finished here? I don't wish to keep you from your plans this evening." Whatever she needed to speak with him about, she looked almost frantic.

"Of course. I'll be done in a half hour—"

"I'll be back then." And with that, she scurried out the door.

What on earth?

Chris blinked several times. The pretty red-haired waitress baffled him.

Looking down, he noticed Sunki watching him. She shrugged her shoulders. "Will you use one of the red ones now?"

"I forgot you told me that you liked red."

"It is my favorite." The soft smile she sent him as she pointed to one of the stones in front of him tugged at his heart. Then she yanked her hand back and snuck a glance at her mother.

He leaned a bit closer to her. "I like red too."

And not just in stones or jewelry.

Julia's nerves had been rattled ever since that gunshot ricocheted above her head. Had she not tripped, she might have been shot! The thought had made her heart race as she'd run back toward the Bright Angel Trail, not even realizing that she'd dropped the helmet and scroll until she reached the well-worn path. When another shot rang out, she decided whoever was hunting must not have seen her, especially since she wasn't on the normal hiking trail, and she didn't want to take the risk of being mistaken for whatever animal they wanted to kill. But oh, what she wouldn't give to be able to show Mr. Miller the scroll and morion right now. Her story wouldn't sound quite so outlandish! Would he even believe her?

She needed to tell someone. Make sure she was doing the right thing. Mrs. Watkins hadn't been anywhere to be found. And Ruth was in the middle of the dinner rush. But Emma Grace was the one who told her the legend. She and her husband spoke very highly of Mr. Miller. In fact, Mr. Watkins had raved about his integrity and honesty and how he wished there were more men like him.

That was enough for her. At this point, her choices were very limited. The desperate need to trust someone rushed through her middle. Someone who knew what they were doing because she was in over her head.

Pacing the rim just outside the Hopi House, Julia smoothed the front of her clean skirt and shirtwaist. It had taken her all of three minutes to get changed, then another ten to figure out where to hide the rest of what she'd found. She didn't want to risk carrying all of it around with her, so tucked inside the pocket of her skirt was only one of the pouches.

Twenty steps one way and then twenty steps the other. Twelve times she'd gone back and forth. Still no sign of him. Surely it had been thirty minutes already?

The only option she had was to wait.

And pace.

So, she started another count and took long strides. Her legs ached from the hike today, but she'd made sure to sign up for the tub tonight. A long, hot soak should help. *After* she figured out what to do. Until then, she wouldn't be able to relax anyway.

The thing that worried her the most was Elizabeth. Her roommate had been kind to her, but they really didn't speak much. They rarely even saw each other. Was there a chance she would go snooping around in Julia's things? What if she did? Especially after what Florence said yesterday. Her roommate may not trust her.

Were the rest of the pouches hidden enough?

The urge to run back to her room made her stop in her tracks. Elizabeth hadn't spoken to her when Julia had come into their room last night. And she'd been in the middle of the group of girls listening to the newcomer's words. Laughing along with the rest of them.

Maybe she should go back and get the other pouches. At this point, she wasn't sure if she could trust any of the women other than Ruth. And Tessa.

With a quick turn on her heel, she headed back toward the hotel.

"Miss Schultz?" Mr. Miller's words stopped her in her tracks. He jogged over to her. "My apologies, I hope I didn't keep you waiting." He looked at his pocket watch.

"No." She put a hand to her forehead. "I thought I had forgotten something." Hopefully she was overreacting. Her imagination was getting the best of her.

His smile calmed her. "Would you care to take a walk?"

"Yes, please." She stepped closer to him and scanned the

area. Lots of people milled about. "Perhaps this way?" She pointed to the east. "Thank you for seeing me, Mr. Miller."

"Of course. And please call me Chris."

"I'm Julia."

"Lead the way, Julia. I've asked Chuma to keep an eye on my things in the Hopi House for now." He tucked his hands into his pockets.

"Chuma?" Her heart pumped. Good heavens, she needed to calm down. Otherwise she'd never get out the story.

"You haven't met her yet? Oh, she's delightful. I believe Mrs. Watkins knows her quite well."

"Oh . . . good." She quickened her pace as they passed several guests from the hotel.

The poor man jogged again to catch up to her.

"Sorry. I walk fast when I'm nervous." Her own breaths were coming in gasps. Her corset pinched. But she kept plowing ahead. After several minutes of hightailing it as fast as she could, she didn't see anyone else around them.

She came to an abrupt stop and poor Mr. Miller ran directly into the back of her. He grabbed ahold of her arms, probably to try to keep her from toppling over.

"My apologies." He took a deep breath.

She forced herself to do the same and turned around with a nervous laugh. "It's my fault. No harm done." She looked over her shoulder and then over his.

"Are you worried someone else might overhear us? Because I haven't seen anyone else for a bit." He craned his neck in different directions as well. His brow furrowed, and he crossed his arms over his chest. "I believe we are quite alone, Julia."

She put a hand to her stomach. Steadied her breath. "I need your help."

His eyebrows shot up almost to his hairline. "My help?"

"Yes." She glanced over her shoulder one more time and then around his. "I found something today. You're the only one I know who can help me."

"Now I'm really intrigued. Normally I'm not the man most women come to for help."

Reaching into her pocket, she grabbed onto the pouch. "You have to promise me that you won't tell anyone what I'm about to tell you."

"As long as it doesn't break the law in any way or sin against God, I promise."

She couldn't think of how it could do either. "I went hiking today and explored a couple of caves. In one of them I found these." She pulled out the pouch and dumped the contents into her hand.

Twenty large gemstones filled her cupped palm.

"Oh my." He stepped closer and stared. "May I?" He reached forward.

She gave him a nod.

In the still of the evening, he examined each one for several moments. "These are exquisite."

"I thought so too but I don't know anything about gems. You're telling me they're real?"

His nod was emphatic. "Yes, they are very real. But I am quite perplexed. You say you found them in a cave?"

"Inside a morion." She swallowed.

A deep *V* appeared in his brow. "I'm afraid I don't know what that is."

"It's a metal helmet. Worn by the Spanish. Several hundred years ago."

From the look on his face, she had to assume that he didn't believe her. But for once, she wasn't telling a made-up tale. This was real. How could she convince him?

"Emma Grace—Mrs. Watkins—told me about a legend of buried treasure from the 1500s." As the story spilled out of the expedition party finding the canyon in the search for Cibola, excitement built inside her. Hopefully she was getting the details as accurate as possible. She couldn't gauge what he thought of her at the moment, but she continued on, hoping she could convince him it was all true. She had the proof, didn't she?

He nodded and put a hand on his chin. "That's fascinating. . . . I know that the Spanish expedition did come here. But they were looking for treasure? Why would they *leave* treasure?"

She bit her lip. "Legend has it that the two brothers were convinced that something as glorious as the Grand Canyon must actually hold a secret to finding Cibola. They returned to Coronado's expedition keeping their secret to themselves and traveled with him for a couple of months and then decided to head out on their own. They paid several of the other men to accompany them and spent six months looking for the canyon again. By this time, winter was upon them. Some sickness hit their camp just after finding the canyon, and everyone except the two brothers and their guide died.

"The guide convinced them they weren't going to find the cities of gold in the winter and that he was going home. Alone and without help, the brothers decided to listen to him but made him promise that when they returned in the spring he would help them. They paid him in jewels and said there was more for him if he would wait for them. The brothers hid the rest of the treasure they brought with them, knowing that they needed to lighten their loads so they could make it back home to Mexico. With only a horse for each of them and some meager food supplies, they started the long trek south. Never to be heard from again. The guide waited for them at the appointed place the following spring. After a month, he went looking for the treasure himself and didn't find it. On his deathbed, he told his son. And the legend has been told ever since."

Chris pointed to the stones. "These *are* quite old, I can attest to that by the cuts. But that's a story that is hard to even fathom."

"Legends usually are." She hated that she sounded defensive. But she needed him to believe her.

"It doesn't bother you that it seems far-fetched?"

She studied his eyes. They weren't mocking her or belittling her. In fact, they seemed genuine. Sincere. As if he wanted to believe her and was trying to wrap his mind around all he'd just seen and heard. "It *is* far-fetched. I'll give you that. But I've always loved a good story. And these stones right here are enough to convince me. Like I said, I found them in a cave, inside a morion, and there was an old scroll with the Roman numeral two on it. Even if the legend isn't the full story—I'm sure it's changed over the generations—we know that there's some bit of truth in it, otherwise I wouldn't have found what I did. Would it help for you to see the morion?" She'd drag him down to where she'd dropped it right now if she had to.

"I would love to see it. Do you have it with you?"

"Well, no. I dropped the helmet and the scroll on my way back."

His eyebrows raised at that. Great . . . he'd never believe her now.

She held up a hand. "Please. It's true. There must have been some hunters down there because I heard a couple of gunshots. I'm a bit skittish, so I raced to get back on the trail and didn't realize I'd dropped them." Reaching out, she touched his arm. "You believe me, don't you? I need your expertise here."

A smile stretched across his face. "You don't need to try and convince me. I believe you."

She released a breath and let her shoulders relax. "You do?"

"Yes." He reached for the pouch in her hand and gently tugged on it. After replacing the stones, he pulled the drawstring tight and set it back in her hand, closing her fingers over it. "You need to put these someplace safe. Luckily, it's just one small pouch of jewels. That will be pretty easy to keep secret."

"Actually . . . there was more than just one pouch inside the helmet."

His jaw dropped this time. "How many more?"

"There were five bags total."

Chris examined her for several seconds and blinked several times. "Wow. They would be worth a great deal of money."

Biting her lip again, she wanted to jump up and down. It sounded like he was getting excited about it. Exactly what she'd hoped for.

"That leads me to my next question. Do you think I'll be able to keep it? The treasure? I mean, there's all kinds of people panning for gold down at the river, and Mr. Owens was just talking the other day about how the president had named this area a national game preserve and protected land. I mean, I'm the one who found it. . . ." The last part just sounded like she was a whiny child. Good grief, she was a grown woman who had legitimately found that treasure. She lifted her chin a notch.

"I know there was a big ruckus last year about the president's Antiquities Act, but I have no idea what it means. I wouldn't get my hopes up if I were you, but I could do some digging around to find out what the laws are."

"Would you?" She clasped her hands under her chin. "I wouldn't even know where to begin."

"Of course. When I get back to Williams, I'll check into it and let you know what I find out." He watched her for several seconds. "If you *do* get to keep them, what do you plan to do with the jewels?"

The question was one she'd tossed around the last couple of hours. "Well . . . first, I'd like to donate a few of the stones to be displayed in the Hopi House here. The Harvey company has been very good to me over the years, and I think a nice display here with the legend and story of how I found them would be a big attraction for the visitors."

"That's a great idea. And very generous of you." His eyes crinkled at the edges when he smiled.

It might be generous, but she had other reasons. Ones that involved a past she didn't wish anyone to know about—especially a new acquaintance who looked at her with respect in his eyes.

Respect. Oh, how she longed to have the respect of her peers. She could redeem her name. Something she wouldn't want to admit out loud, but it was true nonetheless. "After that, I was wondering if you would be willing to help me sell them or use them in jewelry in some way? This is all out of my realm of knowledge as a waitress."

"I'm honored that you would ask me." He paused and clasped his hands behind his back and paced a few steps. "I've never worked with stones that old. I'd have to recut them all to have them work in modern settings."

"Is that a lot of work?"

"It's part of what I do, and yes, it can be time consuming, but the history behind the gems makes them even more fascinating." He stopped pacing. "You know, I think it's something that would entice the clientele here. They are exactly who we'd want to sell to."

"You mean rich people." She quirked an eyebrow at him.

He grimaced. "You aren't wrong, Julia. Not that I would want to say that out loud, but it's more than that. People come here to see the canyon. Doesn't it make sense that they would get caught up in the legend as well and want to bring home a tiny piece of the treasure themselves? What a story they could tell all their friends."

She couldn't help but be giddy with the thought. Bouncing on her toes, she nodded at him. "I love how you think, Mr. Miller—Chris. That's brilliant. *If* I can keep them, would you be willing to make jewelry for me out of the stones? For a portion of the profits?"

"I would love that privilege."

She offered her right hand. "So . . . will you be my partner in this?"

10

Without missing a beat, Chris clasped her hand between both of his. "I would be honored to be your partner."

The grin he sent her made her want to stare at him longer. He was a handsome man. Only about an inch above her height with blond hair and brown eyes.

"Would you care to join me for dinner now?" he asked. "There's a good deal I think we should discuss."

"I don't think that's a wise idea. I'm a Harvey Girl, after all. We're not allowed to spend time with men in a courtship-like atmosphere without permission from the manager, and I wouldn't want it to look untoward." She pulled her hand free.

"I'm sorry. I didn't think about your job. I wouldn't wish to put you at risk in any way with your superiors." He rubbed his chin again. "What if I were to order us some sandwiches for a picnic? Would that be acceptable?"

His thoughtfulness touched her. "I would like that, thank you. We could eat on one of the benches and talk about our next hike." She pointed her head toward the hotel and started walking.

He joined her. "Hike?"

She stopped. "The scroll clearly had a two on it. Wouldn't you think that meant there was at least one more stash of the jewels hidden? There were two brothers, after all."

He appeared to weigh the idea. "Perhaps. But it's been hundreds of years. We don't know if anyone found the rest in that time."

"That's a good point. But wouldn't we have heard about it? The legend has been circulating for all this time, and no one has mentioned any of the treasure being found. Wouldn't you like to come with me to search?"

He held up both of his hands in front of him. "No. Not really. I haven't ever done any hiking. I'm much more at home with my tools and a workbench. Besides, I'll need every spare moment I have to work on the jewelry I'm contracted to make for the Hopi House."

"All right. I do have one of the other girls who has hiked with me. I'm sure she won't mind coming along."

"You don't mind her knowing about the treasure you found?" His question was innocent enough.

Taking a moment to think it over, she frowned. If Florence had gotten to Tessa, her quiet friend might not trust her anymore. "I don't know. Maybe I should go by myself."

"Whoa. That's not my recommendation. I don't think that's wise. Or safe."

He was probably right. She'd already broken the rules once today.

Silence covered them for several seconds, and then they continued strolling back toward the hotel entrance.

As they neared the entrance, he stopped and touched her elbow. "Honesty is my one condition, Miss Schultz."

Heat pulsed up her throat. "It's Julia, remember?" She

forced herself to hold his gaze. Had he heard about her penchant for stories? No. How could he? Unless Florence had been in the Hopi House today, which seemed unlikely.

"Julia." His face softened. "Promise me that you'll be truthful with me. As your partner."

If she was allowed to keep the treasure she'd found and then sell it all for a pretty penny, her life could drastically change. This was her ticket to a new life where she could go wherever she wanted. Tell any kind of story she pleased, and people would love her because she was *somebody*. Somebody of worth. Somebody known.

Somebody loved.

She couldn't let this opportunity slip through her fingers. "I promise. And you'll do the same?"

"Of course. You have my word." He dipped his chin at her.

"I'll go see if I can order us some sandwiches and we can discuss the rest of—"

"Miss Schultz!" Ruth's voice pulled her gaze to the hotel. She ran toward them with her skirts hiked up in her hands. Something must be terribly wrong.

Julia rushed toward the head waitress. "Miss Anniston, whatever is the matter?"

Ruth put a hand to her chest as she came close and then hugged her tight. "Thank the good Lord above you're all right."

"I'm fine." She pulled back a few inches and eyed the relief clear on her friend's face. "What happened?"

"Three of our guests were hiking in the canyon and were attacked by a mountain lion."

Julia covered her mouth with both hands. That could have been her! She lowered her hands. "Are they all right?"

"I haven't heard. They were injured pretty severely before

one of the gentlemen shot the animal. When no one could find you, we feared the worst. Especially after last night." Ruth dabbed at her eyes with a handkerchief.

"What happened last night?"

Julia winced at Chris's question. No way did she want him finding out about Florence and her past. Particularly after he asked her to promise to be honest. "Nothing of consequence."

Ruth looked at Chris, as if seeing him for the first time. Her gaze went back and forth between him and Julia. "My apologies, Mr. . . . ?"

"Mr. Miller."

Her eyes cleared and she smiled. "Ah yes. I'm sorry, Mr. Miller. You're the jeweler Mr. Watkins and Mr. Owens told me about. It's nice to meet you in person."

"Likewise." He tipped his hat at her. "Miss Schultz, we can discuss our business later. I'm sure your assistance is needed." Chris nodded at both of them and headed back toward the Hopi House.

"Wait." On impulse, she reached into her pocket and pulled out the pouch. "Take these with you."

He hesitated and then took them with a nod.

Ruth wrapped an arm around Julia's waist and led her toward the entrance. "You can tell me about whatever business you are involved in with Mr. Miller later. Right now, I'm content that you are in one piece."

Julia recognized the mother-hen tone and didn't argue. "I'm fine."

"Now, tell me the truth." Her supervisor stopped and tugged her until they faced each other. "Did you go down into the canyon alone?"

Back at the Hopi House, Chuma locked the doors to the shop and looked over at Chris. "Everything is secure, Mr. Miller, so no one should disturb you."

Trying to act nonchalant while he waited for them to close up for the evening had just about been his undoing. "Thank you, Chuma." He couldn't wait to get a closer look at the stones Julia had found.

"Do you need any help?" The eagerness on her face was clear.

He sent her his best smile. "Not at the moment. The work I need to do is very delicate and time consuming, but I appreciate your assistance earlier today. You are a fast learner."

"I enjoy the work and want to learn everything you are willing to teach. I have always loved making jewelry here, but it was simple. Not like the beautiful things that you make." She clasped her hands in front of her and returned the smile, showing off an empty space on the bottom. "If you do need anything, a few of us will be weaving upstairs." With a nod, she turned and headed toward the stairs. Her soft footfalls were the only sound around him.

Left in the silence, Chris watched her walk away. These people were truly amazing. Maybe he could learn more about them as he taught them more about jewelry. There was probably a *lot* he could learn from them, since they did so much with their hands. The day Mr. and Mrs. Watkins had given him a tour, Chris had tried not to gape at how fast the women could weave.

Ray said they wanted to incorporate the Hopi culture and history. There had to be a way to combine his jewelry techniques with some of the native arts. That was exactly what the Harvey company wanted to grow. Hmmm. Maybe he should spend more time here.

Which meant more time away from his shop.

The shop. It had been everything to him. And he was still determined to save it. Not only had God given him an incredible opportunity here, but Miss Schultz's find was quite extraordinary. Certainly, she'd be allowed to keep the treasure . . . right?

He shook his head. Awful selfish of him since that would be to his benefit. *Lord, don't let me get ahead of myself.*

The excitement remained after the prayer. Sometimes God provided for people in mysterious ways. Who said He couldn't use a legend and a pretty waitress?

Chris chuckled and shook his head. After wiping his hands on a special towel that helped to remove excess oils from his skin, he headed over to the workbench and sat on a little stool. Time to take a closer look at the stones from the cave.

He gently opened the pouch Julia gave him. Cracked and fragile from the centuries in a cave, it amazed him that it was still in one piece. At one time, the leather must have been thick and soft. Well made.

He dumped the contents into his hand. Four good-sized diamonds were in the midst. Point cut in the octahedron style, which was another clue to the ancient time period of the stones. He'd had to study the history of lapidary for his training as a jeweler. Diamonds hadn't been cut like this for hundreds of years. If men left these here in roughly 1540, how old were the stones prior to that?

It would take a good bit to cut them and do anything modern with them. Might be better to turn them into eight diamonds by cutting down the center axis and turning them into a table cut or old single cut to preserve the age and quality. Chris set them aside. He'd have to decide on those later.

The ruby in his palm was definitely the largest one Chris had ever worked with. He moved the magnifying glass in front of it to get a better idea of how to shape it to be the centerpiece of a necklace. The stone was cut into an old single cut, which showcased the depth of color. A simple design was best to show off the beauty of the stone.

An idea began to form in his mind, and as soon as it was clear, he set down the stone, grabbed his pencil and sketchpad, and drew it out.

Another ruby—smaller with a rougher cut—would be more difficult to maneuver. Back at his shop, he'd need the use of his flex shaft and stronger magnifiers.

The next four pieces were golden topaz. They would look lovely mixed with pearls or perhaps with turquoise.

Four emeralds and six sapphires were left. All the ideas bouncing around in his mind excited him. And to think there were more bags of treasure that he had yet to see.

After taking long looks at each of the stones under the magnifying glass, he leaned back and stretched his neck.

When he'd prayed for a way to buy his building, he had no idea how God would provide for him in such miraculous and creative ways.

His thoughts went back to Julia. Her red hair and green eyes had caught his attention the first time they met. But what he found he really loved about her was the animation in her face as she talked. He could sit and listen to her all day. In fact, she could probably make the most boring story worthy of rapt attention.

Chris blinked and looked back down at the stones. What had come over him?

Fascination over buried treasure? Or a legend that was almost four hundred years old? Or could it be the lovely Harvey Girl that was now his business partner?

No matter what kind of reasoning he tried to come up with, the only answer was the honest one. He was already looking forward to spending more time with Julia.

He pulled his pocket watch out and studied it. If he called now, perhaps it wouldn't be too late to bend the ear of Gramps' old friend the judge. The sooner he could give Julia some news, the sooner he could see her more often.

11

The hum inside the El Tovar dining room at six forty-five in the morning invited Chris to enter. The smell of coffee mixed with the sweet and savory smells of breakfast. Everything he'd eaten so far had been spectacular, and his stomach rumbled as he followed the host to a table.

When he'd asked to be seated at a table served by Miss Schultz, the host had frowned. Was that improper of him? Hopefully he wouldn't get her into any trouble. But as he gazed around the full dining room, realization dawned. Requesting a specific waitress was probably unwise of him when they were so busy.

The host smiled as he stopped at the only empty table, pulled out the chair, and presented Chris with a menu. "It seems you are in luck. Miss Schultz will be your waitress." The man gave a slight bow. "Enjoy your breakfast, sir."

"Thank you." Chris watched the man weave his way through the tables back to the hall that gave entrance to this incredible room. Ray had given him vouchers for all of his meals whenever he came up to the canyon. In addition to what he was making off the jewelry and what he was being paid to teach jewelry-making techniques, this was easily the most fortuitous job he'd ever had.

Julia approached with a pitcher of water in one hand and a carafe of coffee in the other. Her green eyes sparkled with a smile. "Good morning, Mr. Miller."

"Miss Schultz." He nodded

She filled his water glass. "Coffee, I assume? Or did I guess wrong?"

"Coffee is wonderful, yes, please."

After she filled that cup as well, she raised her eyebrows at him. "Do you know what you would like to order?"

He glanced down at the long menu. "Perhaps give me a few minutes to decide?"

"Of course. I'll be back shortly." She turned on her heel and went to greet another table.

The long black dress of the Harvey Girl uniform accentuated her trim figure. It was flattering and feminine. Pristine. Especially with the clean and bright white apron over top with a neat bow tied in the back. All of the waitresses were dressed the same, but only one caught his attention.

The clatter of silverware hitting a plate at the table next to him broke the spell of the moment and made him put his attention back on the menu.

He was here for breakfast. His stomach chose that moment to rumble loudly. Breakfast. Right.

Chris blinked and studied the long list of food.

Winter Cantaloupe, Baked Apple, Marmalade, Stewed Prunes, Guava Preserves, Sliced Oranges

Beef Tea, Cream of Wheat, Rolled Oats, Grape Nuts, Shredded Wheat Biscuits, Force

Broiled Smelt, Salt Mackerel

Minced Capon on Toast, Salt Pork with Fried Apples, Frizzled Beef in Cream

Eggs as Ordered, Omelets any Style

Broiled Chicken

Sirloin Steak, Calf's Liver and Bacon, Lamb Chops, Bacon, Veal Cutlets, Ham

Baked Potatoes, Minced, Browned, Sliced in Cream

Graham Muffins, Hot Rolls, Toast, Sweiback, Buckwheat Cakes, Maple Syrup

With a glance up, he found Julia across the room and watched as she worked her way back to him. When she reached his side, he blurted out, "You look lovely this morning."

Pink tinged her cheeks. "Thank you, Mr. Miller. Are you ready to order?"

"I believe I am." What had come over him? He put his focus back on the menu. "I'll have the frizzled beef in cream, toast, and winter cantaloupe."

"Great choices. I'll be right back with your breakfast."

He opened his mouth to say something else, but she was gone before he could get a word out. He'd have to be quicker next time.

Drumming his fingers on the table, Chris took a moment to view the room. Several men read newspapers as they drank their coffee. Conversations buzzed. But no one else sat alone. Hmmm. He should have brought a paper in for himself. Or perhaps his small sketchbook.

Dining alone had never bothered him. In fact, he preferred being by himself. Living with Gramps the last few years had been great. They'd become quite the pair of bachelors.

It had taken time to get used to the loss of Gramps. Not that they had much to say. Gramps was also a man of few words and saved most of them for his customers. But the companionship, Chris missed. After watching Ray and Emma Grace Watkins the past few weeks, something had begun to niggle at his mind and heart. A yearning for something more.

Maybe God had sent this unique situation to him so that he would pay attention. He'd been so focused on making sure that Gramps' legacy survived that he'd left little time for anything else. Perhaps it was time for that to change? Time to pursue a relationship?

He shook his head of the thoughts. He only had three-and-a-half weeks left. After he saved his building and shop, he could think about other life changes. Not now. He needed to focus.

Julia appeared at his side with steaming plates. Her beautiful red hair was pulled back with a white ribbon. His heart sped up just a touch.

Focus, sure. Easier said than done.

Watching Chris's face as she set his plates of food down, Julia's stomach did a little flip. While being a Harvey Girl presented many opportunities each day to receive admiring glances from customers, there was something different about this man. "Would you care for anything else?"

He glanced down at the food in front of him. "This looks amazing, thank you."

"The chefs here are the very best." She needed to get back to the kitchen to serve her next guests, but for some reason, her feet refused to move. Something about being around Chris made her feel more . . . normal. With all the upheaval she'd felt since Florence's arrival and the glances from the other girls this morning, she wasn't sure which way was up half the time.

"Do you have a brief moment?" He reached for his napkin and laid it in his lap.

She licked her lips and clasped her hands in front of her. What was it about his brown eyes that drew her? They were filled with a sort of . . . light.

Joy.

Something she wished she had. Where did it come from? "Of course. What do you need?"

"I will be returning to Williams today and starting work on our little project. I was a little excited last night and called an old friend of my grandfather's. It sounds promising that you'll be able to keep what you've found. Would you be willing to come down to my shop and bring the rest of . . . the items? I'd love to show you around."

A little thrill of excitement bubbled up. She'd done her best to not think too much about the treasure. But to keep it? She dared hope. Oh, wouldn't that be incredible?

None of the girls could know . . . well, other than Tessa. She'd said that Florence was an instigator and she didn't want anything to do with her. Thank goodness her friend hadn't been swayed by Florence. What was even better, Tessa said she'd love to hike some more. But she also said that she'd have to go to town on her next day off because she needed a pair of shoes. That might give Julia the perfect opportunity to let her hiking friend know what was going on. It would be nice to have a confidante.

Quiet, unassuming Tessa was perfect.

Julia chewed on her lip for a moment and nodded. "As much as I want to go hiking soon and search for the rest, I'm a little hesitant after hearing about the mountain lion. Even though the one that attacked the guests was killed and they don't believe there is any risk for the guests on the trails, I'd rather be safe than sorry. Besides, you'll need time to find out if I can keep it for sure anyway. So, yes"—gracious, she'd rambled a lot—"I think coming to your shop will fit into my schedule quite nicely. Is it all right if I bring a friend?"

"Certainly. Just let me know which day you're off. As long as it's not when I'm up here, it shouldn't interfere with anything else." His smile was warm and genuine, and it caused his eyes to crinkle again at the corners. Something she found attractive. She liked this man.

"Thursday is my next day off. Does that work for you?"

"Yes, it does. Thank you. Now, we should probably discuss our percentages. Just in case. I want to have this all out in the open before I do any work."

Why hadn't she thought of that? Hopefully, he wasn't thinking that she would take advantage of him. "Oh, yes. What do you think?"

"While it will take some work and materials on my part to create jewelry out of the stones, you *are* the one who found them and they are worth a great deal. I propose you take seventy-five percent and I'll take twenty-five."

"Is that enough to cover your materials and labor?" That seemed awfully generous. In fact, in her mind, she was expecting him to offer a fifty-fifty split. Especially after listening to her parents haggle with people. It wasn't like she'd paid anything for the treasure, and she didn't want him to resent her once he started the work. She needed him.

"I counter your proposal." Maybe this would even give

her some leverage later on. "Since I believe this will be more labor intensive on your part and it's only fair that you receive fair compensation for your time and materials, how about seventy-thirty."

His furrowed brow and narrowed eyes told her he was weighing the options in his mind. They stared at each other for almost a minute. She knew because she counted the seconds. "I accept."

She let out her breath. Had she been holding her breath that whole time too?

The dining room clamor grew around her. "Gracious, I need to get back to my other tables. But do let me know if you need anything else, Mr. Miller."

He nodded, and she took off. Moving fast was mandatory in her line of work, but the excitement within her helped her to feel like she could run around the entire rim of the canyon and still have time to finish her shift.

The thought brought a wide grin to her face. She'd never had money. Never had anything to look forward to other than work and entertaining with her stories. But now? A whole new future seemed to open up in front of her. Not that she cared all that much to be rich and famous. It wouldn't be a bad thing. Maybe. But to be known. To *be* someone. Anyone. Other than orphan Julia Schultz.

Florence passed her at the head waitress's station. There was no hateful glare or rude look. Instead, she completely ignored Julia.

Julia wasn't sure which would hurt worse. Of all people, why did Florence have to get transferred here? It wasn't fair. And even though Ruth had warned the girl, she obviously wasn't listening. Julia had avoided being around the others as much as possible, but even so the glances from several of her coworkers this morning had made Julia feel insecure and alone. The exact same feeling she'd had as a child as the new orphan in the orphanage or with a different family fostering her.

"Miss Schultz?" Ruth quirked an eyebrow at her.

Julia headed for her supervisor. "Yes, Miss Anniston?"

The older woman's lips tipped up into the hint of a smile. "I've called a meeting with all the girls this afternoon in between shifts. Your promotion is now permanent. Mr. Owens approved it this morning. Make sure you are downstairs for this honor."

Everything in her wanted to jump up and down, but instead, she dipped her chin in a small nod. "Thank you. I will." It took her biting her tongue to keep from squealing or flinging herself at Ruth.

"We have a busy dining room, so best get back to work. Your new attire will be ready when we move your room today."

New attire? And a new room?! How glorious. Julia spun around, grabbed a couple baskets of bread and plates of butter for two of her tables, and practically floated across the room.

Eight hours later, all the Harvey Girls were gathered in the amusement room in the basement. A sea of black-and-white uniforms along with lively chatter bouncing off the walls greeted her as Julia snuck in and leaned against the wall. Her feet ached, and she still had the dinner shift to go. But she was more than a little thrilled to hear what Ruth was about to say. Things were finally looking up for her. Promotion. Her own room. The treasure.

"Ladies!" Ruth held up her hands from the front of the room.

Everyone quieted.

"Thank you for coming so promptly. I have some exciting news to share. Miss Schultz has been promoted to assistant head waitress. Please join me in congratulating her." Ruth put her hands together and clapped. "Please come up here." She waved to Julia.

With her head held high, Julia stepped forward. But she noticed that it was timid clapping. No whistling or cheering. No hugs or gleeful handshakes. Still, she wouldn't let that get her down. Not today.

When she reached Ruth, her friend hugged her and turned her around to see everyone.

There were smiles. But none seemed sincere. Julia's eyes were drawn to Florence. As soon as they connected gazes, Florence lifted her hands a little higher and clapped while tipping her head at her, a smirk on her face. What was she up to?

Never mind. She was going to be thankful for this moment.

Ruth stepped forward. "Now, I'm sure that all of you understand that Julia is now in a supervisory position. You will give her the same respect you give me. If I am not on the dining room floor, that means she is in charge. Is that understood?"

"Yes, Miss Anniston," a chorus of thirty women responded.

"Good. You are dismissed. I am going to assist Miss Schultz in moving her things into her new room. May I get another volunteer or two?"

Charlotte's hand shot up without hesitation. Then Tessa's. But theirs were the only ones. Everyone else started to move and talk in groups of a few here and a few there.

Ruth snagged her elbow. "Let's get you moved." The smile on her face was a bit forced, but that was to be expected. She'd have to be oblivious to not notice the tension in the room.

Back in her room that she shared with Elizabeth, Julia packed up her things, making sure to bury the stones beneath her undergarments so no one would see them. Charlotte and Ruth helped her haul them down the hallway. She placed her hands on her hips in the new room that would be all her own. "I've got one more trip. I'll be right back."

"All right." Ruth's cheery voice as she and Charlotte put linens on her new bed reminded her that she had a friend in her supervisor. An actual, real friend. As long as she didn't mess it up. Then there were Charlotte and Tessa. Even after Florence's spilling of Julia's past, the two seemed to have stuck by her. Having friends was a first for her. Something she never wanted to take for granted.

Julia walked down the hall to her old room. The door was open, and Elizabeth sat on her bed. They hadn't talked a lot, but she should at least tell her roommate thank you and give her a hug. "I guess you'll have the room to yourself." She pasted on her warmest smile. "Thank you for having me."

Elizabeth picked at a piece of lint on her apron and shrugged. "Miss Anniston said there's a new girl arriving tomorrow."

"Oh. Well, that will be nice. I hope you two get along." Taking a leap of faith, she sat on the bed, leaving a couple of feet between them. "I'm sorry we didn't have the chance to really get to know each other."

"Florence has told us plenty about you, Julia."

What did that mean? "Ah, I see."

"You were chummy with your last head waitress too, we hear." The hurt was evident in Elizabeth's voice.

"Well, uh, yes, I guess I was. But Sue was in fact my only friend."

"Is that what you do?"

Julia gulped. "I don't think I understand what you mean." Maybe saying good-bye to Elizabeth had been the wrong idea.

"I've been here since the hotel opened, and I have worked myself to the bone. Not once have I been looked at for a promotion." She stood. "I wanted to be your friend, I really did. Even hoped that we could be like sisters. But every time I invited you to join us, you remained aloof. You refused to open up and tell me anything about yourself. Kept your distance. It's because you knew from the very beginning, didn't you? It all makes sense now. I bet you lied your way into Ruth's good graces." Her voice rose in volume. "Did you tell one of your outlandish stories to Mr. Owens too?"

"Elizabeth. No, that's not what happened at all. I—"

"I don't want to hear it." She stomped out of the room and slammed the door behind her.

Tears flooded Julia's eyes. Exactly *why* had she tried so hard to bite her tongue, not tell any stories . . . to tell the *truth*? It's not like it did her any good.

She might have the promotion, but thanks to Florence's presence, she wouldn't make any friends. Would she be able to keep the ones she had? The fragile thread connecting her to the others seemed as thin as a spider's web, all things considered.

Julia swiped at her cheeks and picked up the last of her belongings. It was a good thing she found that treasure, because she'd have to leave this place too.

Her heart squeezed at the thought. Why did that have to feel awful? It's not like she had anyone here. Not for long. If they knew who she really was, that thin thread of friendship would vanish. The negative thoughts stampeded through her mind.

Maybe she was destined to be alone forever and she just needed to accept that. At least she wouldn't be hurt by anyone that way. But the idea didn't help her feel any better.

As she left the room, she took long, purposeful strides to her new room.

Even though the hall was filled with other waitresses, she didn't look at any of them, imagining that they were all thinking about what a fraud she was. How she must have lied to get her position.

When she walked into her new room, Ruth held out her arms wide. "Congratulations on your promotion, Julia!" She, Charlotte, and Tessa surged forward and wrapped her in a hug.

The older woman pulled back. "What's wrong?"

Julia didn't say anything for several moments.

Charlotte went to the door and shut it. Wringing her hands, she huffed. "It's Florence, isn't it?"

Julia clenched her jaw. She wouldn't cry. Not again. Maybe if she pretended she wasn't hurt, it would go away.

"What is this about Florence?" Ruth's narrowed gaze as she crossed her arms over her chest told them she meant business.

Charlotte looked to her and then back to their supervisor. "If Julia won't say anything, I will. Florence has gotten a few of the girls riled up over Julia's promotion, telling them that Julia lied to get it. Says it's proof enough because of all the stories she told in the past. Even though you told her not to be gossiping about Julia anymore, they've huddled together several times like a bunch of cackling hens. To make matters worse, they've also picked on several of the other girls. Telling them they are Goody Two-shoes, or . . . in my case, making fun of me for my fear of heights."

"What?!" Julia exclaimed. It was one thing to pick on her, but now they were going after Charlotte? "That's not right. Just because Florence dislikes me doesn't mean she should be taking it out on anyone else."

"Excuse me, ladies." Ruth headed toward the door. "I need to take care of some business." The door shut with a sound thud behind her.

Charlotte's eyes were wide as she turned back to Julia. "I'm so sorry. But I had to say something." She reached for Julia's hands. "I volunteered this afternoon because I want to be your friend. You reached out to me and encouraged me when I needed it. I haven't known how to say it or how to show it, but somehow I'm not feeling afraid anymore."

"You're not worried that you can't trust me?"

"No. We all have things we regret in our pasts. But I've been watching you. You've been reserved here. You've worked hard. And even though you're obviously very talented at weaving tales, I haven't heard you do that here. You're the only one who hasn't tried to push me to do something I didn't feel comfortable doing. Well, other than Ruth. I think that says something about you."

Someone actually noticed her. Saw the struggle. "Thank you, Charlotte." She did her best to hold the tears at bay. "I appreciate your friendship and your words more than you can imagine."

Charlotte leaned in and hugged her. "And I yours." She pulled back and her eyes lit up. "I think you should put all that creativity to use. Have you ever thought about writing children's storybooks? I bet you'd be great at that."

Tessa stepped up from the spot in the corner where she'd been standing. "I agree. I'm your friend too."

In that moment, Julia's heart felt like mush. These girls actually sought her out to be a friend. They understood her and wanted her to thrive.

She hadn't told any crazy stories to get attention.

She hadn't put on a façade.

She hadn't done anything at all.

She felt like . . . she was someone special.

12

Ruth stepped into the bathroom, closed and locked the door, and then leaned against the wall.

Six girls had been gathered together in Florence's room. Six.

Not even trying to hide the fact that they were gossiping, slandering, and just plain ol' being mean.

A couple of them had left Florence's room in tears after Ruth's severe scolding. The disciplinary action she'd had to take was harsher than any she'd ever had to lay on her girls. But the others? The hard looks in each of their eyes told her more about the true state of their hearts.

She wanted to fire every last one of them.

Every. Last. One.

But the rules set in place said she must give them one more chance to mend their ways. First, they'd been warned. Second came disciplinary action. If it happened again, they'd be dismissed.

Florence knew those rules. Apparently she didn't care about Ruth's harsh threat the first time she crossed the line. And the girl had just arrived! The audacity of young women these days.

Mr. Fred Harvey himself would roll over in his grave if he knew. And Mr. Owens? The man would turn beet red, and she could almost envision steam spewing out of his ears. But he would advise her to follow their policy. Which she was doing. It was a good thing the man didn't understand what really went on in the basement.

Ruth went to the sink and splashed cool water on her face. Staring into the mirror over the vanity, she shook her head at the reflection she saw. "You're getting too old for this." Why couldn't young ladies see the damage they inflicted with their tongues? It was without a doubt the most violent weapon known to man.

If only they could go back to the good ol' days. Before the turn of the century. Back when being a Harvey Girl meant you toed the line. She'd never had problems with her girls like the last few years. It had created more than one headache for her.

Maybe she should have taken one of the hundreds of proposals she'd received over the years. Of course, none of the men had met her expectations, her standards. But she wouldn't be in this predicament now if she had married and settled down.

She examined herself in the mirror. At thirty-two years old, she would most likely be viewed as a spinster, even though she'd always appeared younger than her age. Her small stature didn't help with that. What was it that Frank said to her last time? That she could pass for a little girl? It had made her swat at him and giggle, but her longtime friend always knew how to cheer her up.

Frank. Thoughts of their last chat brought her mind back to Julia. The poor girl was carrying a heavy weight. The thing she couldn't understand was *what*. It obviously had something to do with her parents. While it wasn't Ruth's job to fix all of her girls' problems, there was something about Julia that begged her to pay attention.

Frank had met with her as promised to talk about Julia and how to reach her, but they hadn't settled on any concrete answers. One Bible passage had stuck out to both of them, but how could she share it with Julia in a real and meaningful way?

Ruth turned away from the mirror and pulled out a folded piece of paper from her pocket. On it, she'd written out the verses, hoping she could memorize them and put them to heart.

She read the words from Titus chapter three. "But after that the kindness and love of God our Saviour toward man appeared, not by works of righteousness which we have done, but according to his mercy he saved us, by the washing of regeneration, and renewing of the Holy Ghost; which he shed on us abundantly through Jesus Christ our Saviour; that being justified by his grace, we should be made heirs according to the hope of eternal life."

With a little huff, she folded the paper and shoved it back into her pocket. She'd quoted scripture after scripture the other day to Julia, and the response had been more questions and lots of confusion. How could Ruth show someone that God loved them no matter what? When they'd never seen real love before?

It challenged Ruth in a way she'd never been challenged before. While she wouldn't say faith was necessarily *easy*, it hadn't ever been difficult for her. Not like what she'd seen on Julia's face.

Boisterous laughter sounded in the hallway outside the bathroom. Ruth straightened her shoulders and sent a scolding look to herself in the mirror. It seemed she had plenty of young women to show the love of God to. A relationship with Him was all anyone ever truly needed.

If only they could see past their superficial world they lived in.

Lord, I need Your help like never before. I don't even know what to ask for, but I know You understand. I'm weary, and I want to punish them like a bunch of five-year-olds. But I feel like even five-year-olds would behave better. Grimacing at her own words, she shook her head. *I know, I know, I'm not any better. Forgive me where I've failed You, Father. Give me the words to say and the actions that speak of You and not of me.*

A verse from John popped into her mind. "Greater love hath no man than this, that a man lay down his life for his friends." Sacrifice. That was it. What Julia needed . . . what *all* of her girls needed to see. Sacrificial love. No rivalry. No conceit. Just humility.

Putting someone else first.

Her heart lifted. Living out a life of sacrifice shouldn't be that hard to show—because they were in the business of serving others. Surely the girls would understand that.

As she unlocked and opened the door, she took a deep breath. It wouldn't be easy. She couldn't just preach at the girls and have them instantly understand. She was going to have to live it out in new ways every day.

Okay, God, I see the path now. But I'm going to need Your divine help to keep me on it.

Chris stifled a yawn. Working into the wee hours of the night the past few days had helped him to create a lot of new pieces, but he was beginning to feel the lack of sleep. As much as Gramps claimed he could live off strong black coffee and biscuits, Chris knew *he* couldn't.

Especially the black coffee part. He'd never been able to drink it straight like that. He always added milk and sugar.

Stumbling into his tiny kitchen, he stretched and then put his percolator to good use by starting a pot of coffee.

A knock sounded at his kitchen door, and he ran a hand through his hair. Who could that be?

He opened the door and found Mr. Holland on the stoop.

"Good morning, Christopher." He held his cane in front of him. "I know it's early."

"Not a problem, I was just fixing some coffee. Come on in and I'll pour you a cup."

"Thank you, son." He hobbled up the step and squared his aging shoulders once he was in the door. "I'll get right to the point. I came to offer my assistance."

"Assistance? You're already doing that."

"I know, I know. But your grandfather and I were good friends. Now that he's gone and my sweet Lucille's gone, well, I'm afraid I don't have much to fill my days. It's downright gloomy." He cleared his throat. "When I heard about Mr. Langford selling all his holdings in Williams and about you wanting to buy the building, I decided it was high time I did something about it."

Chris raised his eyebrows. "Mr. Holland, you've already help—"

"Nonsense. Your gramps helped me out of more than one scrape. When we were back in Albuquerque, before you came along, he often paid for Lucille's treatments at the doctor when we couldn't afford them. Now, he swore me to secrecy, but with him gone, I think it's only fair that I tell ya the truth.

I owed him. He even helped us move here to Williams when I knew that Lucille didn't have a lot of time left. She wanted to see the Grand Canyon." The man choked a bit and pulled out a handkerchief. "Excuse me."

"That's why you took the train up there once a week?" It all started to make sense now.

"Yep. And your grandfather paid for those tickets too. Every week. Until Lucille passed." The words were thick, and tears rolled down his cheeks.

His heart swelled. "I had no idea, Mr. Holland."

The man wept for a minute and then pulled himself together. "That's what I thought. Your grandfather was the best friend I ever had other than my wife. So now you are going to listen to me, and I won't take no for an answer."

Chris sat in a chair at the small kitchen table and dipped his head. "Yes, sir."

"Good for you. Respectin' your elders." A slight smile lifted the older man's lips. "I'm going to come work for you every day so you can spend all your time making jewelry. Not just the days you go up to the El Tovar. And you're not going to pay me one dime until the building is paid for."

Chris shook his head. He couldn't let the man do that. "Mr. Holland—"

"Nope. I said I won't take no for an answer. Do this for me and for your Gramps. I need to feel useful and feel like I'm giving back to the man who changed my life. Don't take that away from me. After you get the building paid for, we can discuss wages if you still want this ol' curmudgeon to hang around with you. Shoot, you might even be able to teach me some of what you do. But no guarantees. I do know how to greet customers and sell things, though."

That was an understatement. Holland Mercantile had

been a long-standing outlet in Albuquerque until Lucille got sick. Mr. Holland sold it so he could take care of her. Chris had been so moved by the love he saw between the two that he'd often asked Gramps about that kind of relationship.

"It's rare, my boy. Rare. But I pray you find it too."

The memory of Gramps' voice brought a wave of grief. And as Chris met Mr. Holland's gaze as the man stood stoically in his kitchen, he knew he couldn't turn the man down. "Your offer is more than generous, but I see the good Lord's hand in it. Thank you, Mr. Holland. I'd be honored to have you help me."

"Good. Now, none of that Mr. Holland nonsense. Call me Fred. You're like family to me, son." The older man stepped forward and opened his arms. "Come give this old geezer a hug, and then you need to put me to work. We have a building to buy!"

By the time the afternoon had rolled around, Chris was on cloud nine.

Not only had he made amazing progress in his workshop since he didn't have any interruptions, but Fred sold three times as many items as Chris had ever sold in a day. It was the most phenomenal thing he'd ever seen. At this rate, he'd be able to give Mr. Langford the money for the building ahead of schedule.

"You know what I think?" Fred's words shook him out of his reverie.

"What's that?" Chris couldn't help but grin from ear to ear.

"I think you should consider going up to the canyon at least twice a week. With me here at the shop, you'll be able to have all those extra hands up there to help make the pieces you want to sell at the Hopi House. Just an idea."

He walked over to the man with a heart overflowing. "It's a great idea." He gripped Fred's shoulder. "This wouldn't be possible without you. Thank you."

"Aw shucks. But you have to realize that this is a gift to me as well, son. So thank *you*."

As Chris walked back into his workshop, his heart soared even higher, if that was possible. God had made a way. It was almost too much to even comprehend.

Julia would be coming tomorrow, and he could tell her the good news about what he'd found out about her keeping the treasure. Then maybe Friday he could head up to El Tovar. He checked the clock on the workbench.

If he called right now, Mr. Owens could surely get everything in place.

He went to the telephone and picked up the earpiece. He'd tried to keep Miss Schultz out of his mind so he could concentrate and work, but the knowledge that he would get to see her two days in a row made his smile stretch.

Fred raised his eyebrows at him. "What's put that silly grin on your face?"

Things had not gone as planned.

First, that nosy waitress had gotten away. And if the helmet and scroll thing were any indication, there'd been something else hidden there. But what? A map? A clue?

It was enough to drive a person mad.

Second, one of those fat and frilly tourists actually shot the mountain lion. Even though the attack had gone just as planned, word now was that everyone thought they were safe since the vicious animal was dead. Well, just wait. After another attack, they would all think twice about traipsing around where they shouldn't.

More time was bein' wasted today. The town of Williams was not Bobby's favorite place. But it was necessary to get the supplies they'd need for the next few months. And Roger was worthless to send on such an errand. He'd spend all their money without getting the important stuff.

Then there was the fact that there were too many eyes in town.

Too many questions.

Too many nosy people.

What happened to the days when somebody could just live in peace and not be harassed by all the Goody Two-shoes?

They needed supplies. That shouldn't be so hard. Except when people stopped and asked questions. Like, "Where are you from?" and "What brought you out to Williams?" and "You got anybody with you?"

Why were they such busybodies? Didn't people have their own business to mind?

Stupid. It was all stupid.

Walking down the street, Bobby spied a couple standing outside the jewelry store. The man looked like the jeweler who owned the place. Whatever they were talking about had the lady's face quite animated. She looked familiar . . . but from where?

Dagnabbit! The waitress with the red hair!

"You truly think there's more?" The jeweler wasn't that tall of a man. Maybe only the same height as the girl. But he looked young and strong.

The fella's smile stretched. "I'd love to use as many of the jewels as you can find. They'll make beautiful pieces, and I thought of asking Chuma to attach a story with each piece about the legend. What do you think about that?"

Jewels. Legend. That was enough to make Bobby want to stop walking altogether. But that wouldn't be wise. Now someone else knew. Best to keep going . . . one slow step at a time. Ears tuned in.

The conversation came to a halt as the two went into the store.

Blast! It was obvious the girl had found something. Jewels—if what the shop owner said was true. And if she knew about the legend, then whatever she found down there belonged to Bobby. Plain and simple.

Well, they would just see about who this lady thought she was and where she found the jewels. Then she'd have to be disposed of. Such a pretty thing. She'd be missed, but there wasn't any other way. Their mountain lion trap had worked once before. Might as well use it again. Scare the tourists for good if it happened twice.

No one had a right to that treasure. No one.

Except Bobby.

13

The train ride back to Williams was completely different than when Julia first came up to the canyon. This time, she had Tessa with her and her stomach wasn't all wrapped up in knots about starting a new job at her dream place. While Tessa wasn't much of a conversationalist, she had started coming out of her shell a bit more. In fact, she'd responded with actual sentences a few times, which gave Julia hope that her hiking buddy just might open up one day.

When they'd arrived, they parted ways so Tessa could go find a pair of shoes. In their line of work, a good, sturdy, comfortable boot was a must. And poor Tessa's pair was almost worn through.

Chris had met Julia at the station, and she enjoyed chatting with him as they walked the short distance to his shop. Her excitement had grown the more she talked to him and saw his enthusiasm about what she'd found.

But once she entered his store and looked around, she was speechless.

"What do you think?" His grin was wide, his face eager

for her response as he removed his coat and placed a thick leather apron over his head.

She blinked several times and tried to gather her thoughts. "I'm . . ." She put a hand to her waist. "I don't even have words."

An older gentleman behind the counter walked toward her. "Good day. Fred Holland at your service. You must be the lovely Miss Schultz I've heard so much about."

Her head bobbed up and down.

"Takes your breath away, doesn't it?" Mr. Holland winked. "Christopher is the finest jeweler I've ever seen. Even more talented than his grandfather, which is saying a lot."

"Fred." Chris shook his head. "I don't think that's true."

"Oh, I think that's *definitely* true." Julia couldn't hold it in any longer. "You *made* all of this?" She sucked in a breath. "I've never seen anything more beautiful in all of my life. I mean, wow. And I've seen a lot of jewels on customers over the years, especially recently at the El Tovar, but nothing—and I mean *nothing*—like this." The words tumbled out. What was it about this place that struck such a chord with her? There were bold pieces. Delicate pieces. But everything was so . . . unique.

Mr. Holland wrapped an arm around Chris's shoulders. "Exactly. You should listen to this young lady. She's smart." The older man went to the hat rack and picked up a hat and placed it on his head. "I'm going to run a quick errand, but I'll be back in a jiffy."

"All right, Fred, thanks." Chris turned back to her. "My favorite part about making jewelry is the design. I have a sketchbook where I draw what I picture in my mind. Usually a stone will inspire it, or I just visualize something new. I like mixing stones and colors." He strode over to a cabinet and pointed. "Like this one right here. I thought it would be interesting to mix the aquamarine stones with the rose quartz."

"It's breathtaking. Truly." She walked beside the glass case so she could see everything up close. "Oh my goodness, what is this one?" She pointed at a necklace and set of earrings that were most unusual. The stone wasn't clear and crystal-like, like the aquamarine or diamond. It was opaque, with colors that flowed together. "It's almost creamy-looking."

His face looked quizzical. "Creamy. That's not a term I would have used, but it makes sense."

"Like paint being mixed. And it looks so shiny, as if the paint is still wet. The reds and oranges mixed with the greens and browns. I've truly never in my life seen anything like it. What is it called?"

"Bloodstone. The red of the stone is usually quite prominent, thus the name. I enjoy working with it because every stone is unique and displays the colors in different patterns. And frankly, it reminds me of this beautiful land we live in." He seemed genuinely happy that she was excited over what he did.

It lifted her heart to think that he cared about what she thought of him. "You do magnificent work, Chris. Honestly, I'm over-the-moon amazed." If her words were encouragement to him, she would be thrilled, because she doubted he understood his own talent.

"Thank you." A bit of red crept up his neck.

"My goal isn't to embarrass you, but you are very talented." She couldn't wait any longer. "You said outside that you would use as many stones as I could bring you. Does that mean that I can keep the treasure?"

His eyes sparkled. "Yes. I asked the sheriff and a judge.

The president's Antiquities Act was put in place especially to help protect Native American artifacts, which the gems are not. And even though the Grand Canyon is protected as a game preserve now, there's no law against you finding treasure there and keeping it."

She clapped her hands together. "That's the best news." Letting out a deep breath, she put a hand to her chest. "I don't even know what to say."

"Well, I also spoke to Mr. Owens. Since I signed a contract with the Harvey Company as well, I wanted to ensure that everything was aboveboard. I didn't tell him *who* had found the treasure, since I wasn't sure you wanted that information out there. I also didn't want any ne'er-do-wells learning the information and putting you in danger. But he was quite excited and loves the idea of our selling jewelry made out of the treasure at the Hopi House, along with a story of the legend. He also asked that if there are any artifacts they could display there. Like you thought, it will be great for tourism and the hotel."

"Thank you for not giving him my name. Maybe eventually, but I hadn't even thought about needing to speak to him. Thank you for being so thorough."

"Thank you for trusting me with your secret and allowing me to work with such beautiful stones. Come, let me show you what I've been working on." The expression on his face reminded her of a small child excited to show off a new toy.

She followed his brisk pace to the door in the back of the shop, which opened up into his workspace. Wooden tables lined the walls and filled the room. Each one was covered with an assortment of tools, all with wooden handles. But it wasn't a mess. Not in the least. The tools were lined up or in holders. Black cloths lined an open section of each table, and there were magnifying glasses that hung over each workspace. "Wow."

"This is my workshop. If you haven't figured that out already." The sheepish grin on his face was cute. Made him look young and innocent.

"Tell me about your work. I don't think I've ever truly thought about how a piece of jewelry comes into existence. And all these tools . . . Gracious. It's a lot to take in." She plopped herself down in a chair. "But I want to learn. Will you show me?"

His brown eyes crinkled with his smile. His blond hair, normally so neat, had a shock that fell over his forehead. He pushed it back with his hand. "Forgive me. I've been hunkered over the jewels all morning, I must be a mess. But no matter." He grinned as he stepped behind her and pushed.

The floor passed by as her chair rolled! She gasped and gripped the seat as she looked down at the wheels underneath the legs. She'd seen these chairs on wheels but had never sat in one. "This must make it easier for you to get from one workbench to another." Laughter bubbled up and out.

"I find it saves me a lot of time, and I don't have to take off my jeweler's glasses. Now, over here, these tools are all pliers." He picked up a few. "This one is needle-nose pliers, these are flat-nose pliers, and these are round-nose pliers."

She giggled. "Such creative names."

"I know, right?" The light in his eyes made her want whatever it was he had. She'd seen it on more than one occasion, and she wished it was contagious. "I use these round-nose pliers to bend and shape and pinch. But all of them obviously are used to pinch." He tilted his head. "Which makes the name of this one humorous." He held up the tool. "These are pinching pliers."

"Of course they are."

"Then there's the stone-setting pliers. I use these to bend the tiny prongs over the stones in the setting."

She picked up a ring with a lovely green stone. "Like this?"

"Exactly."

"What kind of gem is this? Is it emerald?"

"Good guess. It's actually beryl—the green variety is emerald, the blue is aquamarine, clear is goshenite, pink is morganite, yellow and yellow-green are heliodor. Then there's red, but it's just called red beryl."

"It's beautiful. I've always loved green and red."

He nodded. "Me too. Probably my favorite two colors in stones. Over here, as you can probably guess, are more pliers. Jump-ring pliers and bending pliers."

Placing the pretty ring back on the black cloth, she followed him to the next area and picked up another tool. "These don't look like pliers. What do these do?"

"Those are flush cutters. Helps me get into small spaces. See how the one side is a *V* shape and the other side is flat? That way I can cut very close to something flat and very little metal needs to be filed flush." He leaned close as he showed her the tool.

His breath was minty and warm as it washed over her. "I see." Her pulse took that moment to pick up its pace.

As he pulled away, he walked toward another table with tools. Though he wasn't a tall man, he was strong and muscular. Especially his arms. His shirtsleeves were rolled up to his elbows, and the strength in his arms and hands was apparent. But then he picked up the most delicate-looking of necklaces and held it as if it were a baby chick. "I was working on setting the stones in this piece when you arrived."

"I don't even know what to say. You are brilliant at what you do, that's for sure."

He set the necklace down, and his face tinged with red. "Thank you. But I have to give credit to the Creator. He's the one who's given me the gift." He fidgeted with several things on the table and wouldn't look at her. "This is one of my saws. I have to use different size blades depending on what I'm working on."

"Uh-huh." But she wasn't looking at the saws. She was fascinated with his face.

"And these are cutting shears." He cleared his throat. "Barrette files of different shapes, with different fineness of grit, depending on what I'm working on."

"I see."

Then he stopped and looked at her. "This must be boring to you, I'm sorry."

"Not one bit." And she meant it. This man's work fascinated her. *He* fascinated her.

"Well, over here we have a solder pick, a graver, tweezers of assorted sizes, and different liquids that I have to use in the process. And here's another pair of jeweler's glasses."

She held up a hand and rolled her chair closer. "May I try them?" The funny-looking contraptions intrigued her.

"Here. Go ahead." He handed her the spectacles with movable layers.

She put them on as instructed. "Oh my. That's incredible. I can see so close with these!" The stone in front of her was one of the ones she'd found in the cave, and seeing the cuts and the sparkle in the light was mesmerizing. "I wish I had the scroll from the cave with me. In addition to the numeral two, there were some loops and markings that I thought might be letters or initials. These would definitely help me see them better."

A bell jangled in the other room.

"I'll be right back. Let me see who's out front." Chris strode toward the door.

Which gave Julia a moment to watch him. Her heart did a little flip. She'd never met anyone like him. Not just the fact that he was a jeweler. But that he wasn't like the men she'd served in Harvey Houses all these years. He wasn't rough around the edges. And when she complimented him, he almost seemed like he didn't want the attention. At all. He also hadn't tried to propose. Most of the men she knew, after one or two meetings, were ready to get hitched. It made her chuckle. Mr. Chris Miller seemed like a real gentleman.

"Look who I found." Chris beamed at the door as Tessa entered.

Her friend's eyes went wide as she looked around the room.

"It's so interesting, Tessa. Would you like to look around and learn about the tools?"

Her friend blinked several times but didn't say a word.

"That's okay. You can just sit and listen with me." Julia grabbed her hand and led her to the chair she had occupied. "What's next, Mr. Miller?" She turned her attention to Chris.

"Well, actually, I was going to speak to you about these jewels."

"The ones from the cave?"

"Yes." He grimaced. "I'm sorry—"

"No. It's fine. I've been wanting to tell Tessa all about it, but I haven't had the chance." Julia took a deep breath and turned to her friend. After the train ride down, she felt pretty certain that Tessa hadn't been swayed by any of Florence's stories.

She seemed as steadfast as ever. "I have something to share with you, but I'd like to ask you to keep it a secret for now."

A brief nod from Tessa. "I can keep a secret."

Another entire sentence. Wow. "Good. Because I'm hoping you'll help me."

The bell jangled again.

"Excuse me, I'll be right back."

Julia took that moment to tell Tessa the beginning of the legend. But when she got to the part of the two brothers, male voices from the front of the shop seemed to be getting louder. Closer. She frowned at Tessa. "I'll tell you the rest when we're alone."

Her friend's head bobbed up and down in agreement.

The door to the workshop swung open. "I thought I heard the musical tones of a woman's voice." A well-dressed man with slicked-back hair entered. He bowed dramatically in front of them. "Jeffrey Connors at your service."

Tessa blinked.

Julia stared. Something about this man didn't set well with her. "Miss Schultz." She refused to offer a smile.

"What do you think of my shop?" The man smirked.

"This is *not* your shop, Jeffrey. I own this store. This is all *my* work." Chris's jaw clenched.

Ah. So she was right. Mr. Connors wasn't a good man.

A fake smile stretched across the man's face as he gripped Chris's shoulder. "I'm sorry. No offense, my good man. But we all know it will be mine soon enough." He turned back to Julia. "Mr. Langford, the owner of this building, is selling."

"Yes. He's selling the building to *me*. We have an agreement." She hadn't heard such force out of Chris's mouth before.

"You'll never come up with the money in time and you

know it." Connors' laugh was downright insulting. Who did this man think he was? A fire lit in her belly.

"Mr. Connors." Tessa stood up. "No offense, but you've interrupted an important meeting. If you don't have an appointment, I suggest you make one to meet with Mr. Miller at a more convenient time." With her hand on the man's elbow, she ushered him through the door.

Julia's jaw dropped. Not only had Tessa spoken more words than Julia had ever heard out of her friend at one time, but she'd deftly maneuvered the man out.

With a glance to Chris, she noticed his mouth was open as well. He looked back at her. "How did she do that?"

The bell jangled over the door, and a few seconds later, Tessa rejoined them. She dusted her hands together as if she'd just disposed of trash. "I can't abide men like that. If you allow them to stay, they'll only dig in their heels deeper. Best to just get rid of them immediately."

Julia lifted her brows and stared. There was more to Tessa than she realized.

"What?" Her friend glanced between the two of them. "I'm ready to hear the rest of the story."

Two weeks and three days were left. Every once in a while, when Chris thought about it, it overwhelmed him. But God knew better than he did. God had a plan. It was his job to do his very best and glorify God in the process.

The train chugged its way north from Williams, and he leaned his head back. A yawn overtook him. Once again, he'd stayed up much later than usual to finish making pieces for today. By next week, he should have some of the jewels from the legend set into jewelry. He couldn't wait to see what the tourists thought of them.

Even though his body was exhausted, his time with Julia and Tessa yesterday exhilarated him.

If he were honest? The time with Julia was what did it. Even though meeting her quiet hiking partner was nice—especially when she dispatched Jeffrey Connors with such skill—he had to be honest with himself. Miss Julia Schultz intrigued him. More than intrigued him. But he couldn't allow his focus to go there. In two and a half weeks, the story would be different.

He shook his head. He'd promised himself to take a nap on the train today to make up for his lack of sleep. Then he should be fresh to teach some more lessons and pray that they sold lots of his jewelry today.

Mr. Langford had stopped by yesterday after the ladies left and was beyond happy to hear that Chris was well on his way to purchasing the building. Apparently, Jeffrey and his father had been trying to convince the building owner that there was no way Chris could pull it off. Well, Langford said, he would no longer listen to those men. A comment that thrilled Chris.

Now he just had to follow through. The next two weeks would be rough, but he could persevere. He could.

As he closed his eyes, a charming redhead smiled at him in his mind. Once he bought his building, he could allow himself to pursue the lady. It would be fun getting to know her better. His lips tipped up, and he drifted off to Julia's smile and the swaying of the train.

The dining room at the El Tovar once again hummed with activity. Chris followed the host to the table where Ray and Emma Grace Watkins sat.

"Chris! It's so good to see you!" Ray stood and clasped his hand in greeting. "You look a bit like you're burning the candle at both ends." He pointed to the chair, and the men sat.

"I have to admit that your observation is correct, but I'm hoping it's only for a little bit longer. Good to see you, Mrs. Watkins." Chris dipped his head.

"Please, I thought we already said that you should call me Emma Grace. As much as I love being Mrs. Watkins, seriously, we are all family here." She smiled as she took a sip of her water and looked for their waitress. "Now, I am famished."

"It's no wonder, my dear. You are eating for two." The loving look Ray sent his wife was special.

Chris looked down at his menu.

What would it be like to have that kind of relationship? He'd had several ladies attempt to get his attention. Then there were the ones his mother had sent his way. Not that they weren't attractive or nice people. They were. But nothing had sparked within him. Other than the feeling of *how do I get out of here?*

There were plenty of times, though, that he yearned for a soulmate. A helpmeet. Someone to share his life with. And while he aimed to keep his mind and body pure, he knew God hadn't called him to be single. But as shy as he tended to be—Gramps even called him a hermit because he could stay holed up in the back designing and making jewelry—that created another set of issues. How was he supposed to find the one God had for him? He wasn't one to seek out relationships. Or people for that matter.

In fact, since Gramps died, he couldn't say he had any friends. Plenty of acquaintances and great men of faith at church. He studied once a month at a gathering the pastor called Men of the Word, but Chris was the only single man in attendance. A fact he tried not to think about too often.

"Hello, everyone. It's so good to see you." A familiar voice came over his shoulder. Everything inside him warmed.

"Hello, Julia." All of a sudden his mouth went dry. Like the desert. Parched. He swallowed, but it wasn't any better.

Thankfully, the other gentleman saved the day. "Our favorite waitress." Ray smiled.

Julia narrowed her gaze at Mr. Watkins. "You say that to everyone, admit it."

Chuckles rounded the table as she set down her water pitcher and went over to hug Emma Grace.

Chris stared at the water and licked his lips. But they were dry too. What was going on with him?

In a swift move, Julia picked up the pitcher and circled the table, filling all of their glasses with water. "Coffee or tea?"

As soon as his was filled, he lifted it and took a sip. The cool liquid helped. Maybe now he could at least speak in her presence.

The dining room was full, and as she moved around the table, she positioned cups for the Cup Code. For some reason, Chris felt smarter just knowing that little fact.

"Now, do you know what you would like to order?"

A rare moment of boldness overtook him, and he spoke up first. "I would love the beef stroganoff."

The smile on her face seemed to be just for him. At least that's how it made him feel. "An excellent choice. It's one of my favorite dishes." She gently laid a hand on his shoulder for a fraction of a second. An intimate gesture that Harvey Girls did *not* do. Maybe that smile *was* just for him. After their day together yesterday? "Would you like anything else?

Perhaps the glazed carrots, or the asparagus with hollandaise?"

"How about the glazed carrots. And I do have a hankering for some of that coconut cake today." He handed her his menu. "Thank you, Julia." He stared at her, and as their gazes collided, something stirred within him. Something he'd never felt before. *Are you trying to get my attention, God?*

If only he had more time today to spend with her. But there were numerous projects he needed to finish and then get back to Williams. Besides, she was working too. His urge to pursue Miss Schultz would have to wait.

Ray cleared his throat, which broke the moment.

Julia blinked several times. "You are most welcome." Then she turned to Ray and Emma Grace and took their orders.

Chris didn't hear a bit of their conversation.

After their waitress left, Ray chuckled, and Emma Grace lifted one eyebrow in his direction.

But she didn't say a word. She didn't have to.

14

The trail Julia had taken with Tessa this morning had disappeared. Of course, it hadn't really been a trail per se. More like a narrow path through brush that some critter had taken. Stopped on a steep slope, she placed her hands on her hips.

"What do you think? Should we keep going? Or go back and try to find another way?" Before they'd set out this morning, they'd chatted about their options. Going back to look for the helmet she'd dropped or searching for more treasure. Driven by the excitement of the hunt, they chose the latter. Besides, it was a huge canyon and they were on foot.

Her friend took the same stance and looked around. "I'd still try to get over there . . . if we can." She pointed to the small opening they'd been headed toward. It appeared to be a cave, but from this distance, they couldn't really tell.

Julia smiled. "All right. But be careful. Some of this ground is quite loose, and it's a *long* way down." In a relative manner of speaking, she knew where they were. In her pack was a small sketchbook and pencil. They'd marked their trails and made notes along the way. Not that it was an exact science.

But at least they could try to remember the caves and paths they'd tried so far.

A nod was her friend's response, so Julia planted her hiking stick in front of her and headed toward what she hoped would be another find. Ever since she told Tessa the whole story, her heart had been lighter. Not only was Chris on her side, but now her hiking partner was too.

When she'd shared the legend with Chris, a thrill had gone through her. She wasn't telling an elaborate story to elicit a response. She was sharing a secret with someone. Their partnership created a new type of relationship. One she wasn't quite sure how to categorize.

Then, when she shared with Tessa, she almost felt like a rosebud beginning to bloom. Opening up a petal at a time. It was a new sensation. Something that made her feel good.

Being real with people and telling the truth was wonderful. Something she never expected.

The only damper in her life was, well, her past. And all the stories she'd told. It would be incredible to put it all behind her and move forward. But Florence stood in the way of that dream.

As they crept along without saying a word, the hike became more of a climb, one where they had to watch every step with a careful eye to make sure they didn't fall into the abyss. The two of them huffed and puffed their way, getting closer and closer to what Julia hoped was a prize.

Her thoughts bounced all over the place. Ever since Ruth stood up for her with Florence, she'd had the urge to tell the head waitress everything. Her childhood, her parents' deaths, her almost adoption . . . everything that made Julia who she was. Maybe it was time to share . . .

Her mind took her back to that awful day when she was

eight. She could almost smell the dirt and the mean woman beside her as the wagon whisked her away from the sight of her parents' hanging.

What would people think of her if they knew about her lineage? That her parents were hanged because they'd killed two people while robbing a bank? It wasn't the first time they'd committed a crime. Just the first time they'd been caught.

What would people think if they knew what *she* did? Over the years, she'd tried to eliminate those memories. Telling herself that it wasn't her fault. Her parents had forced her to do those things. But the older she got, the more she realized how very wrong it was. . . .

Trying to push the memories aside, she focused her eyes on what she hoped was a cave ahead. It didn't work. Because the images kept coming back.

Her mom and dad had loved her. Made her laugh. Or maybe that was what she *wanted* to remember? There were very few actual memories of her childhood before they . . . died. Just snatches here and there.

There were plenty of the event and *after*.

Being tossed from family to family. Hated and loathed for being an orphan. And worse, people cringing whenever they heard who she was and where she came from.

Hope had sprung in her young heart and mind when the family in Texas wanted to adopt her. But it had been short-lived. They'd died of some horrible sickness before she'd even spent her first Christmas with them.

She didn't belong to anyone.

No wonder she always dreamed of being chosen. Accepted. Loved.

It was a shame. No child should ever have to feel abandoned, uncared for, unworthy. But that had been her lot in life.

For some reason, she'd been gifted with lots of imagination and creativity. It had been her only way to survive for many years. Her companion. She probably shouldn't have taken to lying so much about her own parents and past, but stories were what she did best.

Charlotte's suggestion came back to her, about using her talent for creativity to write children's storybooks. The thought had made her giggle the first time. Who was *she* to write stories for a living?

But letting it take root now made her—

Nah. It was ludicrous. She didn't have any talent. Not really.

Her only hope was to find more of the hidden treasure. If that didn't make her popular and respectable enough here then she could run away somewhere. Start over. Again.

That thought didn't sit well in her stomach. Start over? Again? Did she have to?

For the first time, she had a few friends. Actual friends.

Couldn't she stay?

No. Not if Florence did. And eventually people would believe the bad. They always did. That woman was full of hatred, and she was aiming it straight at Julia.

It had been a struggle. Wrestling with the weight of her new position, not wanting to run to Ruth like a tattletale every time she heard the rumors Florence shared with the girls. Not wanting to give any of the girls more fuel to the fire that she had connived her way into the head waitress's good graces. For once, she'd tried to stand on her own two feet, with the merit of how well she did her job. And it wasn't making any difference whatsoever. At least not with anyone outside of her teeny tiny circle. Was it worth it trying to sway the majority just so she could keep a few friends?

Sad, really. The first time she had a chance at something honest and real—the first time she *was* honest and real—she might have to give it up. Ruth and Sue always talked about their God. Their faith. Well, this kind of irony just made her think that God was up there somewhere laughing at her.

The cave opening was just ahead. She needed to banish all the other thoughts from her mind. It wasn't doing her any good to think past tomorrow.

Two hours later, they'd gone into four different caves, but found nothing. Most of them weren't any more than six feet deep and had been shelter for an animal or two over time.

"Where did you find the first treasure?" Tessa's voice broke the silence, and Julia almost jumped it startled her so much. "Is it anywhere close?"

She let out a light laugh with her hand over her heart. "It's a good bit from here. But everything is."

"I thought it would be nice to see *something* today—you know, to inspire us for next time. Maybe there's some other clue?"

"I did leave in a hurry. It's entirely possible I missed something. We should have plenty of light left, as long as your legs are up for it?"

The look that crossed Tessa's face was comical. "If they had an opinion, they'd tell me no. But that's not about to stop me."

She couldn't help the grin that stretched into her cheeks. "Okay. I've been wanting to go back and look for the helmet anyway. As long as some wild animal didn't make off with it."

More than a year they'd been searching and had come up empty. Then somehow that Harvey Girl just stumbled upon it? As easy as that? Well, something had to be done about it. That's for sure.

While Roger set out to capture another mountain lion in their trap, Bobby set up watch for that snoopy redheaded waitress. Lately, she'd dragged one of the other waitresses with her on her outings.

The other one never said much. Didn't look like she had much substance either. It should be pretty easy to get her out of the way.

Best to just watch and wait. They'd been on this particular trail before. The two were bound to head this direction again.

Off the beaten path, Bobby crouched. And waited.

And it paid off too. It wasn't more than an hour before girlish chatter filled the air.

Perfect. Must be the waitresses.

When they came to the bend in the trail, Bobby peeked around a boulder and studied. Yep. It was her all right. But it obviously wasn't a two-sided conversation. The other girl seemed content to follow and listen while the redhead jabbered on.

Then they disappeared.

Now, where in tarnation did they go?

The voice echoed back to Bobby. Might as well follow.

It took ten minutes to catch up with them and find a hiding spot within hearing distance.

They'd gone into a cave.

"This is where I found the helmet. I'm disappointed we

didn't see it along the trail. I thought for certain I had it when I left."

Yeah, the one she dropped. Along with that old scroll. Why couldn't she have dropped the jewels? Rather than the worthless piece of metal.

"Tessa, will you help me look around? I know it's here. It's got to be."

"Sure." That was the first the other girl had spoken so far. And her name was Tessa. That might be useful later.

"I've been thinking it's not fair to ask you to help with my treasure hunt without you getting a share."

The scrawny girl giggled. "We haven't found anything yet. I would never ask that of you, Julia. This was all your idea. You're the one who found it in the first place—"

"Don't argue with me. I want to share with you. Of course, after Mr. Miller gets his share for his work."

Miller. The jeweler. Bobby was going to have to find out how much Mr. Miller knew. Was he going to be a problem too?

"I'll be glad to split the money with you when we sell them at the Hopi House. *If* we find anything else . . ."

"Okay. I hope we do."

Fool girl. That's all she had to say? Bunch of idiots. The lot of them. This is why no one else deserved the treasure.

Lots of scraping and digging sounds covered up any other conversation for the next several moments.

Bobby waited until the shadows in the canyon grew. What was taking them so long?

"Sorry for such a long day. I hate to leave empty-handed." The redhead appeared outside the cave entrance and brushed her hands against her split skirt. "But I'm sure there's more. I'm certain of it!"

"There's always next time." The mousy girl shrugged. "It was fun."

Redhead—*Julia*—looked up to the rim. "We are going to have to hike quick. I didn't realize it was getting so late. Don't want to lose the light."

Without any more words, the two headed back up the pencil-thin trail that connected with the Bright Angel Trail a good ways up the canyon. They kept one hand on the rock wall beside them and placed one foot in front of the other, like they were walkin' across a log.

Once they were out of sight, Bobby chewed on a piece of grass.

There were now two of them to get rid of. Two waitresses. Three people total, counting the jeweler.

Perhaps a new plan was in order. One where a tragic accident took the lives of two waitresses. *After* they'd done all the dirty work and found the treasure.

Roger could still be useful. Since he liked dressin' up in his fancy duds so much, maybe he could snoop around, find out where the waitresses' rooms were, and take what they found.

Why work themselves to the bone when there were others who would do it for 'em?

15

What's that?" Tessa yanked on Julia's arm.

She spun around and looked at where Tessa was pointing. "Good heavens. I was so worried about where to put my foot for the next step that I would have completely missed it." That cave just begged to be explored. Julia looked at the horizon and then at the watch pinned to her shirtwaist. "Do you think we have enough time to check it out?"

A wide grin spread across her hiking partner's face. "Oh yes. Let's."

As carefully as she could, Julia scurried to the red rock wall, where she could almost reach the base of the opening. "Hey, do you want to give me a boost and then I'll pull you up, or would you rather me boost you and you pull me?"

"I better give you the boost. My arms aren't very strong."

Julia had wondered as much, since Tessa was such a slight little thing, but she thought giving her the chance to voice her opinion was the best idea.

Tessa laced her fingers together and leaned over so her hand cradle was about a foot off the ground.

"All right, on the count of three." She counted out loud and stepped into her friend's waiting hands. With a grunt and a heave, Julia soon found herself lying on the edge of the cave. She reached down and grabbed Tessa's arms, then pulled with all she was worth. Landing in a puff of dust, they giggled and stood up, patting the dirt from their skirts.

Without saying a word, Tessa pulled out a candle and lit it. She ventured forth, and Julia followed for about twenty seconds until she ran into the back of her friend.

"What's wrong?"

"Too dark." A shiver shook her slim shoulders. "How about you go?"

Julia took the candle and nodded. She wasn't a fan of the dark either, but this was her crazy idea after all. And she'd dragged her friend into it, so she should probably be brave about it.

Her heart thrummed in her ears. Why was it when there was no other noise that the pumping of her blood grew so loud? But only when she was in scary situations? It didn't make sense.

No wonder she liked telling scary stories to the other girls. It had always been fun to watch them almost jump out of their skin.

Huh. Another reason behind her love of storytelling? She liked being in control—especially during scary stories. As long as *she* wasn't the one being scared.

Her boot hit something, and it clanked. Like metal!

Crouching down with the candle, she let out a little squeal. "Tessa, look!"

The girl was already beside her, and she reached for the morion. Julia grinned and watched her face as she reached into the upside-down helmet. She pulled out a scroll and unrolled it. Her eyes widened as she held the scroll close to the candle. There was another burnt etching in the thick leather!

"Three," Julia whispered. The Roman numeral was clear in the center, with more of the same swirly designs in the bottom corner. What if they were the initials of the brothers? Some sort of signature? It could prove to make it even more valuable, couldn't it?

Not that she was out to become the richest person around. But after all the years of storytelling, the idea of having a legitimate legend behind her was rather appealing.

"You were right." Tessa knelt there shaking her head. "There *was* more."

Allowing a giddy giggle to escape, Julia leaned over the helmet and peered inside. This one held one, two, three, four, five, six . . . *seven* pouches! All appeared larger than the last ones she found, but she didn't want to get her hopes up. Maybe she was in shock that they'd found more of the treasure. She swallowed and looked at her friend. "I promised to share this with you. Thank you for believing me. And for coming with me."

Tessa leaned toward her and hugged her. "I almost didn't believe it." She put her hands over her mouth and covered a squeal of delight. Then tears sprang to her eyes. "Thank you, Julia. . . . Thank you so much for letting me be a part of this." Tessa hugged her again.

Heart still pounding from the discovery, Julia stared at the pouches and then opened one to show Tessa. "Aren't they glorious?"

"Oh, wow. Let's get out into the light so I can see them better."

Julia whipped her head to the cave entrance. "Speaking of light . . . yikes, we better head back. I can't believe how late it is."

Tessa grimaced. "We can look at them back at the hotel."

"Good idea. We're going to have to run up the trail if we possibly can. I don't want to be caught out in the dark with whatever wildlife roams the canyon."

They crammed the items into their packs and headed toward the cave entrance. Once they'd slid on their backsides out of the opening and found sure footing, they headed up the trail at the briskest pace they dared. They could still see the sun above the rim, but not by much. Pretty soon, the canyon would be covered in shadows. And not long after, the sun would go down on the horizon.

Julia did *not* want to find out what the trail looked like in the dark.

Two weeks were left.

Three times, Chris had counted what he had put aside so far. He was almost there. In fact, he hoped to be able to pay Mr. Langford right on time. What a burden that would relieve!

Fred locked up the front door of the jewelry store. "Do you need me for anything else, son?"

The endearment had become precious to him. "I don't think so." He couldn't hide his yawn as he stood and stretched. "I'm just going to finish up a couple pieces here and I'll turn in for the night."

"Sounds good. You look like you could sleep for a month." Fred gripped his shoulder and plunked his hat onto his head. "I'll head on out, if that's all right."

"Yep. Good night." Chris placed a tiny piece of solder where he needed to secure the rest of the setting on the legend ruby piece. He couldn't wait to get these up to the canyon.

With Mr. Owens' approval, they could start selling them at the Hopi House. Which meant he had even more of a chance to get his building paid for in time.

The back door closed behind Fred, and quiet surrounded Chris like a warm blanket. What was it about the shop that made him feel like Gramps was sitting in the corner, smoking his pipe and talking to him about break facets, crown facets, and star facets? He'd drilled in Chris the need for practice. Over and over and over and over. So much so that he believed he could probably cut stones in his sleep with a blindfold on.

He chuckled.

Oh man. He missed his grandfather. Some days the grief was stronger than others. It didn't get easier per se, but it didn't always hurt as much as it once did.

As he put the finishing touches on the beautiful necklace, he wondered what Gramps would think of all this. The man loved a good story and the outdoors, so he would probably want to join Julia in hiking and exploring.

Chris leaned back in his chair when he was finished and looked at the workbenches around him. Like he'd told Julia, he was not much of an outdoorsman. He spent much of his time in here. Doing just this.

Gramps hadn't been that way. Yes, he'd loved the store and had spent thousands of hours making and repairing jewelry, but he'd also been an avid fisherman and hunter. Had often spoken of wanting to hike up in the Rockies and climb a fourteener. Something that would have never entered Chris's mind.

He stood up and removed his thick jeweler's apron.

Perhaps that needed to change. Maybe he should have taken Julia up on the invitation to hike. He'd heard many of the guests at the El Tovar rave about venturing down into the canyon. He could sacrifice a little of his time now that he was doing so well toward his goal, couldn't he?

The phone rang in the front of the store.

Chris jogged over to it. Who would be calling at this hour after the store was closed? "Hello?"

"Chris?" The line was filled with static. But it couldn't hide the identity of the caller.

"Hello, Julia. How are you this evening?" For once, he didn't mind the interruption to the silence.

"Oh, I can hardly catch my breath." Muffled sounds came over the line. "You won't believe it. We found more."

Even though he knew it was possible, the statement pushed his brain into overdrive. The legend was real. And they'd found another. "With a helmet?"

"Yes! And the Roman numeral for three!" Her delight was clear even through the staticky phone line.

That meant there could be at least one more. "Wow."

"Is there any way you can come up to the canyon?"

His thoughts exactly. "I can come up tomorrow. It's not my normal teaching day, but I do have several items to put up for sale in the Hopi House."

"Great! Tessa and I both have to work, but maybe we can chat on our breaks?"

"Whatever works for you." Maybe he could even attempt one of the trails. Hiking had never been his thing, but if Julia loved it, perhaps it was worth a try. Especially if there was more treasure to be found.

"Thank you so much! I'll see you tomorrow. Good night!"

"Good night, Julia."

The line clicked.

Lists started filling his mind. He'd need to wrap up the rest of the jewelry pieces this evening so he'd have time tomorrow morning to catch the train. And he'd need to let Fred know his change of plans as soon as possible.

Another little thrill went through him. If he sold all the pieces tomorrow, plus the money he knew was waiting for him already, he just might have enough for the building.

Wouldn't that be amazing to pay it all in full and early to boot? What a relief that would be.

Thinking of all he needed to do and in a short amount of time, Chris moved around the shop as fast as he could. He'd better bring a good pair of shoes that could handle a trail into the canyon just in case. What else did Gramps bring with him when he hiked?

The question tumbled around in his mind. Then he stuck his index finger up as he remembered his grandfather's words. A canteen. That was paramount. A revolver—which wouldn't do a lot of good with bears, but it might scare them off, and it was very handy with rattlesnakes. Of course, Chris didn't think bears would be a problem. But rattlesnakes, yes. He'd already heard several stories. Maybe mountain lions? Although he hadn't heard of anyone having trouble after that first attack. Maybe that one was just starving . . . or sick. What other wildlife lived in the canyon?

Perhaps he should bring a different set of clothes too. It looked like one could get pretty dirty venturing out on a hike.

A thought that he didn't mind one bit as long as Miss Julia Schultz accompanied him.

Roger still wasn't back. Stupid fool. He was always holding everything up. Something that riled Bobby up more and more each time he was late. But at least he'd found a way into the hotel so he could snoop around.

Well, it was a good thing that mountain lion trap was pretty much intact. They just needed to reinforce the latch and put some bait in there.

Too many rich tourists ventured into the canyon every day. It was stupid. Why would they do it? It's not like those wealthy people needed any more money. So what were they looking for?

The canyon wasn't all that interesting. It was just a big hole in the ground. Big deal. Lots of rocks. And a really dangerous roaring river at the bottom.

People were dumb. Plain and simple. Well, Bobby would make sure that less of 'em would come down here. Didn't need anyone else going after what wasn't theirs.

The waitress wouldn't give up so easily. Not now that she got a taste of treasure huntin'. But by eliminating the extra witnesses, Bobby would have a chance to get down to business.

They could follow those snoopin' girls and steal the treasure.

Ensure that a tragic accident could happen. Roger could even die. What a shame.

No one would be the wiser.

16

What a long day.

Ruth always had a soft spot for trying to help her girls reform. But she'd never had to deal with anything like this. Petty arguments, yes. Tardiness, yes. But cattiness and outright ugliness? It was unheard of here. The women who were granted the position of Harvey Girl at El Tovar were the cream of the crop. What was happening to their society?

If it were up to her, they'd all be gone. Yesterday.

The only problem was, Mr. Owens didn't want to dismiss the perpetrators until the new waitresses arrived. It was the height of tourist season, the hotel was sold out every night, and they were in a remote location.

The troublemakers knew it too. Oh, they'd perform their duties to perfection. But as soon as they were off the floor, they got together. It wasn't producing a good environment here. And that was paramount. Especially since there wasn't much outside of the culture that was their home here at the El Tovar. A family atmosphere had been vital to maintain.

A knock on her door made Ruth jump. Good heavens,

she was tired. But she put a hand to her hair and went to the door and opened it.

Julia and Tessa stood there, covered in red and gray dirt, huge smiles on their faces.

Ruth put her hands on her hips. "Well, this looks like an interesting story. Come on in." After they were through the door, she poured fresh water from the pitcher into the basin. "Looks like you might need to wash up a bit."

"It's okay. I'm going to take a bath in a minute." Julia sent Tessa a conspiratorial grin. "But we just had to tell you something."

"All right." She sat on her bed. "But you're going to have to stand there. I don't want to get any of that dirt on my bed or chair."

The girls giggled. Julia pulled off her pack. "We don't mind. You know that ever since Emma Grace—Mrs. Watkins—told me the legend, well . . . I've been a bit obsessed with finding the treasure."

Ruth laughed along and shook her head. "You do beat all, Julia." She turned to the other girl. "I assume she's gotten you all excited about finding treasure too?"

The girl nodded, then blurted, "Julia found it."

Ruth glanced back. Twice. "What did you say?"

"Look." Julia reached into her pack and pulled out an old metal . . . bowl? But handed it to Tessa. Then she held out a pouch and dumped the contents into her palm.

Now, that was something she hadn't expected to see. Ruth put a hand to her chest. She hadn't imagined the legend to be real! As she stared at the jewels, all she could do was shake her head. Back and forth. Back and forth. "You found it today?"

Julia bit her lip and winced. "Actually . . . I found some a couple weeks ago."

With a hand to her forehead, Ruth closed her eyes and then pinched the bridge of her nose. "And exactly why didn't you tell me about this? You *promised*, Julia." Then it hit her. "That's why you were speaking with Mr. Miller. And he said you had business together." Why hadn't she followed up on that? Probably because she was overwhelmed with the troubles of thirty women.

Her new assistant head waitress's face fell, and her eyes glistened. "I didn't lie to you, Ruth. Honest. In fact, the only reason I didn't tell you was because I was afraid you would think I was making up a story. I had to make sure that it was all right for me to keep it, and I wanted to show you the proof with the morion and the scroll. But I dropped the first ones."

It was true. She probably would have accused Julia of lying. But the proof in that pouch made the far-fetched legend real. What had Emma Grace started? She took a deep breath. "Why don't you start from the beginning."

"I found a morion like that one—a Spanish metal helmet—in a cave a couple weeks ago. The day I went by myself. And I haven't done that again. I promise . . ."

Ruth listened to the girls fill in all the details. Both of their faces were alight with wonder and excitement. The fact that Tessa jumped in with several sentences was impressive. The girl was blossoming in front of her.

Fifteen minutes later, Julia lifted her shoulders in a shrug. "That's it."

Tessa lifted her hand and piped up, "Julia's telling the truth, Miss Anniston. I've been with her. Mr. Miller checked into all the legalities and even spoke with Mr. Owens a while back."

How beautiful to see the quiet girl stick up for her friend. It thrilled Ruth's heart in a way she couldn't even capture.

It was all a bit surreal, but the proof was in front of her. "I'm excited for you both. What a wonderful find!"

"I've told Tessa that I would split the profits of this batch of treasure with her since she helped me find it." Julia's face beamed. "And I want to donate the helmet and scroll for a display at the Hopi House."

"That's very generous of you, and I'm sure it will be greatly appreciated. What's on the scroll?" As tired as she was, Ruth knew it would be a while before she would be able to go to bed. The girls were entirely too giddy. And there seemed to be something else that charged the air around them. What was it?

"The Roman numeral for three." Tessa sported a large smile on her face.

Ruth raised her eyebrows. "Ah. So you're hoping there's at least one more to be found."

Julia nodded. "At first I thought I wanted to find all the treasure before Mr. Miller sold any at the Hopi House. But there's no guarantee we will find it anytime soon. But maybe we could keep the legend a secret? I don't know." She looked down at her hands. "I could use the money now, so I asked him to clear it all with Mr. Owens. He's coming tomorrow so that I can speak with him about it. Once they start selling the jewelry with the story attached, there's a good chance others will want to search for the treasure too."

"What is it *you* want to do with the money?"

Silence from Julia.

Tessa clasped her hands in front of her. "My parents don't have much. And they've had to rent a tiny apartment for a long time back home. I'm hoping that I can convince them to move out here and we can buy a small house together. If I keep working here, I should be able to support them."

How delightful to hear Tessa speak with such passion.

Ruth turned back to Julia, but the girl's cheeks were pink and her head was still ducked. So, she got up off the bed and went to stand in front of her assistant head waitress. "You promised me you would tell me the truth, Julia. Are you in some kind of trouble?"

Julia's head snapped up, her eyes wide. "No. Not at all. I haven't done anything wrong, I promise. I've been honest about everything." Tears misted the girl's eyes.

"Then, what is it you're not telling me? Are you planning to leave with the money? Is that it?"

"I . . . I simply feel like maybe I should start over somewhere else. What with Florence here and everything. Everyone knows about my past of telling stories . . . and, well, it's embarrassing. I don't want people thinking of me like that. I've seen their looks when Florence re-tells one of my tales. I want to be somebody. Somebody acceptable. Money will help me do that."

Tessa wrapped her arms around Julia. Tears streamed down the other girl's face. "You can't leave me, Julia. You can't. Florence won't last long and you know that. She's just a gossip trying to stir up trouble." She dropped her arms and her eyes went wide as she looked back at Ruth. "I'm sorry, Miss Anniston. I shouldn't be saying things like that about another Harvey Girl."

Oh, how her heart broke for these two. They each held deep wounds. Frank's words came back to her. She couldn't miraculously fix things. Only the love of God could do that. *Oh, Lord, give me the words, because I feel like I'm at a loss here.*

With a deep breath, she reached for one of each of their hands. "I think it's time we had a long chat. Wash your hands and faces and listen, all right?"

Red tinged both of the girl's faces as they went to the basin and did as they were told. But Julia's expression looked closed off. How could she reach her?

Ruth situated herself back on her bed and tucked her feet up under her. "Money isn't going to solve your problems, Julia. It's not going to make you acceptable in the way that you want. It'll make you just as acceptable as your lavish stories did. They were entertaining, but people liked you on the surface because they liked to be entertained. The same thing will happen with people if they think you have money. But there won't be any real friendships to come out of that. Money can't buy you friends."

"But it can buy me a new life. A way to start over." Julia sniffed and wiped at the tears on her cheeks. "You have no idea what's it like. What I've had to endure because of my parents—" The abrupt clamping of her lips ended that sentence.

It told Ruth all she needed to know. Whatever the secret that involved her parents was . . . it was much worse than any of the wild stories she'd told in the past. "Rather than having to move away, you could use your new funds to do some good here. Help other people. If it's respect that you desire, you have to earn it—not buy it."

"Please don't leave." Tessa's voice was quiet. "I am finally feeling comfortable here. I enjoy hiking and exploring with you. You're my friend."

The two girls hugged each other and cried. "I don't want to leave," Julia sobbed into Tessa's shoulder. "But I think I have to. It's my only choice."

"No." Ruth's voice was firm. "It's not your only choice."

"How can you say that? What about Florence?"

Ruth clasped her hands in her lap and lifted her chin.

"Florence is on thin ice. I'm not saying she can't turn things around, but just like Tessa stated earlier, do you think Florence will be here forever? What if she left? Would you still want to leave?"

"Maybe . . . well, I don't know. The damage has already been done with the other girls."

"You don't think you could change their minds by just being yourself? Showing them who you really are? The girls here didn't know you as a storyteller. Most of them thought of you as quiet and restrained. Why don't you give them a chance?"

"Don't you get it?" The utter defeat on Julia's face tore at Ruth's heart. "You don't know who I am or where I came from or what I've done! Who I really am. I've been trying to figure that out for years. I don't even know the answer! I'm not worth anything."

"That is not true. You are priceless in my eyes and in God's eyes." Ruth looked between the two. "Both of you."

"God doesn't even know I exist. I'm sure He's got way too many other things to keep Him occupied." Julia pushed back her hair from her face and twisted it into a knot.

Ruth grabbed her Bible. "You know, this morning I was reading in the book of Luke. Listen to this: 'Are not five sparrows sold for two farthings, and not one of them is forgotten before God? But even the very hairs of your head are all numbered. Fear not therefore: ye are of more value than many sparrows.'" She thumbed back to the book of Matthew. "And what about this: 'Behold the fowls of the air: for they sow not, neither do they reap, nor gather into barns; yet your heavenly Father feedeth them. Are ye not much better than they?'"

"No." Julia shook her head vehemently. "How am I any better than birds? Why do I deserve God to take care of me?"

Ruth wanted to cry. Then and there. She'd never struggled with sharing her faith before. Had always been strong in this area. But she'd come at it all wrong. *Oh, Father, please. Help.*

For several moments, she just stared at the two faces before her. One strained and hurt. The other eager—almost yearning to hear what she said next. She closed her eyes and thought of all the passages of scripture she'd memorized over the years. Oh, that was it! She opened her eyes and went to the book of Galatians.

Before she read the passage, she cleared her throat and took a deep breath. "You know . . . I don't tell many people this, but I was adopted. My parents were killed in a fire when I was a baby. I don't even have any memories of them. But there was another set of parents that took me in and loved me. It was through their love that I came to understand God's love."

Julia's brow creased into a deep *V* as she frowned.

Best to just keep on going. "My new mom shared with me this passage in Galatians. It says, 'But when the fulness of the time was come, God sent forth his Son, made of a woman, made under the law, to redeem them that were under the law, that we might receive the *adoption* of sons. And because ye are sons, God hath sent forth the Spirit of his Son into your hearts, crying, Abba, Father. Wherefore thou art no more a servant, but a son; and if a son, then an *heir of God* through Christ.' He loved us so much that he sent His son to die for us—to be the sacrifice in our place—so that He could adopt us. All because He loves us and *wants* us to be His children."

Tessa leaned forward, soaking up every word. "Why would He sacrifice His own son for me?"

"To show us how much He loves us. There's a verse in the book of John where Jesus says, 'Greater love hath no man than this, that a man lay down his life for his friends.' He said this right after telling everyone that they needed to love one another just as He loved them. I hope both of you know that I love you. It's not because I'm so great of a person, but because God loves me. I would gladly sacrifice myself for you."

Tears streamed down Tessa's cheeks, but her lips tipped up in a smile. "Please. Tell me more."

"I think God uses this word *adoption* in His scripture to help us understand His love better. I probably grasp it better than most because I've been adopted. Many people have been surprised when they find out they are expecting a child. But you can't adopt by accident. It's not a surprise. It's intentional. The parents *choose* to love and care for you—to cherish you—forever. God chooses us."

But as Ruth shared from her heart about her own story with her family, and how Jesus had done a mighty work in her life, she saw Julia's frown deepen.

How do I reach her heart, Lord?

Uncomfortable. That was the only way to describe how Julia felt at this moment.

How could Ruth tout the love of God being like adoption? Sure, Julia had parents choose to adopt her too, but then they died. No one else wanted her after that.

None of this made sense. Willing to lay down her life for her friends? Who sacrificed like that?

Not anyone she'd ever known.

But Tessa seemed really moved. Julia couldn't trample

over what Ruth was saying at the cost of another friend. So it was best to keep her mouth shut.

Maybe one day her questions could be answered. But she didn't see how.

Tap tap. "Ruth, it's me." Mrs. Watkins' voice sounded through the door.

Ruth hopped to her feet and went to the door to open it to the very pregnant Emma Grace. "Goodness, what are you doing up and around at this hour?"

"The baby is having a boxing match with my insides, and Ray is meeting with Mr. Owens. It wasn't comfortable sitting up in the Rendezvous Room all by myself, so I thought I'd come see how you were doing." The beautiful blond woman scanned the room. "Looks like you girls are having a party without me." A smile stretched across her face.

"Come on in. Let's see if you can find a comfortable position on the bed with me." Ruth tugged her friend in and then closed the door. "Now, where were we?"

To be honest, Julia had tuned them all out the last few minutes. So, when Tessa started asking more questions, she dipped her head and picked at the dirt on her split skirt. Her mind whirled with the possibilities in front of her. While it healed so many places in her heart to hear that Tessa wanted her to stay and called her friend, it couldn't fix her current predicament. It seemed no matter what, her stories would find a way to follow her.

More than anything, she wished they could get back to why they'd come to Ruth's room in the first place. If she could change the subject . . . ? No. That wouldn't be kind to Tessa. No matter how much she wanted to share the treasure excitement with Emma Grace. But all this God talk was too much. How could a loving God exist somewhere up there and give up everything for her? She wasn't worth even having earthly parents want her.

"Julia." Emma Grace's soft voice washed over her.

She glanced up. Where had Ruth and Tessa gone?

Obviously seeing the question on her face, Emma Grace filled her in. "Ruth took Tessa out to pray with her."

"Pray? About what?"

"Tessa wants to give her life to God." The joyful and serene look on the married woman's face was something Julia wished she had.

Give her life to God. Another foreign phrase to her. It just didn't make sense. God seemed so distant and far away. Almost unreal. She shrugged. "Okay."

"Why don't you ever want to speak about your parents?" No tiptoeing around difficult subjects with Mrs. Watkins.

Julia stiffened her back. "Because people have looked down on me when they found out who my parents were and what they did. It's bad enough that I have to overcome my own failings. But to add theirs? It's been truly awful. The thing is, I know my parents weren't perfect. But they loved me. And I loved them."

"Look. It might just be the fact that I'm getting close to delivery and so I don't have a lot of patience left in me to give, but please don't be offended by this. . . ."

"All right." Another shrug. It wasn't like Emma Grace had tried to hurt her in the short time they'd known each other.

"I'm sure what you've been through is bad. Terrible, even. But we love you. We care about you. And we want to be your friends. If you keep pushing us away, you're just going to hurt yourself even more."

Julia shook her head. "That's so easy for you to say because you have a wonderful life with an amazing husband

and a baby on the way. You don't understand what it's like." She couldn't keep the hurt from her words.

But Emma Grace laughed. "I can see how you would think that. But my own father had me kidnapped as a child so that he could gain sympathy from his peers and get control of a railroad spur that he wanted."

"What?" That was not what she expected to hear. From all outward appearances, Emma Grace had the perfect life.

"It gets even more complicated. I ran away. Lied about my age and my name."

"Really? You lied?"

"I'm ashamed to say that, but yes, I did. I became a Harvey Girl and hid for over five years. Always thinking someone was after me. Always living in fear. It was awful. Until I came here. Well, things escalated and got much, much worse before they got better, but I found God here. And He changed my life for the better."

Julia blinked several times. Would this sweet God-fearing woman be able to look past all the ugliness in her own life? For a moment, she really wanted to believe it. Maybe she *could* tell the truth.

No. No, she couldn't. Not as long as Florence was still here. Imagine what horrible things would be spread about her then.

No. She couldn't risk the truth. Maybe not ever.

17

The train's whistle signaled the morning arrival. Just in time for luncheon. Julia's heart thrummed with excitement. She couldn't wait to show Chris everything they found. But it would have to wait until her break this afternoon. He would be talking with Mr. Owens soon and then at the Hopi House. Would it take long for her jewels to get sold? The thought of changing her life and her reputation made her imagination swirl.

Heading back to her tables with bread and butter, she passed Florence. There wasn't any way to avoid it, their paths were always bound to cross in the dining room. But something about the other waitress's face was unsettling.

Normally, the girl ignored her, looked at her with condescension or derision, or sent her an expression of downright distaste. But today, Florence's face was pale and she looked . . . hurt.

Good. It was about time the other girl had a taste of her own medicine.

As soon as the thought took root, a horrible feeling passed through Julia. The hateful thoughts toward Florence made her feel pretty rotten. Shaking her head, she pasted on a smile and looked to her next table. It wasn't her business what was wrong with the other Harvey Girl anyway. Why should she even care?

Lunch passed in one plate after another after another after another. So many people were at the canyon, and everyone wanted to dine in the El Tovar's grand dining room. But today was the first day that she almost confused customers' orders because there were so many of them. Thankfully, she'd caught herself at the last second, but it had been close.

Of course, it wasn't just the amount of people. Not if she were honest. Since she hadn't been able to speak with Chris when he arrived, he didn't know that she'd been debating about selling the jewelry with the story of the treasure just yet.

But now the hotel was abuzz with the legend and the jewelry. From what she'd heard, people were fascinated with the story and had bought *all* the pieces at the Hopi House. That was exactly what she'd been hoping for, right?

Sell the jewels. Make money. Start a new life.

But she hadn't been excited. Instead, she was disappointed. In all honesty, deep down she'd hoped it would take a bit longer to find the treasure. Give her a chance to spend more time with Chris and Tessa. Charlotte and Ruth.

It hadn't helped that Ruth's words last night wouldn't leave her alone. Or the fact that every time she saw Tessa, her young friend was practically glowing and couldn't stop smiling.

And now the hotel was abuzz with speculation about who it was that had found the treasure. Mr. Owens seemed pleased with himself as he spoke with guests about the legend.

If people were so intrigued by the person who found the

treasure . . . maybe they would be fascinated with her? Think she was someone special? That was what she wanted after all, wasn't it?

To be highly esteemed. Respected. Found worthy.

Maybe Ruth was correct and she could stay here and do philanthropic work. Hang out with the wealthy people.

Florence passed by. Their eyes connected. The hatred and disdain there stabbed Julia in her very soul.

Who was she kidding? Highly esteemed. Respected. It was laughable. That wouldn't happen if everyone knew her parents had been hanged for killing men while they robbed a bank. What kind of person would they think she was after finding that out? She'd be shunned for sure.

Maybe her original idea of starting over really was the best. In another country.

Even though she hated the thought of leaving Tessa, Ruth, Charlotte, Emma Grace, and . . . Chris.

As she trekked back to the kitchen, her feet ached. Had she tied her boots too tight this morning? She passed a customer showing off her prize from the "treasure collection," and Julia frowned. Why wasn't she smiling? Every piece of jewelry had sold. That should amaze her! With that kind of sales, she should be champing at the bit to hear from Chris about the profits.

As she turned around, the man in her thoughts appeared in person. A broad smile across his face. Eyes crinkled. He waved at her as he walked toward her.

No. She couldn't tell him about her past. She could imagine the look on his face when he found out.

The disappointment. The disapproval.

That was something she never wanted to see.

"Good afternoon, Mr. Miller." Her stomach fluttered.

Yes, there was something special about him. No use trying to convince herself otherwise.

"Good afternoon, Miss Schultz. I asked the host if I could speak to you. Apparently today, I have a bit more clout."

Her depressing thoughts melted away. "Because you're the man of the hour, I'm sure. I hear your jewelry is a big hit." She glanced around the room. "If you'd like to have a seat at the table in the corner, when I'm done, we can take a walk and discuss our business."

"I would be honored." He gave a slight bow. "May I help in any way?"

What a puzzling man. A customer and yet offering to help a waitress. She let out a small laugh. "It's kind of you to offer. But the dining room will be closing soon. Would you like me to bring you some coffee?"

"That would be wonderful. Thank you." He nodded at her and headed for the empty table.

Mr. Owens was in front of her before she could take another step. "Miss Schultz, I understand you need to discuss business matters with Mr. Miller. Why don't you use my office once you are done with your duties here?"

Shocked couldn't even describe the feelings that jolted through her. The manager had barely said two words to her since her arrival and now he was smiling at her and seemed eager to share her secret. Of course, he was pleased with the profits, no doubt.

"Miss Schultz?"

Shaking her head, she focused on him. "Yes, sir. That's very kind. Thank you."

Half an hour later, she sat in the plush and immaculate office of Mr. Owens. "I heard that you sold out of all the jewelry you brought today?"

"We did! Chuma writing up the legend to go with each piece was a brilliant idea. Of course, I think that lady could sell sand in the desert." Chris relaxed and leaned forward. "Here." He reached into his coat pocket and pulled out an envelope. "This is for you."

She took the envelope and peered through her lashes at him. "What's this?"

"Your share of the profits." His eyes drew her in. And that smile. It made her melt just a little.

She blinked and looked down. Focus, she needed focus. Opening the envelope, she looked inside.

"Oh my goodness gracious." She lifted a hand to cover her mouth. Her gaze bolted back to his. "Really? All this?"

"Yes." His eyes crinkled again, and her stomach flip-flopped.

"And you already distributed the profits to Mr. Owens and yourself?"

"Yes. It's all yours."

In an instant, the appearance of Mr. Connors in Chris's shop ran through her memory. "Do you have enough?"

His head tilted to the right, and he stared at her with a puzzled expression on his face. "It's split just as we agreed."

"No, I mean . . . that nasty man who came into your shop, he said that your building was being sold and that you wouldn't be able to pay for it." She held out the envelope. "Do you need more?" Now she was a bit glad she hadn't been able to speak to him this morning. How selfish of her! She'd completely forgotten about what Mr. Connors had implied.

"That is very kind of you, Julia, but I'm fine. I not only sold out of the pieces I made out of your gems, but they've sold everything I've brought up here so far. God has been good. I almost have the full amount to pay for my shop."

His smile softened. "It was very sweet of you to think of me." The air seemed to warm around them. The moment was . . . intimate.

As she stared at him, no words came to her mind. Other than how nice he looked in his suit. Or how perfect the part was in his hair.

Well, this was awkward.

Another moment passed.

No matter how good-looking the man was, nor how much his eyes and smile made her turn into a puddle, she had no reason to think that he thought any more of her than just their business arrangement. She cleared her throat. "I have more jewels for you to use. Plenty more."

Chris leaned back in the chair. "I'd love to see them."

"I can go get them now."

He stood. "How much longer do you have before you need to be back in the dining room?"

She checked the clock behind Mr. Owens' desk. "About forty-five minutes."

He held out his arm. "Then there's no rush to get the stones now. Would you care to join me for a stroll?"

So much for keeping her mind just on business. "I would love to, but we're not allowed while we're in uniform."

"Oh, I see. My apologies." The disappointment behind his smile was clear.

"But Mr. Owens knows we are together and has given us permission to be in his office. We could continue to chat in here for a bit?"

With a nod, he sat back down. "I realized on the train ride up that I don't know a lot about you. Do you have family?"

"None living." That was the easiest explanation. "How about you?"

"My parents live in Albuquerque."

"Do you get to see them often?"

"I try. But it's been harder since Gramps died." He looked down at his strong hands.

Julia watched him for a few seconds. "You were very close to your grandfather, weren't you?"

"Yes."

As Chris opened up about the man who'd given him the dream of becoming a jeweler, Julia found herself caught up in the story of family. Sacrifice. And legacy.

What would it be like to have that kind of love?

The train ride back to Williams had lulled him straight to sleep. Now that he was back, Chris hoped to put in a few late hours in his workshop. If he could keep his mind focused.

Which was more difficult than he imagined. Because Julia was front and center.

He'd even had a dream about her on the train.

Funny. He never dreamed. Well, at least rarely. And even though he didn't know her very well, he was drawn to her. Felt a nudging toward her. Wanted to get to know her and spend time with her.

He went to the workbench and put on his apron. As much as he would like to keep thinking about the lovely Miss Schultz, it was time to put some dedicated effort in. He was so close to having enough to pay Mr. Langford. And until that burden was off his shoulders, he really should put all his efforts into buying the shop.

Every piece of his jewelry had sold. Not just the ones from last week, but all the ones he'd brought up today. It shocked him. Chris added up all his funds. Only twenty-five dollars more to go. How incredible! By this time next week, he hoped to pay his landlord a visit.

Thank You, Lord. Wow. He would have never imagined he could pull it all together when Mr. Langford first told him. But look at what God had done.

He tucked the money away in the lockbox. He couldn't wait to bring it to his landlord and sign the paperwork. What a great feeling that would be. He'd worked hard and would own his own building! Wouldn't Gramps be proud? He'd built this business from nothing, and to see it thrive now was amazing.

The chatter all day around the hotel had been focused on the legend and its treasure as the wealthy strolled around the rim and showed off their unique pieces they'd purchased at the Hopi House. Chuma did a great job as saleswoman. Goodness, the woman could weave an exciting tale, and it impressed him how no one could possibly tell her no after she shared about the legend that went back almost four hundred years. Everyone wanted a piece of the beautiful history.

Even though today wasn't a teaching day, he enjoyed seeing how the Hopi people improved in their jewelry-making skills every time he visited. Their excitement to create unique pieces that captured their heritage was contagious. He'd begun studying more and more of their art each time.

As he turned on another lamp, he looked at the stones lying on the black velvet. He'd been meticulous in cutting some of the old stones into more usable gems. He'd saved five of the smaller and most beautiful emeralds to the side.

Wouldn't they look lovely on Julia? It would bring out the

exquisite shade of her green eyes and contrast beautifully with her red hair.

That was what he should do. He owed her so much for coming to him and entrusting him with the jewels. He'd loved working with these legendary stones. They'd made so much money already. Surely she wouldn't mind if he created a special piece just for her. Then she'd always have something to remember the historic treasure hunt. Something to remember him by.

But he wanted more than remembrance. If he were honest, he would like to pursue more. Wouldn't his mom and dad think that was a hoot? He'd own his own shop *and* he'd be courting a lady. Maybe he could convince them to move to Williams after all.

He sat back down at his workbench and pulled out his pencil and sketching notebook. The piece would need to be unique. Special. Something that captured the exuberance and animation of Julia.

He loved how she talked with her hands when she was really excited. How her eyes filled with sparkle and light when she talked about the legend. What it all came down to? He knew her face.

There was something about her that drew Chris.

But . . . he stopped what he was sketching. Something in him hesitated. Even after their chat today, there was really very little that he knew about her.

He shook his head. He should still make the gift for her. She would appreciate his thoughtfulness and their partnership. It would take him a long time to use all of the stones, so they'd have lots of time to hopefully get to know each other better. She was charming and full of life. And once he paid for his building, he would have more time to spend up at the canyon. Because then he could negotiate with Fred to continue working in his shop, and he'd have the money to pay the man a salary.

It was sound reasoning. One step at a time.

He'd make a necklace for Julia.

And he'd just have to pray for the Lord to guide his steps if Chris was to pursue more with the lovely redheaded Harvey Girl.

Stupid women. Why weren't they scared of venturing down here? It was bad enough all them frilly tourists kept coming down into the canyon, chattering up a storm about the legend. Nothin' was going according to plan. Nothin'. Them fool Harvey Girls were responsible and were selling off the treasure. A week had passed, and it was their day off. Roger had snooped enough to find that out. Worthless as he was. Their change of plans would have to work. Somethin' had to be done.

"Now, when they come out, make sure you get the flour sack over one of 'em, and I'll get the other." Bobby watched Roger's face. Furrowed, with a set jaw. Good. He was listenin'. "Then we'll tie 'em up. Make 'em tell us where the treasure is. Or keep 'em with us until they find the rest. No more games."

"I heard ya the first ten times ya told me. I'm not stupid." He straightened his tall frame. Lifted his shoulders. Where did all this newfound confidence come from? And why was he always talking back now?

"Just cause ya got yerself a fancy suit and snooped around all them rich people don't mean you can talk to me like that.

Do what I tell ya without the lip. Got it?" Infuriating man. Lately, he'd taken to acting like he was in charge and could make decisions on his own. Like that would ever happen.

Bobby allowed a smirk. Fool. But his time would come. "Quiet!"

The chatter of the redhead sounded like it was getting closer They must be done looking for the day. Finally.

"Now!" Bobby's whisper-shout accompanied a shove to Roger's back.

It only took a second to overtake the two girls, and they had flour sacks over both of them in record speed.

A loud thunk and a moan from Roger made Bobby turn and watch as he fell several feet down the crevasse.

The redhead in Bobby's grip started screaming and wriggling up a storm. There was only a split-second to make the choice. Bobby let go of the girl with one hand to be able to pull out the pistol. But as soon as the revolver was out, that mousy girl had the sack off her and had slung her brown satchel at Bobby. The next second passed at a turtle's pace. Almost like the world stopped spinning as the girl stumbled back and Bobby fell from the wallop.

The explosion of the trigger being pulled filled the air.

18

A gunshot ricocheted up the canyon. The echo of the bullet pinging off rock reverberated in Julia's ears. "Tessa! Tessa, are you okay?" she screeched against the thick material over her face. What was going on?

She couldn't feel pressure on her arms anymore, but she heard a couple of thuds, accompanied by a moan and a weird grunt. She tried to get the large sack up and off of her, but panic was setting in and she struggled with the material. She couldn't breathe! Pushing at the fabric, she gasped and cried. This wasn't helping.

She stopped her frantic movements and took several breaths. Forcing herself to calm down. "Tessa?" It was more of a squeak than a word. She hated having anything over her face.

"I'm . . . here." The words were strained. But at least her friend was alive. What had happened to their would-be captors?

With slow movements, she worked the large sack over her head and breathed deep of the dusty air. Tessa lay on the ground in front of her, a pool of red at her side. "No! No no no no no no . . ." Tears pricked her eyes, and she blinked against them as she rushed to her friend's side.

"They're"—Tessa pointed with her left arm—"they're getting away." Then she leaned back and closed her eyes.

Julia looked over her shoulder and saw a lanky figure hobbling off in the distance below them. A rounder, shorter fella shoved at him. She wouldn't be able to catch them now anyway, not that she'd want to after the attack. But at least they were running in the opposite direction. "You were shot?"

Tessa's cheeks were ghostly white as she bit her bottom lip and nodded toward her right arm. "It either went right through me or just grazed me because I heard it hit rock after."

"I heard that too. It was only one shot, right?" After all the echoes and the chaos of the moment, she couldn't recall. But the strange scent of tobacco and lavender stuck with her. What was that from?

Bending over Tessa's slight form, she swallowed against the bile that threatened to come all the way up. Blood had never been something she dealt with. She'd never tended a gunshot wound before, but she knew enough to at least stop the bleeding. At least she hoped.

Julia tore a piece off the bottom of her old-fashioned bloomers she wore under her split skirt, hoping it would be long enough to wrap around her friend's thin arm. "How did you . . . I mean, what did you do to get away? Once that sack was over my head, I was completely disoriented and scared for my life!"

A lopsided grin lifted one of Tessa's cheeks. "I found out a long time ago that no one expects the quiet ones to fight back. Especially ones my size."

"You fought that guy?"

"No." Tessa winced with the movement. "His grip wasn't all that tight once the sack was over me. I stomped on his foot and gave him a hard shove. Caught him off guard. He must've fallen down to the rocks below us. That was when I slung my satchel at the one who held you. I didn't know he had a gun. I'm just glad they fell where they couldn't get to us."

First Tessa had disposed of the slimy Connors and now their would-be captors. Julia was in awe. "You are amazing, my friend."

"Nah. Just wiry and stealthy."

They laughed together, and another wince crossed her friend's face.

"Does it hurt?"

"Yeah."

Julia looked up the trail as she did her best to bandage her friend's arm as tight as she dared. "Do you think you can walk? I don't want to leave you here alone, and it'll be dark soon."

"I don't think I have much choice, do I?"

Julia helped Tessa to a sitting position. "How does that feel?"

"Give me a few moments to let the world right itself. You're going to have to help me."

"Of course. I can carry you if I have to."

Her friend rolled her eyes. "Up the steep trail? I doubt that." She held on to her right arm with her left. "I think it just nicked me. But that was a lot of blood."

With a nod, Julia took a deep breath. "Look, I don't know who those men were, but I really don't want to be here if they come back."

"Me neither." Tessa grabbed onto her with both hands,

winced, and made it to standing. She wobbled a little but then looked a bit steadier. "I'm ready."

"Drink some water first. You're going to need it to replenish your system after you bled so much." Hadn't she read that in a book somewhere? She was no expert, but it made her feel better to say something. Anything to take her mind off the horrendous journey ahead of them. How were they going to get up the trail?

After they both took several sips, Julia took a deep breath and put her right arm around her friend's waist and pulled Tessa's good arm over her left shoulder. "Okay. Lean against me and we can do this." Hopefully her words sounded more confident than she felt.

Perspiration beaded on Tessa's upper lip as she nodded. And they started the trek.

The first ten or so steps were a bit grueling, but once they got into a rhythm and Julia realized she needed to lean forward, they actually made decent progress. It was a long way up to the top, but they could do this. They both had use of their legs. The only real worry was how much blood Tessa lost. She was so tiny to begin with that any loss couldn't be good.

Even though they were going at a snail's pace, her friend was breathing heavily. If Julia were a praying woman, she'd be throwing some prayers toward God at this point. But she didn't know what to say. *God, if You're there . . . help us?* She felt like a fool. But she'd take any help she could get. She had to get Tessa to a doctor.

With each passing step, her worry grew. Were they attacked because of the treasure or because they were women? Both ideas were hideous and made her cringe, but the thought that she'd brought danger to the El Tovar by finding the treasure made her chest ache.

"Tell me a story, Julia." Tessa's plea jolted her out of her thoughts.

A story. She had a love-hate relationship with those words. But she would do anything for her friend. "What kind of story would you like?"

"Oh, anything. I just need to get my mind off the endless climb in front of me. Maybe something truly fantastical."

"Fantastical, huh?" She smiled. "Once upon a time, there was a pair of magical shoes. Made of gold and crystals, these shoes were passed down from generation to generation, mother to daughter. And they granted the wearer one wish. That one wish changed each of the ladies' lives for the better as long as the wish was an unselfish one. . . ."

"I need a magic wish right now." Tessa's voice was low.

"You'll be fine. I'll get you to the doctor and you'll be right as rain."

"No. There's something I need to tell you, Julia. . . ."

Ruth paced outside of the room as the doctor examined the young waitress. The space had been tight, and Tessa had asked for Julia to stay at her side, so now *she* had the wonderful job of waiting. Something she really wasn't all that good at. At least not in a situation like this.

Almost all of the girls were waiting out in the hallway to hear the news. But they gave Ruth a wide berth. And no wonder. It had been a tough evening.

Florence and her little crew had pulled a prank on Charlotte. A mean prank meant to humiliate the other girl. When they were caught, there was no remorse. It was the last straw and their last chance. Ruth had no choice but to fire them all on the spot.

There'd been begging and crying, pleading and ranting. But Ruth had warned them before that there were no more chances. Why that shocked some of them was beyond her realm of knowledge. They knew the rules.

Mr. Owens was furious about the behavior and what this meant for the dining room, but he was also a stickler for protocol. The next train wasn't until morning, so those girls were all packing their bags down the hall.

What she hadn't needed was to have Julia and Tessa return with a gunshot wound and the story of an attack.

Oh, how she wished Emma Grace had never told them that story about the legend. Because now the entire hotel was in an uproar, and Mr. Owens would have to decide how to handle things with the guests. Not that he could stop any of them from doing what they wanted, but he'd have to post warnings and advise against anyone venturing down into the canyon.

Mr. Ralph Cameron would certainly pitch a fit if he didn't make his money off all the people using his trail. The Kolb brothers would lose a lot of money if they couldn't take the tourists' pictures. But how would they keep people safe anyway? First the mountain lion, now someone was shooting at people! It was ridiculous.

She swiped a hand at her hair and realized her bun was nowhere near intact anymore. Pulling it down, she ran her fingers through the tresses and did a simple braid. A lot of the girls were cutting their hair nowadays, but she wasn't quite ready for that kind of modern change.

The door opened, and the doctor stood there with a smile. He was a very straightforward man. One who didn't care about the wealth of the person he was treating. That made her trust him all the more. "The bullet took a chunk of her arm with it, but with a little rest, she should be back to normal within a couple weeks." He handed Ruth a piece of paper. "Here's my instructions for helping her to keep the wound clean and bound. The muscle was pretty torn up, so she won't be able to lift anything for oh, say, ten days. At the two-week mark, I'll check it again and can most likely clear her for her waitressing duties as long as there isn't any infection."

"Thank you, Dr. Collins."

"You're welcome."

Ruth walked past him into the room. Tessa's cheeks had a bit more color now, which was a good thing to see. "How are you feeling?"

"I'm all right." She sat up a little straighter in the plethora of pillows that Julia must have piled behind her. "Ask her," she whispered and nudged her friend.

"Ask me what?"

Julia went straight to the door and shut it. With her hands clasped in front of her, she turned to Tessa and winced. "I'm not sure that's a good idea right now."

"If you don't, I will." The volume from the girl in the bed was louder than Ruth had ever heard.

"Spit it out." Ruth placed her hands on her hips. What was going on with these two?

The girls shot looks back and forth to each other.

"Fine. If she won't say anything, I'll ask." Tessa used her good arm to smooth her hair. "Ruth, will you please go with Julia to find the rest of the treasure?"

"What?!" Of all the ridiculous things to think about right now. "You were attacked today. And shot. No, I won't have any more of this treasure nonsense—"

"Miss Anniston! Please." The shout from the injured girl was enough to make Ruth and Julia both jump backward. "Sorry. That might be the pain talking, but you need to listen to reason."

"I don't see how reason has anything to do with my traipsing down into the canyon." But when Ruth looked at Julia, she clamped her mouth shut. "I'm sorry. Please . . . continue." Not that she would agree to anything, but she could be *reasonable*.

Julia fidgeted with her fingers. "We don't know that the attack had anything to do with the treasure, but I'm afraid that many of the guests will be put in danger if the rest of it isn't brought back. Soon."

"Don't try to play the guests-could-be-in-danger card." Ruth narrowed her eyes.

Tessa took a deep breath. "Julia's covering for me. My parents are being evicted from their apartment. They are packing up everything they own and boarding a train to come here."

There was more to the story, Ruth felt it in her bones. "What is it you're not telling me?"

Tessa licked her lips. "My uncle—my father's brother—owes a lot of money to some people. No one knows where he is. But the people he owes found my parents. They took everything they had. When I received the telegram, Julia and I had just found more of the treasure, so I told my parents to come here, thinking I could take care of them." Tears raced down her cheeks, and she hiccupped.

Julia stepped forward. "Please, Miss Anniston."

While it sounded like a noble reason, it was still ridiculous. Venturing back down there. The girls had probably hoped to play on her sympathies with such a story, but it wouldn't work. "You both know that I cannot do this. Both of the head waitresses can't be gone at the same time. On top of that, we are several girls short now, thanks to Florence." She shook her head. "I'm sorry, but my answer is no."

Julia's eyes pleaded with her. "I *need* to find the rest, Ruth."

"No. No, you don't. You *want* to find the rest. You *want* to feel like you are someone special. But you already are! Don't you see that? Why do you insist on seeing your value in what people think of you?"

19

Just as Chris was heading to the door, the phone rang. He plopped his hat on his head and adjusted the collar of his coat as he went back to the phone on the wall. Late-night phone calls had happened more often after Miss Julia Schultz entered his life. Not that he expected it was her. Again. But he hoped it was. A smile split his lips as he reached for the earpiece.

"Hello?"

"Mr. Miller. This is Mr. Owens."

Something was off. The manager had never called him before. "Is everything all right?"

"Can you come up to the canyon tomorrow? And stay for a couple of days?"

"Um . . . of course. I'll need to call Mr. Holland and make sure he can cover my shop here."

"Good." The man cleared his throat. "We have some . . . *extenuating* circumstances. I need you to assist Miss Schultz in finding the rest of the treasure—*if* there is any more to be found."

And the man thought they could find it in a couple of days? After all these years? That was odd. "I would love to assist in any way that I can, sir, but I'm not a skilled treasure hunter. Or hiker for that matter. I'm a bit confused—"

"Someone attacked Miss Schultz and Miss Smith on the trail today. We are still unsure if it had anything to do with the treasure, but the sheriff has suggestions that I think we should follow, and it would keep the guests safe."

"Are they all right?" His heartbeat thrummed in his ears.

"Yes. But Miss Smith in injured. Look, I know this is unorthodox, but I need someone that I trust. Mr. Henderson and Mr. Watkins are both experienced hikers, but Mr. Watkins is on his way to Kingman, and I have a greater need for Mr. Henderson in the kitchen since the head chef has taken ill. You are needed in these extraordinary circumstances, Mr. Miller."

His gut tightened. "Of course, I will help in whatever way I can. Miss Schultz is in agreement?"

"Yes. In fact, she's right here and has asked to speak with you." Several muffled sounds came through the line. They must be switching places.

"Hi, Chris." Julia's voice. Exactly what he needed to hear to calm his racing heart.

"I'm so thankful you are okay." He kept his voice as steady as possible.

"Tessa . . ." Her voice cracked. "Tessa was shot today. It was just her arm, so she'll recover. It will take a few weeks to heal."

So much for calming his heart. No wonder the manager had called him. They were shot at? The legend and treasure were all well and good while they brought tourists and profits. But if guests were now in danger because of it? "Who attacked you? Were they after the treasure?"

"I don't know. But the sheriff seems to think so. It's the

most logical explanation. Mr. Owens thinks it would be best for us to try and find the rest. I've kept a notebook with where I've searched so far. The sheriff will advise people not to venture down any of the trails for a couple of days. If we don't find anything else, they're going to tell everyone that all of it has been found. For the safety of everyone."

The next morning, he boarded the train to the Grand Canyon and swiped a hand down his face. He hadn't gotten much sleep after the call from El Tovar. To think that someone had tried to grab the two women on the trail and then shot poor Tessa.

Julia had sounded exhausted and discouraged. But that was understandable. What had been hard for him was not being able to do anything to help her right then and there. And he'd wanted to. More than anything. But the distance between them prevented him from doing anything other than wait.

Mr. Owens had gotten back on the phone and put a plan into place. *He* would take over managing the dining room for a couple of days so that Ruth could accompany Julia and Chris. Apparently, Miss Schultz had been quite insistent that she didn't trust anyone else.

Chris hated the plan to lie if they couldn't find the rest. Dishonesty always rubbed him the wrong way. While he understood what the manager and police were trying to do—keep people safe and hope that the criminals would head on to greener pastures—he didn't think that lying was the way to do it.

Someone could have easily found other portions of the treasure and simply never told anyone about it. It *had* been several hundred years, after all. No one knew how many stashes there were in total anyway. Well, other than the two brothers who left them.

No matter how much he tried to substantiate the lie in his mind, he couldn't do it. There had to be a way to keep people safe without being dishonest.

Once he arrived up at the hotel and had a chance to speak with Julia, maybe he'd come up with a way that would appease all sides. *Without* lying.

His heart went out to Tessa. Missing two weeks of work because of her arm would surely hurt her budget. He understood why Julia wanted to help her friend, especially after she'd been injured. He wondered if Julia also felt guilty for bringing her along the first time.

That brought him back to Julia.

She never told him a reason for *why* she had wanted to search for the treasure in the first place, other than the fact that Mrs. Watkins had told her the story of the legend. He'd always been caught up in the excitement on her face each time she spoke about it. Her eyes would light up, those dimples would appear as she smiled, and she would look as if she were bursting with a grand story to tell. He could sit and listen to her for hours.

Another hint that cemented his decision last night in his mind.

He was going to ask Julia Schultz if he could court her.

And since he'd agreed to go searching with her, he should have plenty of time to ask her all about herself. Now that he'd known her a few weeks and had seen her wonderful work ethic, he was even more sure that he wanted to get to know her better. Every time he thought of her—which was a lot—his heart did something funny. Which told him that yes, he wanted to pursue her. In a romantic way. Even though he had no idea how to do that. But the attraction was strong. He finally admitted it last night after he'd hung up the phone. Now that it was out, he wanted to act on it. Which was something else that was new for him.

Thinking of Julia made him feel warm. Relaxed.

A yawn overtook him and made him stretch. So many late nights in the past few weeks. He pulled his pocket watch out and glanced at the time. If he closed his eyes now, he could get a couple hours of rest in. Might as well.

The trail down into the canyon wasn't anything like he expected. Apparently, it received a lot of use because it was well-worn and pretty wide. The switchbacks helped to make it a gentler slope than he'd envisioned. "This is the Bright Angel Trail?" He spoke to Julia's back as she led their little troop. As soon as he'd disembarked the train, the ladies had taken him to the hotel. Frank had come out of the kitchen for a few moments to give them all food for their packs and had taken Chris aside for a quick talk about protecting the women. After Chris had changed and they'd eaten sandwiches, they headed out.

"Yes." She nodded. "We paid Emery Kolb at the trailhead by their house, remember?"

"Well, yes. I remember that. But I wasn't sure if we were still on it."

"We *will* venture off the main trail in a little while, but the Bright Angel Trail is about ten miles or so down to the Colorado River."

Ten miles? Downhill was one thing. He stopped and looked over his shoulder. He couldn't imagine ten miles *up*-hill. Put him behind a workbench with tools, hammers, metals, and stones, and he could work all day long. But hiking?

Maybe he should start doing more of this so he could get into better shape and keep up with Julia.

"Don't worry." Miss Anniston sent him a grin. "You'll do fine. You're young and strong, unlike some of the wealthy folks who never lift a finger for themselves. Those are the ones who usually have trouble on the trails. That's why the good Lord above told us we would eat the fruit of the labor of our hands." She patted him on the shoulder as she passed him. "Sorry, that sounded extremely judgmental against our guests. I didn't mean it to come across that way. Forgive me. I simply meant that I believe we are supposed to do our work heartily as unto the Lord. I never want my own hands to be idle."

He let out a chuckle and picked up his pace to catch up to them again. "I agree with you. We all have work to do, don't we?"

"Yes, and yours is incredible, Mr. Miller. I'm in awe of the gifts God has given you."

"Please, call me Christopher. Or just Chris. I appreciate your compliment. To God be the glory."

Julia turned her head slightly, but the expression on her face was one he couldn't decipher. Were they not going fast enough?

"All right, Christopher. But then I insist you call me Ruth. At least while we're out here. Mr. Owens wouldn't like that very much when I'm on duty." She kept pace beside him, which was quite a feat since she was a good deal shorter than he. She probably took one-and-a-half to two steps for every one of his. "Are you much of a hiker?"

He grunted at that one. "Sorry. I have to say hiking is not something I've ever tried before."

"Oh, well, then this really will be an adventure for you. I

admit I enjoy it, but I don't take enough time to do it. My days off are usually filled with everything else that I need to accomplish. I should take more time to enjoy creation like Julia does. From what I hear, she's been all over these trails. And she's only been here since April."

Hard to believe it had only been a matter of weeks since God had brought him up here to the canyon for the first time. Not only had He blessed him with the new job, but he'd met so many wonderful people. "That's quite amazing, Julia." He pointed his words toward her back as she blazed down the trail in front of them.

She stopped and turned toward them with a shrug. "I really do love it. I had no idea how much I would before I came here."

"Do you always go at such a brisk pace?" He had to ask. Because if he hoped to spend more time with her, he'd better start training.

"Any mention of the treasure, and she's off like a rabbit." Ruth shrugged.

"We're having to go quick because we only have half the day today. Tomorrow we'll have more time." Julia pointed at Ruth and narrowed her eyes. "And no, it's not just about hunting for treasure." She turned back around, settling into the previous rhythm.

"How long have you been here, Ruth?" Chris looked down at the trail. They'd come to a much steeper section, and he wanted to keep an eye on his footing.

"Since the hotel was built."

"Have you been a Harvey Girl for a long time?"

"More than a dozen years now. I love it." Their pace slowed as they maneuvered around some big rocks that had rolled onto the trail. "One of these days, I want to buy myself a camera and take pictures of all this. I just will never get over the beauty."

"It is breathtaking." Chris watched Julia climb over the largest rock with ease. "What about you, Julia? How long have you been a Harvey Girl?"

"Oh, several years." Another shrug. "We're about to get off the main trail. I want to search a few caves and crevices that I spotted the other day."

Was she always this adept at changing the subject?

"All right. We'll follow wherever you lead." He helped Ruth over the boulder that was almost as tall as she was. He got brave. "I know you said you don't have any living family, but what was your childhood like? Where did you grow up? I don't believe you've ever told me—" The little shake of Ruth's head brought a halt to his words.

Then the frown Julia shot him was enough to make him wish he hadn't brought up the subject at all. Her mouth was pinched. Her eyes narrow slits. "I don't talk about that."

She turned on her heel and darted off on a skinny path to the side.

Subject closed.

The previous day had been almost torturous for Julia. And not just because they hadn't found anything. She had led Chris and Ruth into six or seven small caves and crevices. After she marked the entrance to each one and wrote it down in her book so she'd know where they had already searched, they'd headed back up to the hotel before the sun set.

But the hard part had been listening to Chris and Ruth talk about their faith and God over and over and *over* again. It had made Julia feel more alone than she'd ever felt before. At first, it had been endearing. Her two friends had something in common. It was nice to hear about what gave them hope. She'd listened. Closely. Thankful that they couldn't see her face as she led the way down the trails.

Why couldn't she have the same thing? None of it made sense to her. How people with different backgrounds could all be loved by the same God. And they all talked about it like it was a close relationship.

Something else she had to admit that she didn't understand. Had she ever had a close relationship? With anyone?

Even though her parents had made her do some bad things to help them with their robberies, they'd loved her. Of that she was certain. She'd tried to remember moments from her childhood when they weren't in the middle of some kind of scheme, but it was all fuzzy. She couldn't actually remember anything. Were all of her good memories of her parents wrapped up in them bribing her to help them?

There'd never been many toys or money for toys. She'd never had a room to herself. In fact, she couldn't remember staying in one place for long. But there was always a gift for her when they'd asked her to do something, usually in the form of a treat of some sort. Because a starving belly had also been the norm for her.

In that moment, she realized that her memories were in all honesty pretty awful. For years, she'd tried to convince herself otherwise because she'd needed *something* to cling to.

If she was gut-wrenchingly honest, the only real happy memory she had was with her adoptive parents in Texas. They'd taken her shopping and bought her a new dress and a pair of boots that were the right size. They'd fed her well.

Another memory flashed through her mind. They were

sitting in church. She was between her new parents. They'd given her a doll. In her mind's eye, she was that little girl again. Looking up—back and forth—at the two people who clearly loved her. *Wanted* her.

The memory brought tears to her eyes, and she choked back the sobs that threatened to overtake her. She could see their faces! She hadn't been able to remember them for years. Oh, if she could only hold on to that picture in her mind forever.

The words Ruth had spoken to her and Tessa about adoption started to sink in. They made sense.

Ruth had been right. She had been chosen.

Julia *had* been wanted.

The feelings that filled her middle were warm and happy. She had known—if only for a brief moment in time—what it was to feel loved. She must have stuffed it down deep inside her after their deaths.

Chris appeared at her side and broke through the reverie. "I have to admit, my legs might be killing me, but I'm looking forward to more exploring today."

She turned her head to the other side and blinked away the tears in her eyes. Hopefully he hadn't seen them.

Ruth piped up behind them. "You know what, Julia? I've been thinking. Once all this is over, you should write the whole story about the legend and then how you found the treasure. You're such a good storyteller."

Julia glanced at Chris.

He wasn't frowning, but he definitely wasn't smiling. "A good storyteller, huh?"

"I do tend to get animated and dramatic." Hopefully he would think those were positive traits. The trail narrowed, and Julia smiled at Chris. "We better go single file here. I haven't been this way before, so I don't know what to expect."

"Lead the way." His face softened.

What was it about the light in his eyes that made her feel . . . special? Like it was a look just for her.

As her face and neck heated with the thought, she was thankful he was at her back. Chris was a nice man. But he was way too good for the likes of her. Especially with her past. But that didn't stop her heart from dreaming of him holding her in his arms. To be loved by a good and decent man like him would be like she was the princess in a fairy tale. The happily-ever-after kind.

She'd learned from the other Harvey Girls over the years that romance was hard to find. A few of the girls had been swept off their feet with love of the fairy-tale story, but most simply found a companion and someone to share their life with. Which had been a nice thing for her to dream about. A companion was better than no one.

But to dream romantically about a man? It sent a shiver up and down her spine.

The terrain took a sharp turn around the red wall beside her, and she dared a look down. There wasn't much space for her feet. Beyond that was a steep drop-off that appeared to go down several hundred feet. Should she continue on?

Once she was around the jut, about twenty yards ahead was a cave she hadn't seen before. In fact, it was almost hidden by the ledge they'd just come around and a lone tree that was rooted in the side of the rock. How it had grown so tall was beyond her realm of knowledge. She paused, put a hand on the rocky wall beside her, and looked over her shoulder. "I'm headed for that cave over there." She pointed.

"Huh. I didn't even see it until just now." Chris cracked his knuckles.

"I didn't either." She continued forward. This was the slowest she'd ever moved on any of her hikes, but it was also the highest up she'd climbed off the trail. Probably because her heart was racing as she took each step. Hoping that she wouldn't slip and fall into the depths of the canyon.

An ear-piercing screech filled the air and echoed off the canyon walls.

Julia stopped in her tracks. "What was that?"

"I have no idea." Chris's breath was on her neck, and he put a hand on her shoulder. Her abrupt stop had caused them all to halt at a very unsafe juncture.

"That . . . was the scream of a mountain lion. Both the males and females scream to call for a mate. Or to fight over a mate." Ruth's voice sounded a bit shaky. "Even though that sounded a good ways off, I'm glad the sheriff sent you down here with a rifle, Christopher. Let's just pray we don't have the need to use it."

"I've also got a revolver in my pack. Gramps always said to be prepared." His voice behind her sent prickles up her neck.

"You know how to shoot both of those guns?" Julia hadn't intended to sound doubtful, but the situation was a bit scarier than she wanted to admit. She'd never seen a mountain lion before and didn't want to see one in person today.

Chris's stiff chuckle behind her didn't help. "I might not be much of a hiker, but my grandfather ensured I knew how to handle guns safely."

"Good. Because I don't." She grimaced and looked over her shoulder. "Ruth, do you know how to handle a revolver?"

"I do."

"Why don't you reach into Chris's pack and get it while

we're stopped? It might help to have both at the ready." Julia had no idea what it would take to stop a mountain lion. She did *not* want to find out.

Several seconds passed. "All right. I've got it." Ruth's voice was a bit breathless.

"Let's check to make sure I loaded it fully. I was in such a rush when I left. . . ." Chris's voice had moved away. He must have turned his head toward Ruth.

"It's loaded."

"All right, then. Let's keep moving." Julia didn't like the feeling she had in the pit of her stomach.

"On one condition." Ruth's tone was that of her supervisor again. "If we hear another screech, we turn back."

As much as she hated the thought of turning back, she agreed. So did Chris.

For the next few minutes, they made their way to the cave she'd spotted. Once they were directly below it, the shape was more of a tall triangle, unlike the more rounded openings she'd seen before.

A large crack rose from the pinnacle of the cave's mouth. Placing her hands on the lip of the opening, she boosted herself up onto the rocky ledge. This one looked much deeper than the others. Which meant it was probably a good place for an animal's den.

While she waited for the others, she pulled a candle from her bag and looked around for any signs of life.

Thankfully there were none, and she turned to help Chris pull Ruth up.

Wiping off her hands once she came to her feet, Ruth looked to her. "This is a tad bit . . . creepy."

Julia struck a match and lit the candle in her hand. "I didn't find any signs of wildlife in here, and the light will make it better. I promise." It took a moment for her eyes to adjust, but then she stepped forward.

A scream tore through the air around them. Just like the one they'd heard earlier.

"That was way too close for my comfort." Ruth's mother-hen tone was back.

"Maybe we should just hide in here." Julia didn't want to admit how much that screech made her insides turn.

"Nope. Nuh-uh." Ruth tugged at her.

"Wouldn't it be safer for us to stay here? We're hidden. And we're armed." And if what she'd gotten a glimpse of was any indication, they were in the right place to search.

"No. We said we would turn around, and that's exactly what we're going to do." Ruth had her hands on her hips.

"I agree with Ruth." Chris pulled at her other arm. "We can come back another time."

They were right. After what happened to Tessa, she didn't want anyone else to get hurt because of her. "Fine. I did make a promise, after all."

Another scream.

"We need to head up that trail as fast as we can." Chris reached for the rifle slung over his back and held it in front of him. "I better lead. I know you're more experienced on the trail. But I'd rather face it head-on with the rifle."

As they exited the cave and steadied themselves on the narrow trail, Chris's right foot slipped. But he caught himself before he tumbled down into the canyon.

When they reached a wider point in the trail, Julia stepped in front of him. "Let me lead from here. I know a shortcut back to the rim."

He stepped closer to her. Their eyes connected like magnets. He took a quick glance over her shoulder at Ruth. His breath washed over her, he was so near. "I . . . I care about you, Julia. Please don't take any unnecessary risks. Promise?"

She blinked. He cared about her? She'd hoped—had even dreamed of this very moment. Was it real?

"Promise?" he whispered again.

With a nod, she broke the connection and brushed past him.

The next half hour passed in silence as they made their way up the trail. All of them probably afraid to breathe for fear they'd hear the pursuit of the mountain cat. Julia knew it propelled her forward.

Her shoulders and legs ached. She stopped for a break and lifted her canteen to show the others what she was doing.

Ruth and Chris stopped to do the same.

And then she saw it.

The great beast crouched on a rock above them, the lithe muscles rippling as it prepared to pounce.

"No!" she screamed and tried to push her friends out of the way.

The cat sprang onto the trail in front of them.

Chris jumped in front of her on one side with the rifle.

Ruth on the other with the revolver.

The lion put one large paw forward. Dipped its head. Then took another step.

Julia pushed against her friends, but they wouldn't let her pass. She couldn't let them get attacked. *She* was the one who deserved it. Not good people like Ruth and Chris.

She stepped back and went around Chris's right shoulder. With frantic arms, she waved. "Over here!"

In a split-second, the attention of the great predator was on her.

Time stood still.

Julia stopped moving. Fear froze her in her tracks.

She blinked. Inhaled.

The mountain lion lunged toward her.

Shots rang out.

And then Ruth was on the ground in front of her, the big cat on top.

Blood was everywhere.

20

Press gently but firmly." Chris's voice broke through the fog in Julia's head. Her right hand held a cloth over Ruth's face. Her left was on Ruth's thigh.

A pool of blood beneath them stained all their clothes.

The mountain lion was sprawled a few feet away. When Chris had pushed the great beast off, it had still been breathing. He strode over to it and shoved it even farther away. One giant paw swiped at him and missed.

Two more shots filled the air.

Julia watched as the life drained out of the animal's eyes. Something she never wanted to see again.

A pulsing thrummed beneath her fingers. And brought her out of her shock.

Ruth!

She looked down at her friend. "Why would you do such a thing? I was the one who deserved to be killed. Not you." Hot tears ran down her cheeks. It was the first time she'd noticed she was crying.

Ruth's face was pale. "I'm not dead yet, Julia. But if it is my time? I know where I'm going. Do you?"

The question cut like a knife to her heart. All the talk of

God and heaven . . . she wanted to believe. To be good like Ruth. She did. But she had to admit that death scared her. No matter how much she believed she deserved it.

"Oh, sweet girl. Don't you get it? I would gladly give my life for yours. So that you can know what love really is. *God's* love." She closed her eyes and moaned.

"Ruth!"

Chris rushed to her side. He lifted her left hand, which was on Ruth's thigh. "I'm afraid this is where all the blood is coming from. I had hoped it had been from the mountain lion." He took off his pack and rummaged through it. "Can you find me a short stick real quick and then come back and keep pressure on the scratches in her face?"

"Yes." She scurried a few feet down the ravine where there were several trees growing at odd angles out of the rock. "Is this a good size?" She held up a foot-long branch she'd broken off.

"Perfect."

Within seconds she was back at his side and resumed pressure on Ruth's cheek. Her friend's eyelids fluttered, but with a moan, her head flopped to the side.

"She must be unconscious. Which is a good thing. This next part will hurt. I've got to stop the bleeding and the only way to do that is with a tourniquet. Then we're going to have to get to the hotel as fast as we can and hope the doc is around."

She nodded.

He untucked his shirt and used the knife from his pack to cut a wide strip off the bottom. About five inches of fabric, about two feet in length. "Can you move her skirt up above the wound?"

At that moment, all thought of propriety was gone. Julia

knew that Ruth wouldn't mind being exposed when her life was at stake. Pushing the skirt up, she swallowed against the bile rising in her throat. Blood gushed from three deep slashes in Ruth's thigh.

Chris lifted the leg and placed the cloth underneath. Sliding it above the wounds with fast fingers, he tied a half-knot, placed the stick over the knot, and then made another half-knot. Then he started twisting the stick. The fabric strip of his shirt tightened over Ruth's leg.

"Will that hurt her?"

"Not any more than the initial attack did. But we've got to stop the bleeding. It's the only way to save her."

Another nod. She had to save Ruth. She had to.

This was all her fault. She was the one determined to find the treasure. She was the one who insisted that Ruth was the only one she trusted to go with her. She was the one who should be hurt.

Once the bleeding stopped, Chris knotted the fabric over the tourniquet and then cut more of his shirt. He wrapped the wounds tight and knotted the strips. He pulled Ruth's skirt back down over her legs. "Do you think you can handle the rifle and my pack so I can carry her? I'm going to try to go as fast as I can up the trail so I need to lighten my load."

"Sure." She took his pack from him, shoved her notebook inside, and then slung the rifle over her shoulder. "I'll lead the way and watch for anything in the trail that might slow you down." It wouldn't be easy, but they could do it. Moving as fast as she could, Julia scurried up the trail, listening for Chris's footsteps behind her.

When they were almost to the top, she looked at him. "I'm going to run to the hotel and find the doctor."

At his nod, she pushed her legs to the very limit of her ability and gulped for air as tears streamed down her face.

Why hadn't it been her?

The look on Julia's face as they'd made it back to the hotel haunted Chris as he scrambled back down the trail.

The fear in her eyes was almost his undoing. But then the doctor had whisked them all away and he'd been left to pace in the rotunda. When Mr. Owens came to him with frantic eyes, Chris had been willing to do whatever needed to be done.

The manager had no news on Ruth or Julia other than the doctor said it would take a long time to clean the wounds properly and stitch everything. Of course Julia would stay by her friend's side and assist.

Then Mr. Owens spoke about how devastating it was to have two mountain lion attacks in just a few short weeks. In all his years at the hotel, he'd never heard of the cougars attacking people. When the manager asked him if they'd found anything, Chris almost kept what he'd seen to himself but couldn't.

Right before the animal screamed again, he was certain he'd seen the glimmer of something metal in the candle's glow in that cave. It must have been why Julia had been reluctant to leave. He'd seen the interest in her eyes.

Mr. Owens made the request then and there. Go find the rest of the treasure before anyone else got hurt.

Whether it was for the profits the treasure would bring, or to keep the guests from traipsing all over in the name of treasure-hunting and putting themselves in danger, Chris didn't know the man well enough to be able to say. But it gave him something to do.

Ray Watkins had returned and volunteered to go with him. So far, they hadn't said a word to each other. His thoughts kept going back to Julia, no matter how hard he tried to focus on the trail in front of him.

Julia. He'd told her he cared about her.

And she'd looked like a frightened animal. Ready to run.

Had he overstepped?

God, I don't know what You have planned, but show me what I need to do next.

The least he could do for her was accomplish what they had set out to do the last two days.

"You're going just a little fast there, Chris." Ray's voice came from behind him.

Chris halted and leaned over, resting his hands on his thighs. "Sorry. Don't want to waste the daylight." He took off his pack and pulled out Julia's notebook. "Hopefully I can remember how to get there, but Julia shoved her notebook in here when we headed up with Ruth. I know she took notes to help her remember where she'd been and how to get back."

"Good. I was hoping you had your bearings."

"Sorry I took you away from your wife. Isn't she due soon?"

"I'm glad to help. And yes." A huge smile spread across Ray's face as he lifted a canteen to his mouth. "We are beyond excited." The light in his eyes dimmed. "But Emma Grace is very close to Ruth. Even though she's acting strong on the outside for all the other ladies, I'm sure she's quite shook up."

"I can imagine. They've known each other a long time, haven't they?"

"Yep. They've been through a lot together."

Chris waited for Ray to put the cap back on his canteen and then headed back down the trail. Ray kept up with him at his side.

"Ruth has had quite an impact on Miss Schultz as well," Chris said.

"Is now a good time to talk about the interest that is clearly there?"

Chris kept his gaze straight ahead.

"I mean, that is why we're headed back to the cave. Mr. Owens might have asked you, but you're doing this for her." Ray's tone wasn't teasing. It was sincere. Like a friend's should be.

"I admit, I've been attracted to Julia since I first met her. But I've been so focused on paying for my building that I haven't done anything to pursue her."

"Has that changed now?"

"I would like to ask permission to court her. I know she has a contract and there are rules for the Harvey Girls. But I would rather not wait."

"That's understandable. Once the heart gets attached, there's little you can do to convince it otherwise." Ray chuckled. "You haven't told me about how things are going with the purchase from your landlord. I'd love to ensure that we get to work with you for many years. Do you need any assistance?"

Chris held up his hand. "I have enough to buy it. But thank you very much for your offer."

"That's wonderful news."

"Thank you." He kept the pace as brisk as he could without falling down. Speaking about business made him timid. Ray Watkins and his wife came from vast wealth, and their story was amazing.

Chris was impressed by them. So much so that he decided

to keep his mouth shut. But he had a hundred questions. He'd seen the Watkins' home on the rim. It was very modest in size. Not at all what you would expect from millionaires.

"I can see the gears turning in your mind, Christopher Miller. Go ahead and ask. You won't offend me."

For the next half hour, Chris and Ray talked about everything from the Watkins' philanthropic work to what it was like living without people waiting on them hand and foot. Since neither Ray nor Emma Grace even wanted to be a part of their rightful social class any longer, they didn't seem fazed by the life they'd chosen.

If there was ever someone Chris wanted to emulate, it was Ray Watkins. His respect for the man had shot up by leaps and bounds every minute of their hike.

As they reached the carcass of the mountain lion that had attacked them, buzzards and other birds scattered.

Climbing into the cave, Chris breathed deep. This was the least he could do for Julia and for Ruth.

21

I'll take good care of her. I promise." The doctor looked at Julia, a serious expression on his face.

"Can I stay?"

"No. I'm afraid you can't. There's a lot of stitching I need to do after I've cleaned the wounds. It won't be pretty." The man scooted her to the door.

"Please let me know if there's anything I can do. She . . ." Sobs choked her. "She saved my life."

"I know. The best thing you can do is pray for her. Give her time to rest. She's lost a lot of blood, so I doubt she'll be awake any time soon." Another gentle nudge toward the door.

She couldn't leave her friend. She couldn't. The once white bandages over Ruth's face were now red. What if Ruth died because of her? The thought was more than she could bear. Her stomach revolted and she put a hand over her mouth.

"Ju . . . lia . . ." The raspy voice made her and the doc both jerk their gaze to the woman in the bed.

"I'm here." But the doctor held her arms and kept her from moving forward. "I'm here, Ruth."

"Greater . . . love . . . hath no man . . . I love you." Ruth's eyes glazed over and then shut.

A deep breath from the doc. "I think it's best for you to go back to your room, Miss Schultz." His voice was low. Sad. Defeated.

No! Ruth couldn't die. She couldn't! "No!" The wail left her lips as her body went limp.

"She's still alive." The man squeezed her arms where he held on even tighter. "Now let me patch her up." With a final lift and shove, he moved her out into the hallway and then closed the door.

The dining room was closed until dinner, which meant every other Harvey Girl was in the hallway. Waiting. Watching. Not a sound to be heard. Gazing into each face, she felt her stomach revolt again. This was her fault.

Hers.

The assistant chef with a blazing shock of hair redder than her own held his hat in his hands. "Miss Schultz?"

She swallowed. "Mr. Henderson." Gave him a nod. "The doctor is cleaning the wounds and stitching them. It will be a while." The last words she barely choked out.

The man didn't look at her. Just gazed at the door that Ruth lay beyond. A shimmer of tears was in his eyes. With a nod, he ducked his head and walked away.

Julia ran back to her room, locking the door behind her. No matter what anyone said, it was better to leave. To start over somewhere fresh. She grabbed for her pack. But a voice inside her head asked, *"Where will you go?"*

The echo of Ruth's voice answered, *"I know where I'm going."*

Julia froze, her hand suspended three inches above the leather bag. The question of her eternity didn't matter right now. What mattered was what she would do now that she'd almost killed her friend. Where *would* she go? Florence's appearance at El Tovar meant nowhere was far enough away. No matter where Julia went, her past—her lies—would catch up with her.

She covered her face with her hands and fell onto her bed. Sobs welled up from the deepest place in her soul. And as she cried, the voice inside her head turned spiteful, reminding her of why she didn't deserve any better.

Orphan. Liar. Worthless.

And yet there was another voice whispering, one she needed to concentrate on to hear. It called her very different names.

Beloved. Ruby beyond price. Daughter.

The first voice had a thousand faces. The second had only one.

Ruth.

Except . . .

Julia squinted her covered eyes as though it would help bring the image behind her eyelids into focus. Another woman's face floated into her mind's eye. A woman with kind eyes that shimmered with love. It was joined by a man's face with equally kind, loving eyes. And it wasn't her parents.

It was the couple in Texas who, for a few short weeks, loved Julia as no one—not even her parents—had loved her. Love meant sacrifice. Ruth had said the words and backed them up with her actions. If Julia's parents had truly loved her, they would have sacrificed to keep her safe, to do their best to keep her from becoming an orphan. Instead, they deliberately chose to continue the lifestyle that led to their deaths. That condemned her to a life of bitterness.

Like one of her colorful stories, images from her time in

Texas danced across her memory. The Wrights had greeted her with overwhelming joy. Unused to it, Julia shut herself off and waited for the façade to break as soon as they closed their front door and had her alone in their big house. But they were the same there as they were in public. Always loving. Always asking what she needed. Always providing.

They adopted her, making her their daughter, and spoke about how they'd chosen her because she was special.

Memories flooded her mind. Things she hadn't remembered since that time. She'd pushed them away because she couldn't believe anyone was that nice or that anyone could love her.

Then—just as she started to accept the love they were offering—they died. It taught her to never open herself again. To be someone else. To tell stories rather than the truth because, if people rejected her, it wasn't the *real* her anyway. She was safe.

Only, in retrospect, what she'd really done was waste the few short weeks of genuine love and another fifteen years of potential friendships by holding herself aloof.

Was she doing the same to God? Was He waiting for her to turn and accept the love He offered? Was her own stubbornness keeping her from finally finding someone who loved her now and would continue to love her no matter what in the future?

She sat up on the bed, wiped the wet from her face, and looked at the clock. More than two hours had passed. So, she headed back to Ruth's room. The doctor said she needed rest, but this was too important. For her and for her friend.

As Julia walked down the hallway, the snide voice in her head got louder and louder.

Be quiet!

To her utter shock, it stopped. For an instant. And then it came roaring back. Julia kept walking, though she was hard-pressed not to put her hands over her ears as though it would muffle the dreadful names.

She remembered bits and pieces of the Bible verses Ruth had shared over the past few weeks, so she repeated as much as she could recall. They felt false—almost ridiculous—but anything was better than that terrible voice.

The doctor was leaving Ruth's room. "Miss Schultz, I . . ." He narrowed his eyes, as though she was his patient and he was assessing her condition. "Five minutes. No more."

Julia nodded on her way past him. "I promise." Seeing the right side of Ruth's face covered in white gauze almost turned her around to run again, but she'd come this far. She'd been running for too long. She'd see it through. "I need to ask you one more question. About God."

Ruth winced as she shifted on the bed. "I was hoping you'd come back." Her hand reached for Julia's.

It was cold, so she sandwiched it between her own. She looked down at Ruth's legs. Covered by multiple blankets, she tried to unsee the vision in her mind of what the mountain lion had done with its mighty paw. How Chris had desperately tried to stop the bleeding, praying as he went and asking God to spare Ruth's leg and her life.

The slashes from the claws had been deep.

Julia felt as if they'd sliced her heart.

"Julia?" Ruth's voice drew her gaze back. Her glassy eyes were filled with pain. And . . . love.

Now that the moment was upon her, words vanished. She didn't even know what she wanted to ask. She dropped her gaze to the floor.

There was no sound in the room except the ticking of a

clock and the breathing of two women on the verge of a precipice. Julia closed her eyes, and she could see herself on the rim of the canyon. Then she was floating above it . . . like a bird. Staring down at the gray stone walls as they melded into red. Then the river below. But it was filled with blood.

Because of her.

She shook her head and tried to rid her mind of the image.

"Look at me." Ruth's voice was steady. Strong.

Julia snapped open her eyes.

"I meant what I said. I *know* where I'm going. And you are loved, Julia. More than you could ever imagine by the God of the universe. So, the question is . . . where are *you* going?"

She opened her mouth and then closed it. No matter what happened in the next five minutes, there was no going back. Julia knew it in the depths of her spirit. This was it. She would either accept what God was offering now or reject it for the rest of her life. And if she chose the latter, she'd run and keep on running—from God, from Ruth, from Chris, and from anyone else who threatened to crack her heart open.

She took a deep breath to answer the question, except what came out of her mouth was "God can't love me. No one can."

"That's pride talking."

Julia's head snapped up. "No, it's not. If anything, it's humility."

Ruth pressed her hand against her bandaged cheek and shook her head gingerly. "No, my sweet friend. Humility is knowing your worth and choosing to put others ahead of yourself anyway."

Another sacrifice. Why did everything come back to that?

But Ruth wasn't done. "Pride is choosing to believe your own assessment of your worth rather than God's assessment of it. He says you are loved and worth dying for."

Julia shook her head. "You don't know all the things I've done. Or where I come from."

"Why does that matter?"

"Because . . ." Julia let go of Ruth's hand and crossed her arms over her chest as she searched for an answer. "Because they just do." The justification sounded childish to her own ears.

Ruth took a breath and her chest shuddered. But her face was peaceful. "Because God can handle everyone else's appalling choices and shocking past, but somehow yours are the only ones that are too big for Him?"

Put that way, *childish* was a tame descriptor.

"That wasn't a rhetorical question, Julia. He forgives all. Not all *except for* . . . fill in the blank with whatever you think is the worst thing ever." Ruth's face began to pale, a strain in her eyes that went beyond physical pain. "You don't need to tell me your answer, but you do need to tell God. There's nothing you've done that is bigger than God, His love for you, and the sacrifice He paid for you." She tipped her head toward the table by the bed. "Take the book. Read it. I don't have much energy left tonight, I'm sorry. But I'm praying for you."

With a nod, she squeezed Ruth's hand. And then she leaned down and kissed her friend on the forehead. She'd never been good at showing affection. Probably because she'd never had any. Embarrassed by her own action, she shook her head. "I . . . I need to think." Julia turned and fled back to her room.

After she closed the door and locked it, she leaned up

against the door. She held up the Bible she'd picked up from Ruth's room and held it away from her like it was infectious. Maybe it was. She certainly felt ill, although it was a sickness in her soul that had festered for a long time. But the scripture verses weren't the problem. They just exposed the diseased parts of her insides, like a surgeon who cuts away temporary bandages to operate.

But just this morning, as they'd been preparing for their hike, Ruth had hugged her and talked about the fresh start Julia had been given.

Florence and her group of rabble-rousers were gone. Left on the train.

Tessa was on the mend and had become quite a chatterbox. The other girls had flocked around their brave waitress who'd taken a bullet. And Tessa had done nothing but praise Julia up, down, and sideways.

"Can't you see what God is doing? He's paving the way for you." Ruth's words echoed in her ears.

At the time she had laughed it off, anxious to search for the rest of the treasure. But now?

She clasped the book with both hands. Maybe it was time she paid attention.

"All right, God. If You really do love me, I need proof." She set the Bible on the desk, lifted her chin so she couldn't see what she was doing, opened the pages, and stabbed her finger into the paper. She looked down and read aloud, "'For I am persuaded, that neither death, nor life, nor angels, nor principalities, nor powers, nor things present, nor things to come, nor height, nor depth, nor any other creature, shall be able to separate us from the love of God, which is in Christ Jesus our Lord.'"

Huh. Well, that was interesting.

She lifted her chin, closed her eyes, and did it again, flipping the pages in the other direction.

"'I will praise thee; for I am fearfully and wonderfully made. . . .'"

She couldn't read further because tears stung her eyes. She flipped pages again.

"'In this was manifested the love of God toward us, because that God sent his only begotten Son into the world, that we might live through him. Herein is love, not that we loved God, but that he loved us, and sent his Son to be the propitiation for our sins. Beloved, if God so loved us, we ought also to love one another. No man hath seen God at any time. If we love one another, God dwelleth in us, and his love is perfected in us.'"

Again with the love. She read the verses again. Propitiation? What did *that* mean?

All right, God. One more time. As silly as it seemed, she closed her eyes, flipped pages, and stabbed her finger at the book.

"'This is my commandment, that ye love one another, as I have loved you. Greater love hath no man than this, that a man lay down his life for his friends.'" She choked on the last words. Ruth had shared that with her. Ruth had *lived* that out for her.

Was the whole book filled with words like these? It couldn't be a coincidence that she'd found these verses. Could it? For the next hour, she read from that point on. As her heart flooded with an indescribable feeling of worthiness, she let the tears fall.

Laughter bubbled in her stomach, filling her chest and spilling out of her mouth. "I guess that answers that." She looked toward the ceiling. Wait until she could tell Ruth.

22

Bobby's plans had fallen apart.

They hadn't found the treasure.

They hadn't accomplished anything with the mountain lion they'd trapped.

They hadn't grabbed the waitresses when they had the chance.

The trap couldn't even hold the second lion, and it had escaped.

There was no way around it now. Roger needed to die. He was completely worthless. The only thing he'd managed to do was snag a tintype from the redhead. What good was that? No jewels. No money. Nothing. His snooping around at the hotel wasn't doing any good either. The man enjoyed being around all those rich snobs.

That stupid waitress needed to go too. And all her friends.

And that jeweler.

He just had to go back down into the canyon and find more of the treasure with that other man. Bobby would've killed them both but had slipped on the trail right after the men exited the cave. They'd been spooked by the sound and hightailed it up the trail.

They were probably excited that it was all over now. They could tell the police that the treasure was found so that the dumb tourists would be safe. Blah, blah, blah, blah, blah.

Well, that wasn't good enough.

This couldn't be the end. Nope.

Bobby waited a bit and then headed up the trail.

The sheriff had men everywhere. Why? Because of a stupid mountain lion?

There had to be a way to get the jewels. Or the money. Either one would suffice.

Movement to the left caught Bobby's eye.

The redhead!

She was with someone . . . who?

Oh, good grief. It was the poor little injured girl. Too bad that gunshot didn't hurt her worse.

The two walked slowly to a bench near the rim.

Bobby slithered along and perched on a rock just below them.

"Thanks for helping me out here. I was about to go crazy in my room."

"I can imagine. Being cooped up like that is no fun."

The voices were familiar, but Bobby couldn't tell which one was which. The mousy one was the one who'd been shot.

"There's something different about you tonight, Julia. Your face is . . . serene."

What a stupid word. Serene.

Light laughter floated down the canyon. "Well, I have to admit that things are different for me now."

"Oh, I'm so happy for you!"

What? What was going on?

Their words were muffled for a minute.

"It's time for me to tell the truth. Ruth is the first one I should tell, but I'm nervous. I don't know how to start. And I'm afraid she'll think I'm a horrible person after she knows."

"There isn't even a remote chance of that, Julia. I promise." More shuffling. "Why don't you practice on me? I can help you find the right words if you need help." More laughter. "Me. Find the right words." The two laughed themselves silly. *Get on with it!*

"Wait. Do you smell that?"

"Smell what?"

"It's such a distinctive scent, but I can't place it. . . . Never mind. My mind must be playing tricks on me." A long pause. "I don't even know where to start."

"This is about your parents, right?"

A big huff. "Yes."

"Start at the worst possible part. Then you can fill in the details."

Bobby's ears perked up.

The bell jangled above the door of the shop, and Chris heard Fred greeting the customer. It had been hard to focus ever since he came back from the El Tovar. But once he heard Ruth would live, he'd decided to head home. Julia was probably by her friend's side anyway and would no doubt stay there. He'd left a note with Mr. Owens for Miss Schultz telling her that he'd found the rest of the treasure with Ray and would begin working on the jewelry immediately. Mr. Watkins assured Chris that he would let the manager in on the other details.

It was all that could be done. The rest was in God's capable hands. Hopefully the sheriff and his men could catch whoever it was who tried to capture Julia and Tessa. They should be in jail for shooting an innocent woman.

It was more important that he focus on his work. At least, that's what he kept telling himself. Although he would much prefer being back at the El Tovar. For more reasons than one.

"Mr. Miller." Fred came into the workshop. "There's a lady here who is demanding to speak with you."

"Julia?" His heart lifted.

"No, sir." His brows dipped. "This one . . . well, she isn't a very nice lady. And she doesn't speak too fondly of Miss Schultz."

"Then I don't wish to speak with her."

"I'm afraid I already tried that. She refuses to leave until she speaks with you."

He let out a low growl. "Fine. Let's get this over with."

Wiping his hands on his apron, he lifted his jeweler's glasses up on top of his head and ventured out into the showroom. "How may I help you?"

"My name is Florence Nichols."

"What is it that you wish to speak to me about, Miss Nichols?"

For a moment, her eyes appeared confused. "Julia hasn't mentioned me?"

He shook his head. "No. Should she have?"

The lady huffed. "It doesn't matter now, does it?" The smile she sent him was too sweet. Fake. He'd seen hundreds of those practiced expressions on women over the years.

He raised his eyebrows and waited for her to continue.

"How well do you know Miss Schultz?"

"I can't say that's any of your business, Miss Nichols, now, is it?"

She continued as if she hadn't heard his response. "So I'm guessing you don't know about her past?"

The fact that he didn't know *anything* about Julia's past bothered him, but Chris tried not to let it show.

A smirk now lifted the woman's lips. "Ah, I see I've hit a nerve."

He refused to be baited and worked to neutralize his expression.

"I've heard more stories about Julia's past than probably anyone else. I've worked with her for years, you know."

Mr. Holland stood at the counter behind Miss Nichols. He wrote on a pad of paper: *This one is trouble!*

Chris read it and couldn't agree more.

Miss Nichols must have seen his gaze shift because she looked over her shoulder. But Fred had already turned his back.

More than anything, Chris wanted to laugh at the ridiculousness of the situation and whatever Miss Florence Nichols *thought* she was trying to do. But he crossed his arms instead.

"Anyway, my favorite is probably the story that she was a famous singer and lost her voice."

Was the woman daft? What on earth was she talking about? "Who was a famous singer?"

The woman tilted her head coyly to the side. "Why, Miss Julia Schultz. That's one of the fabulous stories she told about her past."

He frowned.

"At one point, she was also a famous actress, and her parents were killed in a stagecoach accident that was meant for her, mind you. Then there was the time that her family was royalty and were killed so she had to flee. . . . What was another one?" She tapped her lip with a finger. "Oh yes. There was a fire at the Savoy Hotel in New York City on Fifth Avenue and she was trapped on the top floor. Her parents died saving her. She's also been bit by a scorpion, a rattlesnake, and attacked by a bear. On one of her hunting expeditions before her parents were killed and all . . . Would you care to hear more?"

"That's quite enough, Miss Nichols. Why would you come in here and tell me such ridiculous stories?"

She put a hand to her throat and fluttered her eyelashes. "Ridiculous yes, but they're not my stories. I told you, they're Julia's."

"I haven't heard a one of them."

"That's because she's probably trying to pull the wool over your eyes. She does that, you know. Everywhere she goes."

Something didn't add up. "I thought Harvey was strict on honesty."

"Oh yes, he was." Her bottom lip jutted out in a little pout. "But Julia's always gotten away with it. Somehow she flirts with the managers and always befriends the head waitress. Every. Time."

Fury built in Chris's chest. How dare this woman come in here and spew that stuff about Julia! The clock chimed.

"Oh, my train will be leaving soon." She tugged at her gloves and adjusted her hat. "I just couldn't bear leaving without making sure that you weren't her next victim, Mr. Miller. You seem much too nice and too . . . honest of a man for Miss Schultz." She dipped her chin and looked up at him through her eyelashes. Turning on her heel, she sashayed her way out the door.

As the bell jangled, Fred growled. "She has it in for Miss Schultz, that's for certain." The man's hands were fisted at his sides.

"She definitely seemed phony. Although she obviously has practiced at it."

"You don't believe any of it, do you?" Fred narrowed his eyes at Chris.

He waved a hand. "No. Not a bit of it." Even though he knew nothing of Julia's past, he couldn't imagine she'd lie like that. Besides, she'd promised to tell him the truth.

All he needed to do was ask her.

23

The door gave a slight creak as Julia peeked into Ruth's room.

Her friend was still quite pale. Her eyes were closed. Beautiful dark hair flooded her pillow.

"Ruth?"

"Hm?" Eyes opened to slits, Ruth turned her head toward her. "Julia." She licked her lips. "Come in."

"Hi." She let the word out on a sigh and put her hands to her chest. "How are you feeling?"

"A little worse for the wear, but I'm all right. I think."

Julia pulled a chair close and patted her friend's hand. "I'm so glad you're okay." Without her permission, tears sprang to her eyes.

"Oh, don't cry over me."

"But you're my friend." She sniffed. "And I have so much to tell you."

"I can see the difference in your eyes. Tell me everything. Besides, I'm not all that good at talking with this bandage all over my face. The stitches are really tight."

"Yeah, the doctor said that it should keep the scarring

down to a minimum. Over time, you might not even see them anymore." That was hard to imagine since Julia had a tough time getting the picture of Ruth's mauled face out of her mind. But she couldn't tell her friend that.

"What's a little scarring?" While Ruth's voice made light of it, Julia didn't miss the tears pooling in her friend's eyes. "Now, tell me your story."

"It's a good one." And it wasn't made up or embellished. She took a deep breath and dove into how God had drawn her into His forever family. She'd finally been adopted. By the best Father ever. Her heart soared the more she talked about it. There was so much she still didn't understand, but she couldn't wait to learn more. "I went and talked with Frank since I know you trust him. He's like the big brother I always wished I had. Every question I had, he helped me find the answers in the Bible."

"I'm so happy for you. Frank is a wonderful friend." Ruth's voice was hoarse as her eyes closed.

Julia watched her friend for several moments. She took a deep breath. It was time to tell the truth. "There's something else I wanted to tell you. . . ."

But a soft snore from Ruth stopped her. The poor woman. The doctor said she had months of recovery ahead of her. Best to let her rest.

Julia stood as quietly as she could and tiptoed to the door. With a smile back to Ruth's sleeping form, she closed the door.

She rushed up to the dining room. With Ruth recovering, the responsibilities in the dining room fell squarely on her shoulders, and she didn't want to let her friend down.

There was always tomorrow to tell her the whole story.

Chris finished a couple of pieces to take up to the Hopi House but couldn't quite focus on anything new. Instead, he fiddled with the necklace he was making for Julia. It was coming along nicely, if he did say so himself.

But Miss Nichols' words kept coming back to him.

Why did they bother him so much? It was obvious the woman was up to no good, telling her stories and spreading gossip.

But what if it was true?

The phone jangled from the other room. Hopefully it wouldn't be another crisis. What he wanted most was to talk with Julia again.

He wiped his hands on his apron and reached for the phone. "Hello?"

"Hi, Chris. It's Julia." Her voice was soft.

"It's nice to hear from you. How's Ruth?"

"She's healing. But it's going to take some time."

"I bet that means work is busy for you."

She sighed. "Yes. Especially since we lost several waitresses recently too."

"Was Florence Nichols one of them?"

Julia gasped and then there was a long pause. "You know Florence?"

"She stopped by the other day and wouldn't leave until I spoke with her."

"Did you?"

"Yes," Chris answered.

"I see."

The silence on the line made his stomach tie into knots. "I have really enjoyed getting to know you, Julia, and partnering with you on this project. I'd like to think that you've been honest with me."

More silence.

"Julia?"

"Yes?"

"Is anything that Florence said true?"

"I . . . don't know what she told you. But I can imagine." It sounded like she was sniffing back tears. "As much as I want you to think good of me, I can't lie to you. I'm sure what she said probably was true. I was really good at making up stories. Pretty much my whole life."

"You lied?"

"Yes." The answer came without any hesitance. And no explanation.

It was almost like the whole world shifted. How could this have happened?

"I've been honest with you, Chris. I have. But my past is a different story."

"How do I know you're not lying now?" His heart ached. His mind whirled.

"You have to trust me."

"I don't know if I can." Without another word, he hung up the phone. Walking back to his workbench, he couldn't get past the hurt in his gut. The Julia he thought he knew wasn't real, was she?

A sound at the door made him turn around.

Fred unlocked the door and entered with a smile on his face. "I saw your light on while I was on my evening stroll, and I thought I'd check on you. Seems you're working late again, aren't you, son? Need some company?"

Chris stood there but couldn't form a response.

"What's going on?" Fred's face shadowed with concern.

He swallowed the bile threatening to creep up his throat and told him about Julia's phone call.

"I see." Fred tapped his cane on the floor.

"It doesn't matter. Tomorrow, I'm going to pay Mr. Langford. The building will be mine, and we can move ahead with our plans. I've got all the work to do at Hopi House as well." Even though he was numb, Chris needed to focus on something else for his own sanity. This was why he didn't allow himself to get close to people. His workbench was a safe place. His tools didn't lie to him. Didn't hurt him.

"Son, it's written all over your face how much you care about Julia. You said it yourself that she admitted in her past she was different. Are you not willing to forgive her?" Fred placed a hand on his shoulder.

Forgiveness didn't seem to be the issue. Or was it? To him, it was about trust. "I don't understand what I'm feeling right now."

"It's called love, my boy."

He swung his head to his grandfather's old friend. "What?"

"It's clear you're in love with the girl. She cares about you too. I saw it with my own two eyes." Fred shook his head. "Don't throw away your friendship with her over a squabble like this. Hash it out. Have the hard conversations. Listen to her side and let her tell you about her past. You're not perfect either, last time I checked."

Bobby stared at the jewelry store. Tonight was the night.

Roger had ventured into the store in his fancy card-playing duds and overheard the owner arranging a meeting with someone over the phone. To *pay* them.

It hadn't taken much to inquire about town and find out that young Mr. Miller was purchasing his building from good ol' Mr. Langford.

It wasn't the treasure. But it was a lot of money, and that was good enough.

Bobby was tired of all the stupid people around, anyway.

"When do you wanna nab him?" Roger's face was entirely too close.

"Get your stinkin' breath out of my air."

The man's face almost looked hurt. Then it turned hard.

Yeah, Roger had to go. Before he did something dumb.

"We will follow him when he leaves. He's made an appointment with Mr. Langford at the restaurant over by the bank. We'll take him into the alley, beat him until he can't fight back, and take the money."

Roger grinned. "Good plan."

Of course it was a good plan. Come to think of it, it was far better than looking for that stupid treasure anyway. When that old geezer had told them the legend and sold them the map, Bobby thought it would be easy. But they'd spent months upon months and come up empty-handed. Till that fool redhead showed up and stuck her nose where it didn't belong. Well, too bad. Tonight they'd turn the tables back in their favor.

A bell jangled.

The two men exited the store. Miller locked the door and stuck the key into his waistcoat pocket. "Good evening, Fred." Hmmm. Maybe once they got the money, they could grab the key and come back for the jewelry store.

The older man gripped the younger man's shoulder. "I'm proud of you, son."

"Thank you, sir." He snapped his fingers and turned back

toward the door. “I forgot the thank-you letter I wrote to Mr. Langford. I better fetch it.”

The older man nodded his head. “I appreciate your good manners. So would your grandfather. I’ll see you in the morning.”

“See you in the morning.” He unlocked the door, opened it, and entered. Bobby thought about following, but Roger wouldn’t know what to do if they changed plans. The idiot.

But only a few seconds later, the jeweler was back out, locking the door behind him. Tucking the key back in the same little pocket. Perfect.

Bobby checked the street. No one was out. At the moment. “Let’s follow. Quietly.”

Roger nodded.

Miller set a brisk pace, and he whistled while he walked.

Pretty soon that wouldn’t be happening.

Only twenty more paces to the alley. They crept up on him.

As soon as the alley opened up beside them, Roger pounced and tackled Miller. Then dragged him farther into the dark.

Roger threw him down and began beating him with both fists.

Several moments passed. “That’s enough.” Bobby looked down at the man. “Where’s the money?”

Roger had a hand over Miller’s mouth, but there was no attempt at a response. Just wide eyes. Staring.

“Hold him down!”

Roger put an elbow into the man’s neck while his other hand stayed over his mouth.

The man attempted to yell, but it didn’t work.

The new plan firmly in mind, with Roger’s focus on their captive, Bobby retrieved the key, then searched the rest of Miller’s pockets.

Jackpot!

An envelope filled with bills.

Bobby kicked the man several times in the ribs and then nodded at Roger.

The stupid man punched the jeweler in the gut and put a few kicks in himself.

Miller stopped moving.

Roger stood up and smiled at Bobby.

Right as she pulled the trigger.

24

Everything in Chris screamed in pain. His skin. His bones. His insides.

He had stopped fighting in hopes that they'd think they finished him off. And it worked.

The gunshot brought all his senses to high alert. At first, he thought he'd been the one who was shot. But hearing the man next to him cry out and seeing him crumple to the ground told him the gun hadn't been aimed at him. Did one of the robbers just shoot the other?

"That's for your stupidity, Roger. And takin' too many husbandly privileges."

Wait. The other was a woman? Chris had stared into the attacker's cold dark eyes. He'd thought for sure it was two men that attacked him.

The man beside him moaned.

"You were supposed to do what you were told. But no . . . you jes' had to go and tell everyone that *you* were the brains behind the operation. Then you started bragging. It's no wonder them fool girls found the treasure before we did. And then you let that scrawny one knock you over. What a weakling."

Were these the two that attacked Julia and Tessa?

"I never shoulda . . . married you . . ." the man beside Chris croaked. "I don't care how pretty you was or all the promises you made."

The woman cackled. "Fooled ya, didn't I? Of course, Pa helped. He knew you were dumb as the day was long."

"I'm not dumb," the one on the ground whined.

Chris tried to keep still. Now that he knew the woman had a gun, he couldn't risk letting her know he was still alive.

More cackling. Then a clicking sound. The cocking of a revolver. "Good-bye, Roger. Good riddance."

"No, don't kill me. I promise, I'll do better," the pathetic voice sobbed. "I love ya, Bobby. I do. I'll do anything you want."

"Sure. And I'm your fairy godmother." It sounded like the woman spit on the man. "This is for your awful curly hair that I hate."

Another gunshot.

Another click.

"This is for that horrible mustache."

Another gunshot.

"And this . . . is because I hate *you*."

Nothing happened.

Chris held his breath.

Something was placed on the ground beside him. Was she searching for something else?

Then footsteps.

Surely people had heard the gunshots and would come help.

But even as shouts rang out and it sounded like footsteps ran by, no one came.

Chris opened his eyes and eased himself to sitting, grabbing his ribs.

The gun! She'd left it on the ground. To blame *him*!

No. He couldn't let her get away. As he got to his feet, he tried to convince himself that the pain wasn't that bad.

He stumbled off in search of the woman.

She had all his money. He reached into his waistcoat pocket. And the key!

The rest of the stones from the treasure were there. He'd lose the store. He'd lose everything.

He blinked several times to focus and looked both directions.

Nothing. But he surged forward anyway, his body aching from the exertion. He could see a doctor later. He couldn't let that woman get away with murder.

She must have been the one who shot Tessa too.

He was a witness. He'd heard it all and tried to cement the details into his brain through the haze of pain. *Lord, help.*

He kept going. Even though he felt his face swelling. Could feel the blood dripping from his lips.

Another block and a deputy ran out in front of him. "Mr. Miller. What happened to you? Do you need help?"

"There's a woman—well, she's dressed as a man. She just stole an envelope of cash from me, took my store key, and shot a man in that back alley." He kept his voice low as he pointed.

The deputy nodded. "Are you sure you're all right?"

"No. I don't think I am." His legs gave out from under him as the pain overtook him.

The breakfast rush had finished, and the dining room was closed again until lunch. In the lull, Julia had all the waitresses detailing the room. She wasn't about to let Mr. Owens and Ruth down.

Julia's heart ached from how her conversation with Chris had ended. Florence—even after she was fired—was still wreaking havoc.

But Julia pushed that thought aside. She wasn't responsible for the other girl's actions, she was responsible for her own.

As soon as Florence and her cohorts had left, the atmosphere with the waitresses had changed. Like fresh air had been let into the room.

It might also have been that God had changed her heart.

She allowed a smile to take over her face. That was probably it.

"Miss Schultz." Mr. Owens entered the dining room followed by two men in uniform.

She frowned and walked toward the manager. As she got closer, she recognized the sheriff and one of his deputies. She raised her eyebrows. "How can I help you, gentlemen?"

"You're under arrest for corroborating in the attempted murder of Mr. Christopher Miller." The deputy seemed all too eager to shout it to the world.

Chris? "What? Is he okay?"

"Can't you take this outside, gentlemen?" Mr. Owens' frustration with the situation was clear.

"Would you rather it be in front of all your guests?" The deputy smirked.

The manager pinched his lips together.

"Place your hands behind your back, miss." The sheriff looked at her with a bit of compassion.

What was going on? "But I didn't do anything. Is Chris all

right? Please tell me he's all right." Her hands were gripped and placed behind her.

"Mr. Miller has been beaten, but he is alive."

She let out a long breath. Tears that she hadn't expected streamed down her face. Chris was alive. *Thank You, God!*

She looked around the room. All the rest of the waitresses watched. Some of them whispered behind their hands.

Charlotte stepped forward. "Julia didn't do this. I promise."

"That's not for you to decide, miss." The deputy behind her seemed all-fired intent on making this as difficult as possible.

As much as Julia tried to keep her newfound faith at the forefront, fear and dread cascaded in.

Tessa stepped forward. "I'm coming with you. I'm not on shift yet anyway." She used her good arm to remove her apron and marched up to the sheriff. "I've spent a lot of time with Miss Schultz. When did this crime occur?"

"Last night."

"I was with Miss Schultz and Miss Anniston last night. Doesn't that give Julia an alibi?"

The sheriff let out a huff. "You can come along and share with the judge. But we still have to arrest Miss Schultz. We have another witness."

A witness? Who saw her do what?

Mr. Owens stepped toward her. "I will come down to Williams as soon as I sort things out here. Miss Smith can be your support for now."

"Thank you, sir." Poor man. Ruth was out of commission, and now her, plus they were still short-handed.

The manager nodded at her but didn't give her any words of reassurance. Instead, he turned to Tessa. "Take care of her. But I'll need you back for the shifts tomorrow if you think you can help?"

"Yes, sir. I'm getting stronger every day."

And just like that they were marched out to the train.

Tessa, with her head held high and her arm in a sling.

Julia in handcuffs.

For all to see.

Three-and-a-half hours later, Julia's hands had grown numb from being handcuffed the whole time. But she'd promised herself she wouldn't cry and she wouldn't complain. Even though all she wanted to do was both. The train came to a stop, and Julia glanced out the window at the very busy, very full platform.

It was bad enough that the sheriff and his deputy would parade her in front of all those people, but she was also still in her uniform. For those who knew anything about the Harvey Houses, they'd recognize that she was not only a Harvey Girl but also a head waitress. Her long black skirt with white shirtwaist and black ribbon at the neck were a sure sign.

Oh, the shame. No wonder Mr. Owens looked like he had swallowed his tongue. He had probably already thought ahead to what would be seen in Williams.

"We'll wait until everyone else is off the train." The sheriff stood beside her. He covered her shoulders with a long coat, effectively camouflaging her cuffed hands behind her.

"Thank you." She swallowed back the tears. She would *not* cry.

The entire train ride her mind had spun. She'd tried to pray but didn't even know what to say. At least she knew that Chris was okay, but someone had tried to kill him! And after their last conversation, he probably didn't even want to see her.

Did *he* think that she had something to do with this?

She stumbled on the platform, and the sheriff caught her.

Not one of their foursome said a word as they walked to the jail.

When they entered, something smelled familiar, but she couldn't place it. She'd never been here before.

Two cells were at the back of the jail. One on the right. One on the left.

The deputy placed a key into the door on the left and opened it. "In you go." He removed the coat from her shoulders, tugged her elbows, unlocked the cuffs, and gave her a gentle shove.

Rubbing at her wrists, Julia looked around her. Was this to be her permanent home?

No. This was all some huge mistake. Chris would clear it all up. Wouldn't he? He might not trust her anymore, but he knew she wouldn't hurt him. Where was he?

As the deputy slammed the cell door closed, he placed his hands on his hips. "When Mr. Miller arrives, we will discuss the charges with you."

Words wouldn't come, so she nodded. She wouldn't cry. She *wouldn't* cry.

She got a whiff of the scent again. What *was* that? An odd combination of pipe tobacco and . . . lavender?

Movement in the cell across the way drew her attention. Just a lump on a bed. A criminal of some sort.

The thought made her gasp. *A criminal.* That's what people thought of her now too. She sat on the clean yet hard bed and wrapped her arms around her middle. What would happen to her now?

An hour later, shuffling sounded down the hallway. Like it was coming from the front door.

"Where is she? I need to see her." The familiar voice soothed her frayed nerves.

"Chris! I'm back here." Julia rushed to the bars and gripped them. She wanted to laugh and cry at the same time.

But the sheriff appeared first. Then, across the way, the lump stood up.

A stout woman, dressed as a man, grinned at her. "It's good to see you, Julia."

"What? Who are you? How do you know my name?" She frowned. There was that scent again. Where had she smelled that before?

The sheriff, his deputy, Chris, and Tessa now stood in the hall between the two cells.

Chris moved toward her, but the sheriff held him back. His face was swollen and bruised, his right eye blackened.

Julia bit her lip. "Are you—"

"No talking," the deputy shouted. What was it with this guy?

"No need to be so harsh, son. I've asked the judge to join us." The sheriff looked down at the watch in his pocket. "Should be here momentarily."

Julia stared at Chris. She had no idea what happened but sure hoped that all of this could be straightened out. Her heart ached seeing him hurt.

She mouthed the words, *I'm sorry*.

He looked away. Studied the woman across the way. Anger filled his face.

Julia took that moment to stare at the woman too. What was going on?

Stomping was heard at the front. "I'm here."

Footsteps accompanied the voice, and a very tall and broad man entered her view. Everyone present had to look up to see his eyes. He removed his hat. A long gray beard was the only hair on his head.

"Let's start with the attack on Mr. Miller last night." The judge pulled up a chair and faced all of them.

Chris cleared his throat. "Last night, I left my shop to go pay Mr. Langford for my building. I had an appointment with him. On the way there, I was accosted by what I thought were two men. They stole the money I was to pay my landlord and the key to my shop. But one of them"—he pointed to the woman in the cell across from her—"was this woman right here."

"When did you discover she was a woman?"

"She'd tried to disguise her voice, but when they thought I was dead, she pulled a gun on the other man and called him her husband. She shot him. Multiple times."

The judge dipped his chin in a slow nod and crossed one leg over the other, resting his right ankle on his left knee. "That is the man we found dead in the street."

"Identified as one Roger Black." The sheriff handed a paper to the judge.

"Continue, please."

Chris licked his swollen lips and proceeded. "When the woman was done shooting the man, I slowly got up and saw that she left the gun on the ground beside me. Trying to frame me for the murder, I'm sure. I tried to follow her, but I was too weak. One of the sheriff's deputies found me a few blocks down and went after her then."

"When was she arrested?" The judge didn't look too intrigued.

The deputy stepped forward. "I caught her in Mr. Miller's shop, loading up everything she could carry."

"And she was also found with the money?"

"Yes, sir." The sheriff handed the envelope to the judge. "And the key to Mr. Miller's store, which I've already returned to him."

"How much is in here?" He pinned his gaze on Chris.

"Fourteen hundred dollars, sir. The sum of what I owe Mr. Langford for his property."

The judge licked his fingers and started to flick through the bills. When he was done, he handed the envelope back to the sheriff. "Return this to Mr. Miller, please."

Julia didn't understand what any of this had to do with her. Her head shifted back and forth between the men.

The judge put one hand on his beard and then stroked all the way down the length of it. "Well, that's one case solved." He eyed the woman across the way. "And this is . . ." The judge glanced back down at the sheet. "Roberta Black?"

"Bobby," the woman barked.

"You do realize the charges we have against you, ma'am?" the judge barked back.

"Yes." The woman lifted her chin. "But *she*"—she pointed at Julia—"is the ringleader."

Julia sucked in a huge gasp, along with Tessa and Chris.

"That's right. She made me do it. It was all her idea."

25

Everyone spoke at once. Voices fought for attention. The volume grew as Julia speared the woman in the other cell with her gaze. "I can't believe you would make up a story like that!" Her heart threatened to pound out of her chest.

The judge stood and held up his hands. "Everyone, quiet! I will allow you to speak when it is *your* turn. Not before. It is Mrs. Black's turn to speak now."

"Don't you ever call me that again." The woman spit at the judge's shoes. Good thing she missed.

Julia watched through the bars with wide eyes. What on earth would this woman say about her? They'd never even met!

The judge's eyes narrowed as he sat down in silence.

Julia held her breath. It seemed everyone else was too. What would the judge do now?

"It's a good thing I'm a patient man, *Mrs. Black*. Otherwise, you might find yourself hanging by the neck sooner rather than later." He stared at the woman for several seconds. "Now, please. Give us the testimony that you told the sheriff last night."

The woman who called herself Bobby sent Julia a smile that made a shiver race up her spine. "You see, I've known Julia since we were young."

"That's not true!" The words burst out of Julia's mouth.

The judge turned to her. "Not another word, Miss Schultz. I will call on you when I am good and ready."

She clamped her mouth shut. What had this horrible woman made up about her?

Bobby continued. "Her parents—back in Colorado—were thieves, ya know."

This time it was Chris who tried to interrupt. Along with Tessa.

Julia's stomach sank. How did this woman know?

In that moment, she realized that it would all come out. And she would look guilty. Even though she wasn't.

"As I was saying . . ." Bobby lifted her chin. "Her parents taught her thieving quite well. When she was just a little thing, they'd send her off to be a distraction while they went and robbed. It was a pretty nice setup. Worked for years. Until they got caught. They were hanged for killing two men and robbing a bank." She nodded. "See? This here's her parents. Such a tragic story really."

All the air seemed to be sucked out of her lungs as Julia stared at the tintype Bobby held up. "Where'd you get that?"

"Are you saying that this picture is indeed your parents?" The judge quirked an eyebrow at her.

"Yes, sir." And just like that, Julia felt like her fate was sealed.

Chris looked at her, but she couldn't hold his gaze. After their last conversation, there was no way he would believe her. She ducked her chin and looked at her shoes.

"What did this have to do with *you* robbing Mr. Miller

last night and *you* killing your husband?" The judge's tone was getting harsher every time he spoke.

"Doncha see? She's the mastermind behind all this. She's been lyin' the whole time. She found the treasure and went into cahoots with the jeweler all so she could rob him. We were just her workers."

Chris stepped close to the woman's cell. "You're telling us that she also *told* you to attack Tessa and herself on the trail that day? That she *made* you shoot Tessa?"

The deputy scrambled forward and yanked Chris back. "That's enough, Mr. Miller."

But the judge stood again. "I'd like to hear Mrs. Black's answers, please." He crossed his arms over his chest. "Well?" He pointed his glare at Bobby.

"Yep. It was all part of her master plan. So that you would feel sympathy for her and then she could rob ya blind."

Tessa put a hand to her forehead. "Could I get some water, please?"

But no one was paying attention.

Her friend got really pale.

Julia yelled, "Chris, catch her!" just as Tessa fainted.

All the men scrambled over to her friend.

Julia glanced at Bobby. A smug smile filled the woman's face. What had happened to her that made her so bitter and angry?

Tobacco and lavender.

That's where she'd smelled the combination before. When they were attacked on the trail. She wanted to scream, "*You won't get away with this!*" But in her heart, she had a feeling that the woman already had.

Julia took a deep breath and looked at Tessa, who was coming to. *God, please protect these innocent people. Forgive me. I know I probably have to pay for my past sins, but keep Chris and Tessa from being hurt by my actions.*

The scene before him was *not* what Chris expected from today.

How had this happened? But every time he tried to look at Julia, she looked away.

What was going on?

He patted Tessa's face again as she moaned and shook her head. When she opened her eyes, Chris sighed. When would all this craziness end?

"Give the young lady my chair, please." The judge was an imposing figure. Especially so when he had his arms crossed over his chest.

Once Tessa was in the chair, Chris kept a hand on her shoulder. "You all right?"

She nodded, though she was pale as could be.

The deputy ran back with a glass of water and handed it to her.

"Miss Schultz, I believe it's time we hear from you in all this. Are you the ringleader, as Mrs. Black states? Did you hire them to attack Mr. Miller?"

"No." Julia's tone sounded strained to Chris's ears. "I would never hurt him. He was my friend."

"Well, then. Let's have the truth." The judge's tone was a touch more compassionate than it had been with Bobby.

They all shifted their gazes to Julia, who looked frail standing in the cell, her white knuckles wrapped around the bars in front of her. She dipped her chin.

Then she lifted her face and stared at Chris. "I did not hire them to do any of this. I promise. I've never even met this woman. Well, other than the day they attacked us and threw sacks over our heads." She shifted her gaze to the sheriff. "I recognized the scent when you brought me into the jail. Pipe tobacco and lavender. It was the same that day. I would never hire anyone to steal from or hurt Mr. Miller. He was my partner. He was making jewelry out of the treasure I found, so why would I want to steal from him? He's . . ." Her gaze connected with his again. There was something more there, wasn't there? "I care about him." She ducked her head back to the floor and shook it.

Chris's heart wrenched. In that moment, he wanted to take her into his arms. It didn't matter what happened in the past. It didn't matter what Florence had said. He believed in her. What an absolute mess all this was. Couldn't the judge see the truth?

"Miss Schultz, is it true that your parents were thieves who murdered two men and were hanged for that?" The judge raised his eyebrows.

Her shoulders raised as she took a deep breath. "Yes."

Chris gulped at the air. *That's* why she never wanted to share about her past.

"See!" Bobby pointed a finger through the bars. "I told ya. It was her. It was *all* her!"

"Enough!" The judge's voice raised in volume as it dropped an octave. The glare he sent Bobby could skin a cat.

The woman narrowed her eyes but clamped her lips shut.

"Now . . ." The judge turned to Julia. "I have one last question. Did you order Mrs. Black to shoot her husband?"

"No, I did not." Julia's voice was soft. A single tear made a trail down her cheek. She turned and looked at Chris, those green eyes drilling into his. "Please forgive me for not telling you about my parents. When I was young, people judged me for who my parents were. So I made up all kinds of stories about what happened to them. I was afraid what people would think of me. I'm ashamed of that now, but I just hope you can believe me. As long as you are all right and you believe me and forgive me, I can face whatever comes my way."

The sincerity in her eyes pricked Chris's heart. Was it any wonder that Julia had told stories about her past? He wouldn't be shouting the truth from the rooftops if that had been *his* parents.

He placed a hand over hers on the bars.

"Do you believe me?" she whispered.

Could he?

She couldn't decipher the look on Chris's face.

All the thoughts of the past bubbled to the surface. She wasn't deserving of forgiveness. She wasn't worthy.

No. That wasn't true anymore. She was adopted by God. He loved her. Even if no one else did. She didn't have to try to be worthy anymore because she was washed clean by Jesus' sacrifice.

"Chris?" She begged him with her eyes. Why did this mean so much to her? Because she cared about him? Or was it more?

He opened his mouth and then snapped it shut.

Tessa stood behind him. "Judge, you haven't heard my testimony yet."

"All right. Are you feeling up to it, young lady?"

"Yes, sir." Her hands were clasped in front of her. Julia wasn't sure what her friend would say, but it did her heart good to see Tessa standing up for her. "Miss Schultz is my friend. We work together at the El Tovar."

"I gathered that." The judge stroked his beard again.

"We were attacked by this woman"—she pointed at Bobby—"and her husband. Like Miss Schultz said, they threw sacks over our heads, and had I not caught the man off guard and slung my bag at him, I don't know what they were planning to do with us. The lady there . . . well, she shot me as I swung my pack at her too. That's why my arm is in the sling, sir."

"All right. Do you have anything else to add?"

"Yes, sir." Tessa swallowed hard. "I got a good look at both of them. It was Mrs. Black and her husband that attacked us."

"Okay. Thank you."

"But there's more, sir. The night before the robbery, Julia helped me walk out to the rim. It's been a bit boring to stay in my room while I'm recovering. That night, I caught that same scent. Tobacco and lavender. But only for a moment. At first, I thought I might have imagined it. But that woman must have been close. Spying on us."

"Why is that of significance?"

"Because that's the night Julia told me about her parents. You see, she hadn't wanted anyone to know about who she was before and where she came from. She was afraid if people found out that her parents forced her to do things as a child that they would think the worst of her. But she's not a criminal, sir. She's not. How else would Mrs. Black know her story?"

The woman in the cell grunted. "That's ridiculous. No one is going to believe that bunkum."

The judge looked from her to Bobby. Then to Tessa. Then

back to her. "If I could meet with the sheriff and the deputy outside, please."

Tessa took another sip of water and then came up to the bars. "I believe you, Julia. I know you didn't do any of this. Thank you for being my friend." She threw a look over her shoulder at Chris. "I'll let you two talk."

"Thank you." Julia smiled at her.

"Oh, save the theatrics. You're nothing but a piece of garbage. Just like me." Bobby shook her head and plopped on her bunk at the back of her cell.

While the words were like barbs to her heart, Julia refused to let them bring her to tears. Those were the kinds of words that had followed her, accused her, shamed her for years.

Chris stepped and stood in front of her. Very close. He covered her hands with his own. "Don't listen to her, Julia. I know it was hard to admit the truth about your parents. I understand why you kept it hidden, I do. But I'm hoping that we can promise to each other that we will continue to be honest?"

"You believe me?" Tears pooled in her eyes.

"I do. I'm sorry I ever caused you to doubt that." He squeezed her hands. "And I will fight with the judge if he comes back and says you have to be formally charged. If I need to pay for some fancy lawyer to come in here, I will. I don't have to purchase my building."

Her heart felt like it was floating. "I can't let you do that for me."

"But I want to do it for you, don't you see that?" His brow furrowed. "I'm making a huge mess out of this." He looked to the floor, took a huge inhale, and then looked back up at her. "I would like to pursue you, Miss Schultz. I want to court you."

She stepped back a few inches in complete shock. What did he just say?

"Don't look so shocked. I'm not good at this kind of thing and I haven't known how to do it, but I'm asking now. Will you allow me to court you?"

"Son, I'm afraid you're going to have to wait for an answer." The judge's voice boomed as everyone entered the small hall again. The sheriff came to her cell door and unlocked it. "You are free to go, Miss Schultz."

Gratitude flooded her heart. She put a hand to her chest. "Really?"

"Yes." The judge grinned at her. "I'm sorry we had to bring you down here like this, but after checking into who you were after Mrs. Black told the sheriff her story, they had to."

"I understand that."

"I'm just sorry that we chased that rabbit." He sent a scathing look to the woman who still sat on her bunk, her lips pursed, a hateful look on her face.

"Thank you." Walking out of the cell, Julia realized she didn't ever want to take another moment for granted. Not her freedom. Not her job. Not her friends. She wanted to pour her life out and be useful.

Chris put a hand at the small of her back and led her out of the jail. It was like a dream. The nightmare was over.

Once they were outside, Tessa lunged forward and gave her a big hug. "I was so worried about you! I couldn't believe that woman would be so awful."

"There are some really awful people out there. But we're all sinners, aren't we?" Julia couldn't believe that she'd ignored the tug of God for so many years. How had she lived that way? In fear? With a façade? Always having to come up with another story.

Chris turned her to face him. "I'm sorry for my part in all of this, Julia. And you don't have to answer my question right away, not if you don't want to—"

"No. I want to answer it. I would be honored to be courted by you, Mr. Miller. But you need to get permission from Mr. Owens first."

"I can do that." The smile that covered his face warmed her all the way to her toes.

"And Miss Anniston."

"And me!" Tessa giggled.

"And probably all the other Harvey Girls too," Julia added. "We're one big family, after all."

He took her hand. "Would you like to go with me as I pay Mr. Langford for the building?"

"I would love to!"

Tessa took up residence on the other side of her. "Count me in too. As long as we go see that Connors fellow afterward. I can't wait to see the look on his face when he hears the news. Can I tell him? Pretty please?"

The thought of Jeffrey Connors facing off with Tessa again made Julia burst into laughter as the trio linked arms and walked down the street.

Ruth gingerly patted the bandage on her cheek. *Lord, give me strength to handle whatever comes.* She'd repeated the prayer too many times to count as she waited for the doctor to arrive.

She wasn't a vain woman. At least she hadn't been before a mountain lion mauled her face. Had she? Now she spent an agonizing amount of time consumed with her appearance and how it affected her future. How many times had she heard how pretty she was? She shook her head. That wasn't the point.

She was thirty-two, a veritable spinster. If she couldn't work, what was she to do? Where could she go? Working as a Harvey Girl had been her entire adult life. It had brought her so much satisfaction. Hopefully, she'd brought God glory through it all. And even when she was younger and struggled when all the other girls were getting married and settling down, the Lord had given her peace.

Now she was the head waitress at the crown jewel of Mr. Harvey's string of restaurants—an accomplishment she'd worked hard to obtain. It was all she'd ever wanted. More to the point, it was the only job she knew. What if she couldn't do it anymore? Harvey Girls made people feel comfortable. They were trained to be efficient. Pleasant. And spotless.

Mr. Owens had bent the stringent Harvey rules for Emma Grace in her time of need. Surely he would do the same for her. Only Emma Grace could still do her job. Ruth couldn't. Not to the Harvey standard. Her leg would take a long time to heal. And she'd probably always walk with a limp. But that wouldn't be as visible as . . . her face. She placed a hand over the bandage and closed her eyes. What would she look like?

Lord, give me strength to handle whatever comes.

The prayer grew frailer with each repeat.

Against the doctor's orders, Ruth began to peel back the edge of the bandage. She leaned close to the mirror, hoping the damage was far less than her fears.

"I asked you not to do that, Miss Anniston."

Ruth turned away from the mirror, her emotions a mix of chagrin for disobeying the doctor's orders and relief that she'd put off the inevitable for a few more minutes. "I'm sorry."

He smiled kindly, the gray in his eyes blending nicely with the silver in his hair. He was such a nice-looking man.

Nice-looking. She cringed. No one would probably ever say that about her again.

"In truth, Miss Anniston"—he stepped deeper into the room and set his bag on the desk—"I'm surprised you haven't removed it already. How are you feeling?"

He wasn't asking about her pain, but she still didn't have a grip on her emotions, so she answered, "Fine. It's itchy more than painful at this point."

He narrowed his gaze. "All right. We'll leave it at that." He snapped open the black leather medical bag and peered inside. "I have an ointment that will help with the itchiness." He pulled out a small jar. "And your leg?"

She bit her lip. Couldn't lie to him. "It hurts. I can't put my weight on it."

"I told you, that wouldn't be possible for some time. It's a miracle you even have the leg. . . . You understand that, don't you, Miss Anniston?"

"Oh good, you're here." Mr. Owens strode into the room, a false smile on his face. But she welcomed the interruption. "How are you feeling today, Miss Anniston?"

Unlike the doctor, Mr. Owens surely wanted assurance that she'd hold up under whatever the removal of her bandage revealed. Ruth squared her shoulders where she sat with her leg propped up and gave him her best Harvey Girl smile. "I'm fine, sir. Thank you for asking. Glad to hear that everything was resolved with Miss Schultz."

"Yes, and she will do a tremendous job in your stead, I'm sure."

Oh, please, Lord. Don't let him replace me already! She banished the selfish plea. "She will make the Harvey name proud."

"She's been begging to see you all day, along with Chef Henderson. Shall I let them know that after the doctor leaves, they may come visit?" The manager raised his eyebrows.

"Let's wait for visitors until later, shall we?" The doctor looked between the two of them. "I want to remind you both that Miss Anniston's wounds are still very fresh. They will be red and swollen today, far beyond what they will eventually fade to. I hope you'll keep that in mind."

Lord, give me strength to handle whatever comes.

The prayer was tissue-paper thin now. Barely holding her together. Her hands were damp, and her heart was beginning to pick up speed. "I'm ready."

And she'd told Julia that lying wasn't the Harvey way. What a hypocrite she'd become.

"Let's get this bandage off, shall we, Miss Anniston?" The doctor pulled a chair closer, the one not facing the mirror. Should she ask to be turned away as well? Or was it better to see the full damage all at once? But the doctor didn't give her a choice. He took the mirror from her hands.

How bad did he expect this to be?

She wiped her hands against her skirt and, calling upon all her training, forced herself to be calm. Under control. "Thank you." It was an automatic response but was she thankful? No. Not for this.

But she *was* thankful for his many visits and his skill. She closed her eyes and focused on that while he eased the bandage away from her cheek.

While he worked, Mr. Owens talked. "I've been thinking about how to ease you back into working, Miss Anniston.

I think it's best if we keep you off your feet as much as possible, don't you, Doctor?"

"She's going to have to until her leg fully heals, and that's going to take some time."

But that wound was hidden. It wasn't ugly and out in the open. Ruth cringed at her own thoughts.

Her manager was still talking. "I'd like you to keep training the new girls, of course, but perhaps it would be best to do that when the dining room is closed so you aren't interrupted by our guests. That way you can also sit and not strain your leg."

Ruth stiffened. Her fears were coming true. He didn't want guests to see her.

"I saw that, Ruth. I know what a workhorse you are, but you are too valuable to Harvey to not let you heal completely. It's for your own good," Mr. Owens continued. "I'm just thinking we should keep you off your feet. But don't think we won't put you to work in other ways. I'd like you to take over some bookkeeping responsibilities. Don't you think that's a good idea?"

No. It was a terrible idea. She had no idea how to handle books. She knew how to handle people. But at least he was offering her work. "That sounds good, sir. Although I'll need to be trained on bookkeeping as it's outside of my—" She gasped as a piece of gauze pulled her tender skin. "Out of my expertise."

With the last piece of gauze removed, she took a shallow breath, then another one."Of course. I'm sure you'll be a quick study. Managing the dining room and kitchen alone is a huge undertaking. With all your knowledge and skill as head waitress all these years, perhaps we could make another arrangement. I find myself overwhelmed a good bit of the time."

Was he trying to make her feel better? It wasn't working. What she wanted was to be able to get back on the floor and do *her* job. Not the books. Not managing the dining room and kitchen.

"But of course, whenever you're ready, my dear." Mr. Owens' voice held a slight edge. Like he was tempering his tone. What did they see?

Ruth closed her eyes, forcing back sudden hot tears. Her manager was as no-nonsense as they came. He didn't believe in false hope or platitudes. He told it like it was. If he was calling her *my dear*, things must be worse than even he expected. Just like the good doctor.

"I believe I should leave the stitches in for another week. Even though they make the injuries look so much worse, it will be best for the long-term recovery. If you would like to keep it covered with bandages during the day, that is fine. But at night, it's best for the wound to be uncovered so it can breathe."

"All right." How bad did it look?

"I think we should leave Miss Anniston alone for a moment."

There was her answer. Yes. Things were much worse than expected.

Ruth opened her eyes and whispered, "Thank you."

The doctor nodded once, his gray eyes wet with compassion. "Take your time. And remember, this isn't how you'll look in a few months. It will get better. I promise."

She swallowed and nodded. The tears she'd held back earlier leaked out, stinging her hot skin. She wanted to say thank you again but couldn't get the words past the trepidation clogging her throat.

He patted her hand, then stood. "Let's go, Mr. Owens."

"But I wanted—"

Ruth imagined the good doctor either grabbed her manager's arm or silenced him with a glare. Either way, she was grateful she didn't have to endure a gasp or horror-filled eyes or any other reaction. Dealing with her own was going to take every ounce of whatever courage she had left.

She sat straight, smoothed her skirt, and took one more shaky breath. As she lifted the mirror once again, she whispered, "Lord, give me strength—"

But then she saw her face.

The prayer perforated, and she fell apart.

Julia sat beside Ruth's bed. "How are you feeling?"

Her friend scrunched up her nose. "Honestly?"

"Yes." She leaned closer and grabbed Ruth's hand.

"Just moving my nose like that hurt." Ruth chuckled. "I'm sorry, I shouldn't joke about it. But it's true." She let out a breath. "My leg was damaged the worst, and it gives me a lot of pain, but I have to admit that I'm concerned about what scars will be left on my face."

"You are such a beautiful woman, Ruth. No one will see the scars."

"You're sweet, but we all know that you are good at stories, Julia."

She shook a finger at her friend. "That's not a story. You *are* beautiful. And those of us who know you and love you will not see the scars. I can promise you that." She couldn't imagine the pain their head waitress was going through.

"That's enough about me. Catch me up on everything

upstairs and tell me what happened. How are things running in the dining room?"

"Well, if you need to be entertained, I can certainly do that." They laughed together, and then Julia dove into all the stories of the past few days. The most humorous being of a family that brought their two-year-old to the El Tovar. The child was charming and cuter than any other little one she'd ever seen. But as soon as any of them got close, food would go flying. After five different waitresses had to change their uniforms, Julia made a rule that none of the staff should talk to the baby.

After they'd giggled together for a few minutes, Julia grew serious and shared with Ruth about all that had happened. She bit her lip. "Which leads me to a question I'd like to ask you."

"If it's about Christopher Miller courting you"—she picked up sheets of paper from her side—"he's already asked Mr. Owens' permission and mine." She waved the letter. "Which we both heartily gave. That is, of course, as long as you are committed to your duties."

A thrill rushed through her. "Oh, thank you! But no . . . that's not the question I wanted to ask."

"All right." Ruth smiled at her. "Go ahead."

"Will you be my Paul?"

Her friend tilted her head. "I'm not quite sure I understand."

"I was reading the epistles to Timothy this morning. I realize that I need a Paul in my life. I need someone to hold me accountable, to help me learn more about my faith. I'm new at this and don't want to stray in any way." She bit her lip, hoping that Ruth would agree to it. She couldn't think of anyone better.

Tears filled her friend's eyes. "I would be honored."

"Oh, thank you." Julia got up from her seat and gingerly wrapped her arms around Ruth. "Thank you."

"Thank you for asking me." Ruth dabbed at her eyes with a handkerchief. "Now . . . tell me all about Chris. . . ."

Epilogue

December 28, 1907

Tessa stood behind Julia and brushed her hair. "I can't believe today is the big day."

Julia's heart skipped as she looked at her friend in the mirror. "Me neither. After all these months."

"Have you decided how you would like me to fix your hair?" Her friend—once quiet and unassuming—had blossomed into a radiant woman. She'd even moved into the assistant head waitress position. And after today, Tessa would become the head waitress.

"I'll let you decide. You always do such a lovely job with the other girls' hair."

Tessa pursed her lips and placed her hands on her hips. "This might take me a while, but we'll see if I can put together what I've envisioned."

"I'm sure I will love it." She smiled at her friend. "How are your parents doing? I haven't seen them in a couple of weeks."

"Mom is still getting over her cold, but they are doing great. They love living out here. Dad walks along the rim every morning and evening."

It made Julia smile. "Every time I see him, he's telling me about some new plant he's discovered."

Tessa wound some of Julia's hair between her fingers. "Have you seen the Watkinses' baby this week?"

"I've been so busy, I haven't been over to see them." The adorable and chubby baby was the highlight of everyone's day. Full of smiles and giggles, the little boy could entertain the staff for hours.

"He has two teeth now. Emma Grace told me yesterday that now she knows why he was gnawing on everything he could get his hands on."

The morning passed as Tessa finished her hair and wound it up into a beautiful coiffure. Several of the other girls came in to see her, leaving little gifts and well-wishes.

A knock on the open door made Julia turn around. "Mr. Owens!"

"I wanted to add my congratulations." He stepped forward.

Julia stood and went to him, placing a kiss on his cheek. "Thank you for all you've done for me . . . and for believing in me."

"You are quite a jewel." The man's face softened. "It has been a joy having you work here."

"Thank you, sir. And thank you for the lovely display at Hopi House. I wasn't expecting anything so big." Mr. Owens had paid the Kolb brothers to take pictures of Julia, Tessa, and Chris with the treasure they'd found and with some of the finished pieces Chris had made. The pictures were large and on display with a short story of the legend, the scrolls, and the two morions.

"We're all looking forward to you finishing the book, Julia. And we will proudly sell copies of it here."

It had been by Ruth's prodding that she'd followed through with writing down the story. As she poured the words onto the page, she discovered how much she had a love for the written word and story. Maybe one day she would write children's stories as well. One day. "Thank you, Mr. Owens. For everything."

"It won't be the same without you here. I'll see you a little later." He gave her a brief hug and then walked away.

Normally not an emotional man, it was clear that he was moved by her request to walk her down the aisle. Her El Tovar family would all be present, and that meant the world to her.

The music room at the El Tovar had been transformed into a beautiful sanctuary. Julia looked around at how the girls had decorated and wanted to cry happy tears. It was perfect.

"Do you like it?" Chris came up beside her and put his arm around her waist.

"I do. It's beautiful." She leaned into him.

"A bit later today, we'll be saying those words to each other. *I do*. I'm almost in awe of it."

What a treasure this man was. She turned to face him. "I can't wait."

He took a long, deep breath and winked at her. "Me neither. I feel like I've had to wait for this day . . . for forever."

"It does feel like it's been a long time, doesn't it? And yet it also seems to have passed so quickly. I've learned so much about who you are and who *I* am in Christ. I never understood who the real Julia was before I came here. I feel like a whole new person. That fresh start I'd been longing for is here and now. Each day is a new beginning."

"Today we start a new beginning together." He reached into his pocket. "I made this for you."

Her eyes widened at the beautiful gold necklace embellished with emerald stones. It was the most beautiful piece she'd ever seen. "It's gorgeous. These are from the ones we found?"

"Yes. I was hoping you wouldn't object to me saving a few for you. I'm glad you like it." He undid the clasp and went behind her to place it around her neck. "I spent months on it. Setting each stone. Praying over our relationship. Praying for you." He stepped back in front of her and reached into his pocket again. "Each stone has a verse that I prayed over you." Chris handed her a card with scriptures handwritten on it. "And it's a small reminder of our first adventure together."

Tears pricked her eyes. "I don't deserve you."

"I don't deserve you."

She stepped into his arms. "I love you, Chris."

"I love you too." He pulled her even closer and wrapped both his arms around her. Their heat melted together, and she leaned her head against his. She couldn't wait to become one with this man.

"Thank you for waiting for me."

He kissed her forehead, then trailed kisses down her temples, to both her cheeks, and her nose. Then he paused for half a second and leaned back to look into her eyes before kissing her passionately.

She tangled her fingers in his hair and pulled him closer.

He pulled away, a bit breathless. "I'm looking forward to more of those. Every day for the rest of our lives."

"Me too." Surely her cheeks were crimson, the heat was so intense in her face.

"I'm glad we've had a few moments alone."

She nodded and kissed him again.

For months, they'd struggled with the passion that had built between them. But seeking to honor the Lord with their bodies, they'd promised to only share one kiss a week—and a small kiss, at that. Which had gotten harder and harder as the weeks passed.

Chris had told their pastor during their sessions that it was hard to restrain himself. She loved that he was honest and forthright and wanted to be held accountable, but it stirred her own feelings that seemed to grow with every passing day.

"I'm looking forward to everything with you." Chris released her but held her hand. "Now I understand what Gramps said about love."

"What was that?"

"That it was the finest gem to be found. It takes time to cut it, mold it, shape it, but in the Master's hands, it becomes a priceless treasure. That's what I want our marriage to be. A priceless treasure. For the glory of God."

That was exactly what she wanted too. When she'd heard the legend, she thought the treasure to be found here was only that. But it wasn't gems and stones. God had given her so much more. He'd given her the truth about who she was.

A chosen and beloved child of God.

And He'd given her Chris.

Priceless treasures, indeed.

Note from the Author

The first time the mystery surrounding the Spanish expedition of 1540 sparked an idea for a story for me, I was standing on the edge of the canyon, reading one of the interpretive signs.

I found it fascinating that the expedition of hundreds of men had to go home without ever finding anything that pertained to the seven cities of gold. But a few of them did get to see the canyon. Which to me is worth far more than gold.

If you'd like to learn more about the history that sparked my imaginary legend, check out these links:

- nps.gov/grca/learn/historyculture/explorers.htm
- nationalgeographic.com/history/article/seven-cities-of-cibola

One of my favorite things about writing this series about the El Tovar is the food! Gracious, if the dining room at the hotel were closer, I would eat there at least once a month. If you get the chance to go to the Grand Canyon, I highly recommend staying at the El Tovar and eating there at least once.

Research for this story was so much fun. Not only did I eat there a lot, but I was able to speak with multiple staff members who have worked there for more than forty years. Their insight and tales were great fodder for my imagination. The breakfast menu I wrote in chapter eleven is straight from a menu I found from 1908. (They even have one posted in a glass case in the hallway to this famous dining room.)

Jewelers fascinate me. In fact, my best friend from college (waving at Christi!) has a family member who owns a jewelry business, and one day when I was in the back looking at the scope of tools, my little author brain kicked into high gear. Come to find out, the majority of the tools they use today are the same as they would have used more than a hundred years ago. My friend Kelly Vaughn is a jeweler today, and she helped me with a lot of research for this story. Lapidary is so fascinating! To understand some of the cuts I used in *A Gem of Truth* here's a fun link: gemsociety.org/article/the-history-of-lapidary

I've hiked down into the Grand Canyon, but it's hard to remember what everything looks like when you are huffing and puffing your way up the trail. I found these hiking pictures (links below) to be ever so helpful to refresh my mind and bring it back to life.

birdandhike.com/Hike/GRCA/BA_Phan/_BA_Phan-u.htm

birdandhike.com/Hike/GRCA/Ba_Igc/_BA_ICG_Tr-u.htm

I am so excited to return to the Grand Canyon and the El Tovar in *A Mark of Grace*, coming January 2023. I hope you will join me for Ruth's story.

Thank you for being a part of my life and joining me for this story.

Until next time,
Kimberley

Acknowledgments

First and foremost, I need to thank God for the gift of story. This is His story. I'm privileged to bring it to you.

Next is my husband. The man is brilliant. A saint for putting up with me. And he's pretty good at brainstorming too. Jeremy, I love you more. Thank you for all you do to encourage, support, and cheer me on.

Josh and Ruth, Kayla and Steven, and Little Man—CJ. Being Mom and Nana is such a joy. I praise God for y'all every day.

Kelly Vaughn—We've shared the love of music, movies, books, cooking, and so many other things over the years. You have been a huge blessing in my life. Getting to watch you become a master jeweler and fulfill your dream was such a joy. I'm so proud of you. Thank you for giving me so much help with this book.

Christi Campbell—oh, my friend—we have been through so much together. Thank you for sticking with me all these years.

To the BHP and Baker teams—wow—thank you. It takes a whole passel of you guys to bring these stories to life. (And to keep me straight, just sayin'.) Jess and Jen, thank you for your editing brilliance. Serena, Brooke, Amy, Noelle, you guys do SO much. Thank you! The design team knocked it out of the park once again with the cover. And everyone else, thank you. It is such a huge privilege to be a Bethany House author.

I wouldn't be where I am today without Tracie Peterson pouring into me. As mentor, friend, prayer partner, writing partner, and a million other things. Love you, lady.

My crit group and Mastermind group—I love you all so much. Thank you for sticking with me and making me better. Becca Whitham, Darcie Gudger, Jana Riediger, Kayla Whitham, Jaime Jo Wright, Jocelyn Green, and Tracie Peterson.

Becca the Tall (Whitham), thank you for all the support and help. You gave so much to this story. Your friendship is priceless.

Becca the Short (Weidel) and Kailey Bechtel, you are both amazing. Thanks for the check-ins, prayers, and encouragement.

I'd also like to thank the incredible people at El Tovar and the Grand Canyon who assisted me over and over again. And the historical private researcher who helped with the Krakow collection—University of New Mexico—Larry Larrichio.

Last—and definitely not least—YOU. The reader. Thank you for making it possible to do what I do.

Kimberley Woodhouse is an award-winning and bestselling author of more than thirty books. A lover of history and research, she often gets sucked into the past and then her husband has to lure her out with chocolate and the promise of eighteen holes on the golf course. She loves music, kayaking, and her family. Married to the love of her life for three decades, she lives and writes in the Poconos, where she's traded her title of "Craziest Mom" for "Nana the Great." To find out more about Kim's books, follow her on social media and sign up for her newsletter/blog at kimberleywoodhouse.com.

Sign Up for Kimberley's Newsletter

Keep up to date with Kimberley's latest news on book releases and events by signing up for her email list at kimberleywoodhouse.com.

More from Kimberley Woodhouse

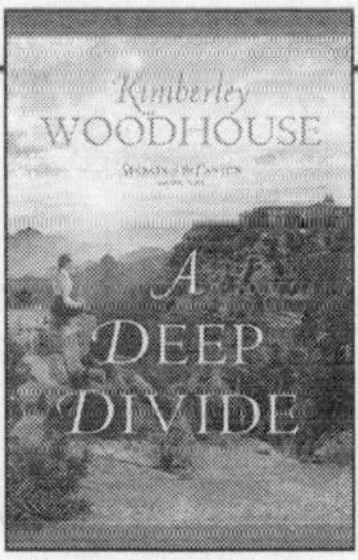

When her father's greedy corruption goes too far, heiress Emma Grace McMurray sneaks away to be a Harvey Girl at the El Tovar Grand Canyon Hotel, planning to stay hidden forever. There she uncovers mysteries, secrets, and a love beyond anything she could imagine—leaving her to question all she thought to be true.

A Deep Divide
Secrets of the Canyon #1

You May Also Like . . .

When her grandfather's health begins to decline, Havyn is determined to keep her family together. But everyone has secrets—including John, the hired stranger who recently arrived on their farm. To help out, Havyn starts singing at a local roadhouse, but dangerous eyes grow jealous as she and John grow closer. Will they realize the peril before it is too late?

Forever Hidden by Tracie Peterson and Kimberley Woodhouse
THE TREASURES OF NOME #1
traciepeterson.com; kimberleywoodhouse.com

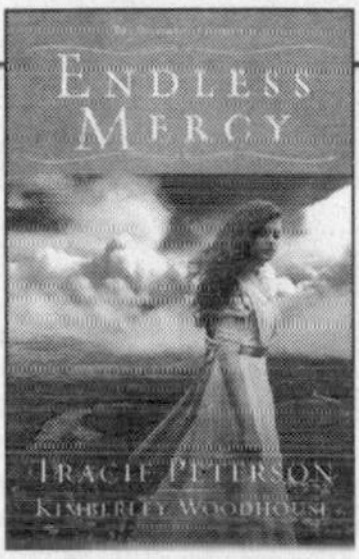

When Madysen Powell's supposedly dead father shows up, her gift for forgiveness is tested and she's left searching for answers. Daniel Beaufort arrives in Nome and finds employment at the Powell dairy, longing to start fresh after the gold rush leaves him with only empty pockets. Will deceptions from the past tear apart their hopes for a better future?

Endless Mercy by Tracie Person and Kimberley Woodhouse
THE TREASURES OF NOME #2
traciepeterson.com; kimberleywoodhouse.com

On the surface, Whitney Powell is happy working with her sled dogs, but her life is full of complications that push her to the edge. When sickness spreads in outlying villages, Dr. Peter Cameron turns to Whitney and her dogs for help navigating the deep snow, and together they discover that sometimes it's only in weakness you can find strength.

Ever Constant by Tracie Peterson and Kimberley Woodhouse
THE TREASURES OF NOME #3
traciepeterson.com; kimberleywoodhouse.com

BETHANYHOUSE

More from Bethany House

When an accident leaves Cassandra Barton incapacitated, she spends her time compiling a book of stories about the men working on the Santa Fe Railroad. But worry grows as revolutionaries set out to destroy the railroad. As the danger intensifies, Cassie and her longtime friend Brandon must rely on their faith to overcome the obstacles that stand in the way.

Under the Starry Skies by Tracie Peterson
Love on the Santa Fe
traciepeterson.com

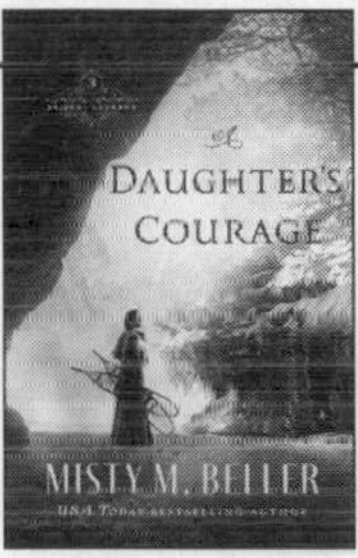

Charlotte Durand sets out on an expedition in search of a skilled artisan who can repair a treasured chalice—but her hike becomes much more daunting when a treacherous snowstorm sets in. When Damien Levette finds Charlotte stranded, they must work together to survive the peril of the mountains against all odds.

A Daughter's Courage by Misty M. Beller
Brides of Laurent #3
mistymbeller.com

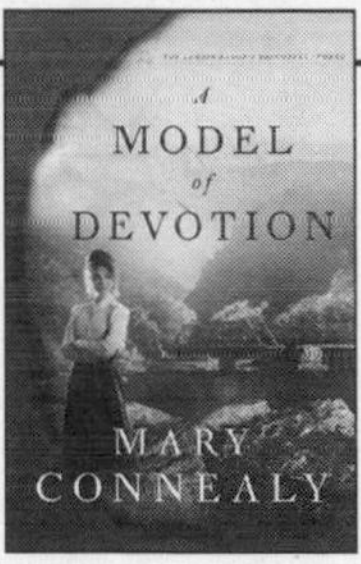

A brilliant engineer, Jilly Stiles sets her focus on fulfilling her dream of building a mountaintop railroad—and remaining independent. But when a cruel and powerful man goes to dangerous lengths to try to make Jilly his own, marrying her friend Nick may be the only way to save herself and her dreams.

A Model of Devotion by Mary Connealy
The Lumber Baron's Daughters #3
maryconnealy.com

BethanyHouse